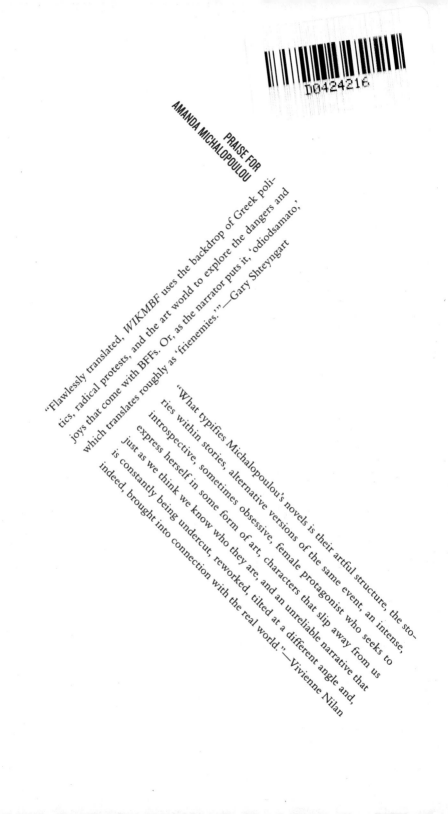

PRAISE FOR
AMANDA MICHALOPOULOU

"Flawlessly translated, *WIKMBF* uses the backdrop of Greek politics, radical protests, and the art world to explore the dangers and joys that come with BFFs. Or, as the narrator puts it, 'odiodsamato,' which translates roughly as 'frienemies.'" —Gary Shteyngart

"What typifies Michalopoulou's novels is their artful structure, the stories within stories, alternative versions of the same event, an intense, introspective, sometimes obsessive, female protagonist who seeks to express herself in some form of art, characters that slip away from us just as we think we know who they are, and an unreliable narrative that is constantly being undercut, reworked, tilted at a different angle and, indeed, brought into connection with the real world." —*Vivienne Nilan*

WHY I KILLED MY BEST FRIEND

AMANDA MICHALOPOULOU

Translated from the Greek by Karen Emmerich

OPEN LETTER
LITERARY TRANSLATIONS FROM THE UNIVERSITY OF ROCHESTER

First edition, 2014
All rights reserved

Library of Congress Cataloging-in-Publication Data: Available upon request.
ISBN-13: 978-1-934824-74-0 / ISBN-10: 1-934824-74-7

This project is supported in part by an award from
the National Endowment for the Arts.

ART WORKS.
arts.gov

This book was published with the support of the Hellenic Ministry of
Culture and Tourism and the National Book Centre of Greece.

Printed on acid-free paper in the United States of America.

Text set in Bembo, a twentieth-century revival of a typeface originally
cut by Francesco Griffo, circa 1495.

Design by N. J. Furl

Open Letter is the University of Rochester's nonprofit, literary translation press:
Lattimore Hall 411, Box 270082, Rochester, NY 14627

www.openletterbooks.org

One

A wild animal charges into the room and knocks me to the floor before I know what's hit me. All I see is an eye glaring fiercely from beneath a tuft of blond hair.

"Niaaar!" it roars. "I'm a tiger! I'll tear you to shreds!"

The first graders and I have been sitting and drawing in a circle on the floor, as we do every afternoon. I've just gotten them under control; my reward is the dry, monotonous scuffing of pencils on paper. Natasha, one of the shyest girls, starts to shriek when she sees me flat on my back on the floor. Panos shapes his fingers into a gun and lets out a string of incoherent sounds, something between machine gun fire and spitting. The tiger pounces on him and bites the barrel of his gun. While he's recovering from the shock, it lunges at me again, trying out a new set of roars. I look over and see Saroglou, the principal, standing in the door, one hand over her heart.

"My Lord, Maria! She slipped right through my hands . . ."

I grab the girl by the wrists to immobilize her. It's a trick I've learned well, how to grab a child by the wrists. "What's going on? How on earth did she—"

"You think I've ever seen anything like it? Spoiled tomboy!"

"What's she doing here?"

"She's new. Her name's Daphne Malouhou. The family just moved back to Athens from Paris. Her parents work long hours, and they asked if we'd let her into the after-school program. Do you think you can handle her?"

The little girl continues to struggle as if possessed. I have her by the arms, but she keeps flailing her feet in the air. She crumples Natasha's drawing with her shoes and Natasha begins to wail inconsolably. By now the rest of the kids are whimpering, too. In hopes of calming them down, I tell Saroglou to leave and close the door behind her. Then I tell the kids we're going on a journey into the jungle, where we'll turn into wild animals and show our hooked claws, just as Daphne did. They start to roar like lions and slowly but surely stop being afraid of the newcomer. To add to the atmosphere, I beat a rhythm on the floor with my fingertips. A stream of memories from Africa floods my mind: suya with peanuts at the beach, imitation Coca-Cola, hide-and-seek with Unto Punto behind the badminton court.

Daphne is still prancing around bewitched, half horse, half tiger. She elbows the other kids out of the way as she takes a victory lap around the room, but her primary target is me, the animal tamer. She rushes at me, grabs both my thighs and squeezes. How strong she is! She raises her head and stares at me intently. I shiver: that same dimple in her chin. The same look in her eye. The same tenacity. All that's missing is a white streak in her eyebrow.

"Are you going to be a good girl now?"

"Not if I don't want to!"

"Daphne, I'm not kidding!"

"Me neither," she says, and pinches my calf.

It isn't so much the commotion caused by her entrance that convinces me. Or even the hard evidence: France, the dimple, the blond hair, the resemblance. It's the pinch that does it.

"What's your mother's name?" I ask.

"I'm not telling."

"Your mother's name is Anna."

The girl jumps back.

"You're a witch!" she says.

"Of course I'm a witch. And if you don't behave, I'll turn you into a tiger for good."

Her mouth drops open. Then she closes and opens it a few times, soundlessly. Like our goldfish, back then, in Ikeja.

Two

I'm crouching on the lawn under the palm trees at our house in Ikeja. I'm eating something green and crunchy, using both hands because, as Gwendolyn says, you can't catch fleas with one finger. Across from me is the stone pond with the goldfish, only it's empty now. We can't bring our fish with us to Athens. Where do fish go when people move? I hope they go down a pipe into the sea to find their long-lost families, and hug by rubbing their scales together since they don't have any arms. When fish move to a new place, there are no suitcases, no tears. Mom and I have the handkerchiefs she embroidered with our initials in case we want to cry, and a shipping container for our things. Unto Punto carries everything out of the house, even my roller skates. Except for Dad's things. Dad's going to stay in Nigeria with the empty goldfish pond.

It's summer and the rainy season has started. We have to leave before the beginning of the school year so I can adjust to the "Greek system." In the Greek system the blackboard isn't divided in half and all the kids in the class are the same age. That's because there are lots of kids of every age. Mom says I won't have to leave for school at five-thirty every morning. In the Greek system the schools are close to your house. So what time will I leave? More like seven-fifteen. But then I'll be out in the heat, I'll be all sweaty when I get to school. Oh, silly, it's not hot in Greece. In winter people wear sweaters, heavy clothes. They go to movies and plays.

Greece is our real home, Africa is the fake one. In Ikeja there are periods of political unrest. Whenever you hear the words "state of emergency," or "Igbo and Hausa," or the name General Ojuku, you know there won't be any school. In Greece there's been democracy for two straight years, so there's no escaping homework. Why should I have to go to school every day in a place where it's cold? What do I care about movies and plays? I'm happy with the squash club and the Marine Club where the U. S. Marines have real Coca-Cola at their parties on Fridays. I don't want for us to lose Gwendolyn and Unto Punto and go and live in an "apartment," as Mom whispers to Aunt Amalia over the phone. I want to ride my bike in the house, do slalom turns around the columns, ring my bell drin-dran-drin and have Gwendolyn say, "You crazy girl! I thought someone was at the door again!" and laugh out loud, holding her belly.

Mom comes up behind me silently, grabs my hair and slaps my face twice, fast. Then she pries my mouth open with her fingers.

"What's gotten into you? Spit it out! Now!"

A green pulp dribbles from my mouth, mixing with tears and snot.

"Haven't I told you to never, ever eat crickets again?"

I eat crickets because Africa is my real home. Greece, the fake one.

I'm on the balcony of our apartment, crying and crying. I stuck my head through the railing and now I can't get it out. I was just playing, I sucked in my cheeks, held my breath, and, oop, popped my head between the bars, which are as hot as the sand at the beach in Badagri or at Tarkwa Bay. Right away the floral-patterned lounge chairs sprang up before me, the banana boats and the bar that sells suya. A two-naira suya, please. With onions! Now my ears are as hot as the suya grill.

Exarheia Square is the ugliest place in the whole world. We live in a building that was designed by someone important. Everyone calls it the "blue building." On the ground floor is Floral, a patisserie where mostly old people sit. The cars rev their engines and honk. At night I can't sleep from the screeching of brakes in the street. The apartment is called a quad because there are four rooms in total. There's a porthole window in the front door. The whole place is the size of one of the rooms in our house in Ikeja, only it's divided into smaller rooms. There are two bedrooms, not five. One bathroom, not three. There's no game room and no storage room, just a tiny pantry off the kitchen. And I'm not allowed to ride my bicycle in the apartment, because there are "people" living downstairs. Besides, even if I were allowed, how can you ride your bike in a quad? There are no columns to do turns around. If I want to ride my bike, I go to the Field of Ares with Mom and her cousin, Aunt Amalia, who's an old maid, like Gwendolyn. But that's where the similarity ends: Aunt Amalia is thin as a rail and very pale, like she's sick. Sure, she knows the names of all the movie stars, but she laughs with her mouth closed. I miss Gwendolyn so much, with her belly laughs and her proverbs! Which one would she tell me now to make me feel better? No matter how wrong things go, salt never gets worms? Gwendolyn equals joy. Joy equals Africa. So I'm crying for lots of reasons, not just because my head got stuck in the railing.

I hear Mom letting herself into the apartment. Her footsteps echo down the hall.

"Maria! Mariiiia!"

When she finally finds me she lets out a shriek. "Maria, why do you do this to me? You're nine years old, practically a woman! It's time you grew up!"

A man saws through the bars and sets me free. As he saws he keeps saying, "You're quite a handful, aren't you?" Mom is pacing up and down in the hall. She's angry, I can tell from the click of her heels. When she sees me come running inside she grabs me with both hands and shakes me, squeezing my wrists. No, I'm not going to cry. I'm nine years old now, practically a woman.

I wait for Mom to lie down for her afternoon siesta, go into my room and close the door. I take off all my clothes, then put on the white uniform from my school in Nigeria so the stewardesses will know I go to school in Ikeja and let me onto the plane. I have a whole bunch of naira in my pocket. How much can a child's ticket to Africa cost? Five naira? Six? Or maybe it'll be really expensive, and since I don't have any money, they'll make me work in the fields until my feet are all callused. I pull my suitcase out of my closet and pack a dress that Mom and Gwendolyn sewed, two monogrammed handkerchiefs, and my colored pencils. I can't find any drawing paper, but that's okay, they'll give me some on the plane. I sneak into the kitchen and take two cans of Nounou evaporated milk, a box of Alsa Mousse, a package of Miranda cookies, and two eggs. If we land in Lagos late and I have to sleep on the beach, I'll fry the eggs in the sand. There'll be plenty of bananas to pick, but I might as well bring a few for the road. I wrap my roller skates in a towel so the wheels won't clatter. *Dear Mom,* I write in a note, *I'm going to see Gwendolyn and Dad for a few days. Come as soon as you can! And bring my bicycle. Love, Maria.* On the bottom of the page I draw the stone pond in Ikeja, with the goldfish flopping around on the ground, out of the water. If she doesn't feel sorry for me, maybe she'll at least feel sorry for our fish.

Lots of busses are passing by. I get on the one the most people are waiting for. The eggs roll around in my suitcase. I hope they don't break.

"A ticket for the airport, please. Can I pay in naira?"

The ticket collector smiles. He looks like Unto Punto, only he's white. Neither one of them has many teeth. "You give someone the slip?" he asks.

"Excuse me?" Giving someone the slip doesn't mean anything to me. My Greek isn't very good.

"Where do you live, miss?"

"In Exarheia, but right now I'm going to Nigeria, to see Gwendolyn and Dad."

"Nigeria? The black people will eat you!"

"Black people don't eat!"

"Oh, they eat, all right."

"Yes, but they eat yams or amala or moyin-moyin, not other people!"

"But you're so small and tender, they'll open their mouths, mmmm, and gobble you up in a single bite, because people in Africa are very hungry. Haven't you heard?"

Heard what? Has there been more unrest? Another state of emergency? Did General Ojuku come back? Maybe the ticket collector is right, and instead of hugging me Gwendolyn will sink her teeth into me, saying, "The fear of tomorrow makes the snail carry its home wherever it goes." How could the world have changed so much in just two weeks? Does salt really not get worms? I get off at the next stop, on the verge of tears. But I'm not going to cry. I'm nine years old, practically a woman.

I sit down on my suitcase and eat my banana as slowly as I can, running my tongue over my broken tooth. The story is that I broke it just now, during my adventures, I'm the heroine of a fairytale who has to endure various trials. I squint my eyes and pretend I'm on our covered veranda in Ikeja, under the bougainvillea. I'm eating vanilla ice cream, my favorite flavor. Gwendolyn is ironing in the shade and telling me my favorite story, the one about the two friends, Dola and Bambi. Dola has a walnut tree and animals are always eating its leaves. Bambi gives her a big pot with a hole in the bottom to plant her tree in, so the animals won't be able to get at the leaves. When Dola starts to make lots of money from selling her walnuts, Bambi gets jealous and wants her pot back. But for that to happen they have to kill the tree, since now it's rooted in the pot. Bambi is stubborn. She wants her pot back! The village judge decides in her favor—Bambi will get her pot. So the poor walnut tree dies. The next year, Dola gives Bambi a gold necklace for her birthday. Ten years later she decides she wants it back. But in order to get at the necklace, Bambi's head will have to come off. They go back to the village judge and he says that since Dola insists, they'll have to cut off Bambi's head, and that's that. Bambi cries a river of tears, Dola takes pity on her, and in the end Bambi lives. No one is jealous of anyone anymore, because jealousy is the worst thing of all.

Two police officers appear just as it's getting dark. They say they'll take me home in their patrol car and ask if I've thought about how my mother must feel. I have thought about that, I think about it all the time, we're not happy in this country and we need to go home soon, while Gwendolyn is still our friend and cares about us and doesn't have the heart to eat us.

Mom has been crying. Her eyes are puffy. She doesn't shake me, doesn't squeeze my wrists, just combs her fingers through my hair.

"I think the eggs in my suitcase broke," I say.

"No use crying over broken eggs," Mom replies, which is almost as clever as one of Gwendolyn's proverbs. Then she hugs me. Her hugs still smell just as warm, just as African as ever.

•

I'm wearing a light blue school smock out of Laura Peiraiki-Patraiki fabric that we bought at Mignon. It has two sashes at the sides that tie in a bow at the back, like Gwendolyn's aprons. I've got my red backpack over both shoulders so I don't get a hunchback. My ponytail bounces up and down, creating a breeze that cools the nape of my neck. Mom and I are walking hand in hand down Themistocles Street. For the first little while she'll take me to school and pick me up at the end of the day, but I have to learn the route in case she's sick one day and can't come. "If you get sick, I'll stay home and take care of you," I say. Mom laughs with her whole body, since she's wearing her dress with the big yellow daisies and the pleats on the front. In that dress she laughs even when she's not laughing.

She drops me off at the entrance to my new elementary school. I wave to her from inside the fence like a tiger in a cage. We're supposed to line up according to grade, so I get into line with the other fourth graders for the annual blessing, the national anthem, and morning prayer. After that we do drills—*at ease! attention! at ease! attention!*—and then finally file into our classrooms, which all have doors that open onto the schoolyard. Mine is D3, a room that's painted green halfway up and white the rest of the way, with a world map hanging from a nail over the blackboard. Whenever we have to write on the board the map gets rolled up to make space. My teacher's name is Aphrodite Dikaiakou and she looks sort of African, which is a good sign. She has short, curly hair and dark skin. I go sit at a desk in the last row, in the empty seat next to a girl with braids who tells me her name is Angeliki Kotaki. She has a mole on her eyebrow that looks like a smushed turd. I feel sorry for her because of the mole and decide to protect her. I'll become her best friend and if people dare to make fun of her, they'll have me to deal with.

"You, new girl, stand up!"

Kyria Aphrodite is talking to me.

"Well, where have you come to us from?"

"From Africa."

"Are you sure you didn't come from the moon?"

The other kids laugh. The boy in front of me turns around and makes animal faces. I gather my courage and cry, "I came from Africa! From Nigeria!"

"Fine, there's no need to shout. Come sit up front so I can keep an eye on you."

I sit all by myself at a desk in the front row. The desk is green, the color of Papoutsanis soap, and covered in doodles and carved notes: lots of names and *love forever*, the names of the soccer teams Olympiakos and Panathinaikos, and then *fuck you* and *fart on my balls*. A high school class meets in the same room in the evening. Someone has written, *I'm Apostolos. What's your name?* In beautiful round letters I spell out the only two words I've mastered in Greek: *Maria Papamavrou*.

Kyria Aphrodite tells us what we're going to learn in the fourth grade and why it will be a challenging year. We're going to have to work our very hardest at arithmetic, grammar, penmanship, and geography. Then she gives us a spelling test by dictation: "The children eat their breakfast and go to school. They are diligent students. Mother prepares the afternoon meal. Father works very hard. At lunchtime they eat all together as a family and then relax. In the afternoon they go for a walk in the park." It's almost right, except that we don't all eat together anymore. Mom and I eat on the balcony with the sawed-off railing. Now that no one is there to see, Dad probably eats on the covered veranda in Ikeja with his tie loosened, without washing his hands. And Gwendolyn, standing at the kitchen counter—"Oh dear, like a goat!" Mom sighs.

Recess is the worst part of the day. The kids gather around me and ask if my father is a black priest, since that's what my last name means. Someone notices that half of my pinky finger is missing and shouts: "Look, guys! A lion ate her finger!" Petros, the boy who was making animal faces, asks if we brought our hut with us from Africa. Angeliki, who I thought would be my friend, says that there's no toilet paper in Africa so people poo in the jungle and wipe themselves with leaves from the trees.

"That's not true!" I say, stamping my foot on the schoolyard cement. "We have three bathrooms in Ikeja, and pink toilet paper, pink!"

"Liar! There's no such thing as pink toilet paper, or a house with three bathrooms!" Angeliki says.

I pull her hair to shut her up and she starts to cry. "You're a chicken, Kotaki!" I say, because chicken in Greek is *kota*. Then I stick out my tongue and run to the other end of the yard where the canteen is. I should really get in line, but I'm so angry I just push my way to the front. The canteen sells zodiac crackers, orange-ade, koulouria, which are like bread only round with a hole in the middle, and . . . rocket pops! For only fifty lepta! Two drachmas of pocket money a day equals four rocket pops! I buy my ice cream and sink my teeth into something sugary that's not at all cold. It only looks like an ice cream pop, it's actually stale marzipan. I throw it in the trash and feel like crying, for the hundredth time since we came to Athens.

As soon as we file back into the classroom, Kyria Aphrodite grabs me by the ear and drags me to the blackboard.

"Why did you hit Angeliki during recess? Why did you tear her sash?"

"I didn't tear her sash. I just pulled her hair a little . . ."

"You pulled out a whole clump of my hair and you twisted my ear and you ruined my uniform, too!"

"Liar! Your uniform was already torn!"

"Now listen to me, Maria. You have the greatest number of mistakes of anyone on your spelling test, and let's not even mention your behavior. I don't know what your school in Africa was like, but this is a civilized country. Go and stand in the corner until the bell rings, and if you ever do anything like that again, you'll get what's coming to you."

So now I'm standing in front of the blackboard, facing the world map. It's the most wonderful part of the whole day. I can stare for hours at Nigeria, which is yellow, like my mother's dress, or like the banana boats at the beach. In the middle is the flag with its three stripes, two green ones that stand for agriculture and a white one that stands for unity and peace. I don't know what's happening behind my back, and I don't care, either. I'll become the worst student in the entire school, so I can spend my days standing and staring at the map of Africa.

"Aunt Amalia, what does 'fart on my balls' mean?"

"Christ and the Virgin Mary!" Aunt Amalia puts her hand over her mouth as if she's afraid something bad might come out. She's frozen in place on the path with the statues, in front of the bust of Manto Mavrogenous, who fought in the Greek War of Independence even though she was a woman. Aunt Amalia brought me to the Field of Ares to ride my bike because Mom is busy. Busy means shutting herself up in her room and crying as she strokes her belly and sighs. At the very most she might throw a glance at the biftekia cooking on the stove, then go lie down on the couch.

Aunt Amalia has her hair in a bun under a net and is wearing her camelhair overcoat with the collar up. I can't stand overcoats. I wear my yellow raincoat and galoshes even when it isn't raining. A bird doesn't change its feathers when winter comes, as Gwendolyn says.

"Where did you learn that, child?"

"It says it on my desk. It's been there since September."

"Those are very naughty words, Maria. It's the kind of thing only good-for-nothings would say. Now listen, I want you to dig a hole in your head, put those words in there, and forget all about them. And tomorrow at school I want you to rub it out with an eraser, you hear?"

Aunt Amalia looks like one of those actresses who plays the role of the old maid in Greek movies. But she's a very modern old maid: she goes to the movies alone, takes off one shoe in the middle of the street to scratch her foot with the heel, whistles old songs like "Let Your Hair Down" or "In the Morning You'll Wake Me with Kisses." When she was young she got an idea in her head: she wanted to marry Constantine, who back then was prince and later became king. She didn't want anyone else. When Constantine married Anna-Maria—who's from Denmark, where they call her Anne-Marie—Aunt Amalia told my parents that she was giving up on marriage: she dug a hole in her head and buried all the bouquets and wedding dresses. Whenever anything bad happens, she digs a hole in her head and shoves it in there. Now she's telling me to do exactly the same.

We're headed to the lake to feed the swans. Aunt Amalia always buys two koulouria, one for me and one for her, but she doesn't eat hers, just crumbles it up and throws it to the swans. "Pssst, pssst," she hisses as if they were cats, but these particular swans understand and waddle over. Then they swim back to their little wooden house, fold up their wings and go to sleep.

"Aunt Amalia, if you dig a hole in your head, how many things will it fit?"

"Oh, lots. Lots and lots . . ."

I imagine a hole that's not very big but not very small, either, maybe the size of the wooden house where the swans live. Only I have to fit all of Africa in there: the goldfish pond, the badminton court, Carnival that isn't really Carnival, the puff puffs at Mrs. Fatoba's house. Then I'll squash it all down and put our apartment on top, and Kyria Aphrodite, and the ice cream that isn't really ice cream, and Angeliki and Petros, and our spelling lessons in school. And I won't remember anything anymore.

Kyria Aphrodite is giving us our first penmanship lesson. We copy out the sentence *"Andron epifanon pasa gi tafos"* in our notebooks with curlicued letters. It's ancient Greek and I only understand the last two words, *gi*, earth, and *tafos*, grave, since they're the same in modern Greek. I would rather write "I hate Angeliki because she's a stupid brat," but I'd get in trouble. So I finish my exercise and write a reply to Apostolos, the boy who sits at my desk during the evening high school. He's my only friend in Greece. Each Monday we erase our notes from the previous week and start fresh. I told him I was in the sixth grade, because Apostolos is in the ninth grade and wouldn't want to be writing to a little kid.

I read over last week's correspondence one last time:

Me: *I don't know. I hope we can at least go to Ikeja for Christmas!*

Apostolos: *Why don't you like Greece?*

Me: *1) It's cold. 2) I'm not allowed to ride my bike in the house. 3) There's school every day. 4) There are too many cars. 5) Our teacher is strict and doesn't have a parrot.*

Apostolos: *Did your teacher in Nigeria have a parrot?*

Me: *Yes, our English teacher, Mrs. Fatoba, had a parrot that talked! And she made us puff puffs, which is round fried dough with sugar on top.*

Apostolos: *Why don't you ask your mother to make some?*

Me: *Mom is sad, she doesn't sew anymore, and barely cooks. Only frozen biftekia and lentils, for iron.*

Apostolos: *Are you going to the Polytechnic on November 17?*
Me: *I don't know. Are you?*
Apostolos: *Of course. Give the junta to the people!!!*

I'm not sure what I'm going to ask him next, but I go ahead and start to erase. Kyria Aphrodite grabs me by the wrist the way Mom does, only harder. The eraser falls from my hand.

"What are you doing, Maria?"

She bends down and reads over my shoulder.

"That's it, go stand at the board! And tell your mother to come see me tomorrow."

Mom and Kyria Aphrodite are standing in the yard, talking. Mom is wearing her denim skirt with the horizontal red stripes, which makes her look even bigger than she already is. Kyria Aphrodite is tiny, half a mouthful, but she gestures as if she's the boss and Mom bows her head. The whole scene reminds me of one of Gwendolyn's sayings: The elephant and the tiger don't hunt in the same place. Mom is the elephant, she's been getting fatter and fatter since we got to Athens.

"What did she say?" I ask Mom when they're done talking.

Kyria Aphrodite said she'd done her research and discovered that I have "relations" with a seventeen-year-old plumber who goes to night school. She also said that at my age I shouldn't be getting involved in politics. I feel like showing off, so I tell Mom all the things I learned from Apostolos.

"But Mom, the dictators killed the students, don't you get it? They ran them over with tanks!"

"That's none of your concern."

Angeliki comes over and tries to kiss up to my mother. When there are no adults around I call her Diaboliki. She calls me Teapot, ever since the first day of school with the toilet paper and the jungle. She says "teapot" over and over until it sounds like "potty." Who's she to speak, with that smushed turd on her eyebrow?

"Are you Maria's mom?"

"Yes, dear. Who are you?"

"I'm Maria's friend, Angeliki."

"See, here's a nice girl for you to be friends with. No more scribbling on desks. Will you promise me that?"

And that's how I lose my only friend, Apostolos. I had no idea he was seventeen years old, and studying to be plumber. Now that I know, I invent a dramatic story in my head. He's Hausa, I'm Yoruba, and we can't get married because we're from different tribes. Apostolos climbs onto the gate of the Athens Polytechnic and shouts: "Give the junta to the people!" Then he pulls me up beside him and I shout: "No matter how wrong things go, salt never gets worms!" The police beat us up a little bit, but the worst that happens is that they break my tooth and cut off one of my fingers, and in the end we win. All the dictators from Greece and Nigeria come pouring out of the tanks and run off as fast as they can. Then we climb into one of the tanks, which turns into a house-submarine, and before we even realize what's happening the current has carried us all the way across the Atlantic and, oops, here we are on the coast of Nigeria. We wring out our clothes, spread them on the sand to dry and eat a couple of bananas. The tank is a tank again and we head toward Ikeja. Dad and Gwendolyn are waiting for us on the covered veranda, under the bougainvillea. Apostolos will help Unto Punto with the plumbing in the house. Until we get married, that is. Because afterward he's going to be a doctor and I'll be a painter and we'll have lots of kids, and Gwendolyn will take care of them. On second thought, we won't have any kids, because one of them might die and then what would become of us? We would pull our hair and cry and eat nothing but lentils and biftekia.

A tear rolls down my cheek, then another. I keep forgetting to bring my monogrammed handkerchiefs with me to school.

When a ripe fruit sees an honest person, it falls, Gwendolyn always said. I decide to forget all the dramatic stories and say an honest person's prayer. I stand in front of Mom's little shrine of icons, cross my hands on my chest the way I've been taught, and say, "Lord have mercy, the Father and the Son, let us go back to Ikeja and I'll never ask you for anything else ever again. Amen."

One Sunday morning when he's probably still lying in bed, like me, without much of anything to do, God actually listens.

"Wake up, Maria! I have a surprise for you!" Mom calls from the kitchen.

I jump out of bed and run into the hall in my pajamas.

"Your father can't come to Athens for Christmas, so we'll go and see him. How does that sound?"

I jump up and down and twirl around in circles and dance a dance I made up myself, singing tourourou and lalala and heyhey. Out of habit, I glance up at the ceiling, too, to see if some piece of fruit might be about to fall on my head.

I'm honest, and Ikeja is my ripe fruit.

I squeeze my eyes shut and swear I'll die. It's another Sunday, we just got back from Nigeria, Mom is making her biftekia, cars are screeching to a stop outside the blue building. I try to hold my breath as if I were swimming underwater at the beach in Tarkwa, only for longer. If I can just die a little, if I can at least make myself turn blue, they'll bring me back to Nigeria for good. But I can't: my cheeks burst and I gasp in air through my mouth, my nose, even my ears.

Christmas vacation is over. Tomorrow school starts again. I feel as if I only dreamed the Mercedes at the airport in Lagos; Dad standing and smiling in the doorway of our house in a new pair of beige shorts and socks pulled up to his knees; Gwendolyn's hugs; hide-and-seek with Unto Punto behind the badminton court; my blue flippers; diving off the dock at Tarkwa; the New Year's pie we cut on the beach. My piece had the lucky coin.

"I don't see what's lucky about it," I said to Gwendolyn. "They're still making me go back to Greece."

"Don't be ungrateful," Gwendolyn had replied without lifting her eyes from the iron. "The big iroko tree sprouts from a small seed."

The coin is as small as a fingernail. It says 1977, and it's supposed to bring me luck for this whole year. Mom hung it on the gold ID bracelet I wear on my wrist. I take it off and as I'm lying there snuggled in bed, I use it to pick my nose a little, then put it in my mouth and suck on it. I have no idea how it happens: it just slips gently down my throat, like a fresh, warm puff puff. Oh no, what have I done? I swallowed my luck!

So it isn't strange that the very next day Anna Horn enters my life.

Anna slides into the other seat at my desk in the front row and winks at me. She's the most beautiful girl I've ever seen in my life! An angel—blond, with eyes like the waters of Tarkwa Bay and a tortoiseshell clip holding her bangs back. She has a dimple in her chin and half of one of her eyebrows is totally white, as if it's been dyed, which makes her look wise and just, exactly how a person should look who's waiting for a ripe fruit to fall on her head. She's wearing a *marinière*, as she tells me with a sort of foreign accent— which is to say, a shirt with blue and white stripes.

"You in the front row, new girl," Kyria Aphrodite says. I'm glad Anna is here so I'm not the new girl anymore.

"Yes?" Anna answers imperiously.

"Make sure to wear your uniform to school tomorrow."

"I don't have a uniform. We haven't had a chance to go shopping yet."

"Perhaps you've come from Africa, too, like Maria?"

"No, I came from Paris."

"What am I going to do with all you immigrants?"

"We're not immigrants, Kyria, we're dissidents. My father had a scholarship from the Institut Français. My mother had me in Paris so I wouldn't be a child of the dictatorship. Now that Greece is free again, we came home. Well, not my father. My mother and I. My father is so busy he doesn't even have time to sleep. He has a huge office with over a thousand books, all in French. And he's read them all twice!"

The words come rushing out in a torrent. Kyria Aphrodite doesn't dare interrupt. You could hear a pin drop in the classroom. Anna is a human bee buzzing around, bringing back stories like pollen: about how beautiful the gardens in Paris are, about eating breakfast on Sundays at Café de Flore, or how kind and funny Melina Merkouri is in real life, how you pronounce the French *r* as if it's coming from the inside, from a well in your chest. During recess all the kids flock to her. But Anna chooses me.

"First, because you're my deskmate, and second, because you came from somewhere else, too. Were you guys dissidents in Africa?"

"Kind of," I murmur as we run hand in hand through the schoolyard. Dissidents resist, and resistance is the opposite of dictatorship. Dictators are bad guys, so dissidents must be good guys, and we're with the good guys, for sure. I holler Apostolos's slogan in a sing-song—"Give the junta to the peeeeople!"—and Anna hugs me enthusiastically. We play a skipping game where you sing this song with nonsense words, only instead of "one franc a violet" we chant our new slogan. When we get tired we sit down on the steps in front of our classroom and Anna tears her sandwich in half so we can share it. I'm not sure I really want it because it smells like rotten cheese but Anna insists. "Eat! Comrades share everything!" Why on earth did I ever want to be friends with Angeliki, the smushed turd, when there are girls like Anna in the world? All of a sudden Greece feels wonderful, African.

The big iroko tree sprouts from a small seed.

Anna isn't speaking to me. She wants to divide our desk down the middle. I'm not supposed to let even my elbow creep over onto her half.

"But what did I do? What?"

"You lied to me. There are no dissidents in Africa. My mother says you're racists who exploit black people."

That's going too far! I blurt out all the proverbs Gwendolyn taught me and tell Anna about the games I used to play with Unto Punto. Anna just puts her hands over her ears and sings, "I'm not listening, I'm not listening, I can't hear you!" My eyes fill with tears.

"Please, Anna . . ."

"It's over, we're through. I won't be friends with a racist."

It's recess and we've stayed behind in the classroom to talk, but now Anna storms off in a huff and goes out to play with Angeliki, her new friend. I cry for a while, then tear a sheet out of my penmanship notebook. At the top of the page I write a line by Dionysios Solomos, our national poet: *Freedom requires daring and grace.* Underneath that, in fancy letters, taking care to stay inside the ruled lines, I write: *Dear Mrs. Anna's Mother, We aren't racists!!! I love Gwendolyn even more than my own life. (And Gwendolyn is very black.) I'm an African. Love, Maria.* In the margin I draw two black tears, or dark blue, anyhow, with my pen. At the bottom of the page I sketch the man-made jetty in the harbor in Tarkwa Bay. I draw lots of tiny black people, too, like ants, stretched out in the sun under the palm trees. The sun is smiling, but its teeth are black. Its rays are squiggly, rastafarian. I fold the page in fours and slip it into Anna's primer. She'll find it when she gets home, and I'm sure she'll be mad, but I bet she'll show it to her mother, too.

The rest of the day is hell. Angeliki keeps hissing "teapot, teapot, teapot" behind my back. Kyria Aphrodite doesn't hear, but she catches me sticking my tongue out and sends me to the blackboard until the bell rings. I'm facing the world map again, but this time I don't even look at Africa. I keep my eyes trained on a country in Europe that's exactly the same shape as Nigeria—a country called France.

"My mom says you should come to our house for lunch, if your mother will let you. Do you want to come?"

Anna is looking at Kyria Aphrodite, but she's talking to me.

"So you believe me that I'm not a racist?"

"Do you want to or not?"

"Okay!"

"Only my mother is a ballet dancer and we don't eat things with sauces."

"I don't like sauces."

During recess we stick together and ignore Angeliki. We share Anna's sandwich—the rotten cheese tastes better today—and swear to be friends forever. I'm so happy my nose starts to bleed. I think I'm going to faint, because I can't stand the sight of blood. But I have to seem strong. Anna uses some of the blood to write our names in her notebook as if it were a single name, Anna-Maria.

"It's an oath, you know, now that it's written in blood," she says.

We go back to our anti-junta skipping game. I'm the happiest girl in all of Greece, and in all of Africa, too! When school is out we walk to her house holding hands, our palms slippery with sweat.

"How far is your house, anyway?"

"I'll tell you a secret. Promise not to tell? We lied and said I live where the bakery is, the one across the street from school. I actually live in Plaka. We gave a fake address because our school is experimental and I ab-so-lute-ly *had* to go there. See?"

"If our school is so good, I wonder what the bad ones are like. You mean there are worse teachers than Kyria Aphrodite?"

Anna laughs with her whole face: with her eyes, her cheeks, the dimple in her chin.

"You're so beautiful!" I tell her.

"What matters most is inner beauty," Anna replies. She must've heard it somewhere, it's the kind of thing grown-ups say. But since it's Anna saying it now, I learn it by heart.

Anna's house is like one of the smaller houses in Ikeja. It has a yard with stone walls. Anna unlocks the door with her own key, tosses her bag on the floor and her mother yells *"Allooo"* from the kitchen. Anna runs in and hugs her. When she lets go, the most beautiful mother in the world suddenly appears before me: plump lips, sort of liquid eyes, like Gwendolyn's, hair braided into a shiny black rope that comes all the way down to her waist. She's wearing a black leotard and burgundy tights. She's barefoot and very skinny, like all ballerinas. She bends down and smiles at me. I can see all of her ribs through the leotard, like an X-ray.

"You must be Maria. I'm Antigone."

So I'll call her by her first name, like I did with Gwendolyn! Anna calls her Antigone, too, only she says it funny, with a French accent. They talk in French for a while as I take off my raincoat.

"Where should I put my backpack?"

Anna gestures toward the living room. I can leave my bag wherever I want? On the floor, on the sofa, on the table by the bookshelf? At our house my backpack belongs only in my bedroom, on the floor by my desk.

"Maria, you told your mother you'd be eating with us, right?" Antigone asks.

I pretend not to hear. I didn't tell my mother, but I won't be here that long, will I? I put my backpack on the table, which is buried in books and electricity bills, papers covered with scrawled writing, overflowing ashtrays. Antigone smokes a brand called Gauloises. The pack is a pretty color. Everything in their house is beautiful and strange. They have African statues, like we do, and huge worry beads made out of amber. The tables all have wheels on the legs, because when Antigone practices she needs to roll the furniture out of the way. There's a poster on the wall of a little boy peeing on a crown, and beside it a long, narrow, black-and-white picture with lots of people. All their faces look the same, they're sad because they're carrying a wounded girl on their hands. She might even be dead.

"Do you like that woodblock? It's by Tasos," Antigone says, lighting a cigarette.

"It's nice."

"Do you see how many people suffered in the name of justice and democracy?"

"All those people suffered?"

"Oh, many, many more . . ."

"When we were in Africa and you were in Paris?"

Antigone nods. Her forehead fills with tiny wrinkles. She doesn't have any eyebrows, she draws them on with a pencil.

"Why don't you put something happier on the walls, now that we have democracy?"

"Like what?"

"I don't know, fruit. Or the old guy with the pipe."

"We have to remember those who sacrificed their lives for us, Maria."

She's right. She's beautiful, but she also has what Anna was talking about: inner beauty.

We eat our lunch backwards. First the main dish, chicken with mushrooms, then salad. And then some strange cheeses and Jell-O with chunks of fruit. Antigone eats the way Aunt Amalia does, absentmindedly, a bite now and again, when she remembers. But Anna and I are starving! Their kitchen is so cheerful, with blue walls and yellow cabinets. Like a nursery school.

"I owe you an apology, Maria," Antigone says while she's doing the dishes. Anna has gone out to bring her a newspaper from the kiosk on the corner.

"What for?" I ask.

"For what Anna said to you. You know, apart from good people like you and your parents, there are also lots of bad white people in Africa. Ones who want to take black people's land away and turn them into servants."

I feel my face getting hot. Gwendolyn and Unto Punto *are* servants. But they don't mind.

"What were you doing in Africa?"

"Riding my bike, mostly. Our house was even bigger than yours!"

"Oh my!" Antigone says and bursts out laughing. "What about your parents?"

"Dad worked all the time. Sometimes Mom would sew me dresses. Or she would go for tea with Miss Steedworthy who had a glass eye because her husband hit her. Now she doesn't do anything. She doesn't have any friends in Athens."

Maybe if Antigone feels sorry for Mom she'll want to be her friend, and convince her to go on a diet so she can wear her dress with the daisies again.

Antigone's face gets all wrinkled again. Whenever she's thinking, her face looks like a crumpled piece of paper. "Do you think your mother might be interested in joining the League of Democratic Women? It's an organization for women on the left."

"What do they do?"

"They talk about their rights, discuss domestic violence . . ."

"If they sew, too, I'm sure she would go."

"Here, let's give her a call together."

Fantastic! Mom and Antigone will meet and become friends, just like me and Anna. Dola and Bambi, minus the jealousy. I carefully dial the six numbers.

"Hi, Mom, Anna's mom wants to know if you want to know about the League of Democratic Women."

"What I want to know, Maria Papamavrou, is where in heaven's name are you? If you think it's okay to go traipsing around wherever you want, you've got another think coming! You'd better come home this instant! Now!" Mom is shouting. I cover the receiver with my hand so her voice won't be heard all the way down in Plaka.

"Well, what does she say?" Antigone asks.

"She says she's not feeling well and I should come home right away to take care of her."

Antigone drives me home in her Beetle—a car that looks like a turtle and shudders all over as it moves. In my head I hear Gwendolyn say: *The fear of tomorrow makes the turtle carry its home wherever it goes.* That's what I want for myself, too. To have a house I can carry on my back, like my red backpack with its shoulder straps. To not live with Mom and have to do whatever she says. Anna and I are in the back seat of the Beetle. She keeps stroking my hand, though avoiding my pinky finger, since it's kind of scary. "Poor thing, I hope your mother hasn't gotten malaria and lost any of her fingers, like you." I lied and told her my finger rotted and fell off because of a terrible African sickness.

Antigone wants to come upstairs to the apartment and bring Anna, too. "Women's solidarity," she says. I tell her my mother doesn't like to have people around when she's sick, and to make it more dramatic I say that sometimes Mom breaks plates when she's annoyed. That's pretty revolutionary, the League of Democratic Women will love it. When we pull up outside our building in Exarheia I shoot from the car like a bullet, I forget to say thank you, and by the time I'm at the top of the stairs to the front door it's too late: Antigone steps on the gas and the exhaust pipe belches a thick cloud of fumes. A tiny hand waves to me out the car window. It's the hand of Anna, my friend!

I'm being punished. Not in front of the world map, but in the kitchen pantry. So I'll learn that we never, ever go anywhere unless we call home first. I'm sitting on a stool, taking an inventory of the food on the shelves. Misko pasta, twenty boxes. Swan tomato paste, twelve cans. Nounou sweetened condensed milk, twenty cans. Alsa chocolate mousse and Yiotis cornflower, three boxes each. If only we had a storage room as big as the one in Ikeja! There you could never get bored. Sometimes it was hard to buy things at the market, so we had our own supermarket at home. It would take days to read all the names of the things we bought at the American base. Of course back then I was practically never punished. Mom was much more patient and at the very most would call me "silly girl," never "Maria Papamavrou," which is what she says when she's mad. Now, though, things are different. The salt might even have worms. I climb onto the stool and open a cardboard box of Kalas sea salt to check. No worms yet. A few cans shift and fall. I lose my balance, the stool clatters to the ground, and suddenly I'm on the floor. I prop myself on one elbow but my other arm, from elbow to wrist, has taken on a funny shape, it's looking off somewhere else. By the time I realize how much it hurts, my mother has unlocked the pantry door and is looking first at my face, then at my arm, and shouting, "Dear God!"

The cast makes me stand out. Even the kids in the fifth and sixth grades who never talk to fourth-graders want to know what happened. "Oh, it's nothing, I just broke my arm," I say with a heroic sigh. "At least it's your left arm," says one of the fifth-grade girls. How is she supposed to know I'm left-handed? Anna is my bodyguard. During recess she clears a path for me to pass, shouting, "Come on, guys, can't you see we've got a wounded person on our hands? Merde, merde!" Merde means shit in French. It's what we call Angeliki, too. Anna told her that "merde" is how you say Angeliki in French and she fell for it. Today I feel sort of sorry for Angeliki. She asked me what my sign is. "Sagittarius," I said, and she didn't make any jokes about natives hunting in the jungle with bows and arrows, just picked two archers out of her box of zodiac crackers and gave them to me.

One big pro of the cast: I'm off the hook during penmanship class, and I get to draw instead. Drawing with my right hand is really hard, especially since I only have four fingers. My circles come out wobbly, my lines tremble, but I'd rather draw than practice my penmanship. Plus this way, if there's ever another dictatorship and we have to fight the tanks and the soldiers break one of my arms, I'll already know how to draw with the other hand. Every day my mother pulls my hair back into a ponytail and cooks food you can eat with your fingers: biftekia, fries, and puff puffs, at last! Antigone drew a peace sign on my cast. Anna wrote "merde," but this time it doesn't mean shit, it means good luck.

"Do you want me to teach you French, now that we can't play during recess?" she asks. "When we grow up we'll go to study in France, Greek universities are terrible."

"Where will we live?"

"In Paris, of course! At our house."

First we learn the numbers and the days of the week. Then how to answer the phone (*haalloooo, qui est à l'appareil?*), *bonjour, bonsoir,* I'm hungry (*j'ai faim*), I'm sleeping (*je dors*). I call hide-and-seek *cache-cache* now, not *dezi* like I did in Africa. Ripe fruit is *fruit mûr,* and honest person is *personne honnête.* Pretty soon I'll be able to translate Gwendolyn's proverbs!

The best French lessons are the ones with music. Anna and I sit on the coffee table with wheels and move it gently with our feet. We pretend it's a magic carpet and that we're revolutionary witches. Our carpet goes wherever we tell it to as we sing songs about the wretched of the earth: "*Du passé faisons table rase, foule esclave, debout! Debout! Le monde va changer de base! Nous ne sommes rien, soyons tout!*" Or we listen to the sad songs of Françoise Hardy: "*Que sont devenus tous mes amis et la maison où j'ai vecu . . .*" A woman is feeling sad because she's living far from home. Just like us.

Anna talks about her dad all the time, about the apartment in Paris, about all the books he's read, about the French and Greek people who used to come over every night with wine and cigarettes to brainstorm anti-dictatorship slogans.

"The smoke didn't bother you?"

"Are you crazy, merde? Smoking helps you think."

We try to light a Gauloises in the kitchen.

"Suck in!" Anna shouts. "You have to suck in!"

I suck in and choke. I do whatever she tells me because she knows all about history and penmanship and how to fly a magic carpet, she knows revolutionary songs and can do all of the exercises in *The Key to Practical Arithmetic.* She has a beautiful, skinny mother with no eyebrows and a dad who thinks all day long. She has the blondest hair in the world. Thank goodness I'm better at drawing. Otherwise I'd be jealous and then there'd be trouble, like with Dola and Bambi.

Carnival in Greece reminds me of the theme parties we used to have in Ikeja. One morning we'd say, Hey, why don't we all wear polka dots to the Marine Club tomorrow, and then next week we can dress up as Robinson Crusoe? Only Carnival lasts a long time, so you get to dress up a lot. For the parties at school my mother dresses me as a nun. The boys decide I'm a Catholic nurse and ask if I want to join their war effort. Anna gets annoyed. She's dressed as a flower child, and no one wants a hippie on the front lines. Whereas I can treat their wounds in the washbasins in the yard. Besides, my cast means I'm a wounded nurse, and *that* means I'm a true heroine. Not to mention my missing finger . . .

"Forget about that stupid war," Anna says, trying to pull me away. "We're going to a protest."

"What protest?"

"For the League of Democratic Women."

She starts pinching all the boys so they'll let me go. Then she insists on us singing the song about Petros, Yiohan, and Frantz working together in the factory. But isn't that what we do every day? War is more original.

"War is what babies and Americans play," Anna says.

With a heavy heart I leave the front line and go back to protesting. Angeliki wants to march with us but she's dressed as a harem woman. Anna tells her that women in harems are the slaves of men and any woman who does men's bidding deserves only pity. Angeliki starts to cry and takes off her fez. Her hair is a mess and her nose is running. I feel like hugging her, I always feel sorry for people when they cry, but Anna gets between us and shakes a finger in my face, saying, "She's crying now, but later she'll be calling you Teapot." What can I say? She's right. A bird doesn't change its feathers when winter comes.

After the protest we drink an orangeade, the kind without fizz. Anna is sunk in thought. "What's wrong?" I ask. She tells me that we should be going to real protests and hanging out with older boys from the working class, like Apostolos the plumber. She makes me write and propose a meeting. *Apostolos, do you want to meet the day after tomorrow, when school lets out?* He writes back, *How will I recognize you?*, and I reply, *I'll be dressed as a nun.*

We wait outside the gate, a nun and a hippie. Apostolos is pretty cute, but he has two chipped teeth, so he could never be my husband. Besides, he pays absolutely no attention to me. He asks Anna who drew the beautiful daisies on her cheeks. "Me!" I cry, but Apostolos just asks about Paris and if she liked living there, as if he didn't hear me at all. Anna goes on and on about the Fourth International, the proletariat, the League of Democratic Women and Georges Brassens, throwing in whatever she knows, and Apostolos gazes at her admiringly. I, meanwhile, am bored to tears. I sit on the curb, eyes glued to my knees, waiting for them to be done so we can finally leave.

Every Friday afternoon Antigone gives us ballet lessons in the living room of their house in Plaka. So I learn even more French words, like *pas de chat*, which means step of the cat. First, second, and third position. *Plié*, to bend. *Relevé*, to lift. In the end Antigone does a split and we clap and shout "*Encore!*" Then we go out for a walk. Antigone wears embroidered shirts and holds us by the hand as if we were both her daughters.

"We're Anna-Maria!" I say, laughing.

"Don't ever say that again!" Antigone says. "That's the name of that fool of a princess."

Sometimes, on the weekend, Mom lets me sleep at Anna's. We take a bath together, then Antigone dries our hair with a towel and does it up in little braids or buns or ponytails. Then she smokes her Gauloises cigarettes or calls Paris, and while she's not paying attention we play house, or sometimes build a fort with a blanket. Anna always wants the houses we live in to have special furniture, special music, a special atmosphere. "You should be thankful, if I had my way we wouldn't live in a house at all," she says, "we'd just fly around on our magic carpet!" The conversations about revolution are kind of boring, but I let her have her way on that, at least. After all, even in the half-light under the blanket, Anna can see right through me. If I disagree, she'll pinch.

Shortly before the end of the school year, Aunt Amalia buys me a game called Little Wizard, a box full of magic tricks. You learn how to make colorful bits of paper disappear or do card tricks or hide plastic animals in a hat with a false bottom. Anna and I climb onto the magic carpet and do magic tricks for an imaginary audience of poor kids. Everything always has to be about the poor. That's why Anna gets mad when Aunt Amalia takes us to see *My Fair Lady*, a movie about Eliza Doolittle, who starts out as a beggar but by the end is a real princess, after an aristocrat takes her in off the street and teaches her how to speak properly. Eliza's name in real life is Audrey Hepburn. She has a very long neck and wears her hair in a bun. Aunt Amalia gets tears in her eyes, probably because she's thinking how if things had turned out differently, she too could have lived like a princess. I want to tell her that the princess Constantine married was a fool, but Aunt Amalia says, "Shhh, don't talk in the movie theater." My favorite scene is when Eliza Doolittle can't sleep because she's in love with the aristocrat. The maid puts her to bed but she keeps popping back up to her feet like a spring. Anna grunts in disgust and says that Eliza was happier back when she was selling flowers in the street and hadn't gotten so hoity-toity. "But she's not!" I cry. "Of course she is," Anna says, "just like you."

"Where is your family going to spend the summer?" Aunt Amalia asks Anna on the way home.

"*A Paris.*"

"I'm going to Ikeja, right?"

"No, honey. You're coming to Aegina with me."

Merde, merde.

Martha and I are sitting on the low wall in the garden, playing beauty pageant. Martha and Fotini are sisters, and they're my summer friends on Aegina. Only today Fotini is grounded: she stole a teacup from Martha's tea set, hid it in the yard, and won't say where. Her punishment is that she has to stay in her room until it's time for the live broadcast of the Thessaloniki Song Festival. The girls have an older brother, Angelos, who is in high school, but he doesn't talk to us. Each summer Aunt Amalia rents a room on the ground floor of the girls' house, where their grandfather used to live before he died. She and I sleep together in the double bed. We leave the windows open and the bougainvilleas outside shape the shadows of junta fascists, or the grandfather's ghost. One night I got scared and woke up Aunt Amalia, who sleeps with curlers in her hair. "Oh, Maria, there's no reason to be scared, with these curlers I'd frighten even a ghost away!"

In the mornings we have breakfast together. The girls' mother, Kyria Pavlina, has a goat and makes her own yogurt. The only bad part is that we eat it at their kitchen table, under a strip of fly paper covered with dead flies. Kyria Pavlina doesn't like to kill flies with a fly swatter. She prefers for them to get stuck on the paper and die on their own.

After breakfast we go down to the beach to swim or to dig deep holes in the sand. Fotini and Martha are always singing a song by the child star Manos: *You don't live in my time, Mom, you don't live in my time, Dad . . .* I like it a lot but I also know it would annoy Anna. In fact we do all kinds of things that Anna wouldn't like. We watch *Little House on the Prairie* and wear cherry lip gloss during our beauty contests. There are three titles, one for each of us: Miss Beauty, Miss Inner Beauty, and Miss Youth. Fotini always ends up being Miss Youth because she's the youngest. Martha likes being Miss Beauty, and I'm happy with Miss Inner Beauty, so it works out just fine for us all.

"Girls, the festival is starting!" Kyria Pavlina calls. Martha and I abandon our beauty pageant in the middle and run to the television. Fotini comes, too, since her punishment is over. We're rooting for a girl, Roula, who sings in the commercial for Roli cleaning powder. *Please tell me, Dad, is love good or bad? Today he gave me my first kiss, and I cried with bliss . . .* Her father gives his approval and Roula gets as excited as Eliza Doolittle: *Well, then, I'll say it, I love a boy, I love him and I want him tons!*

This summer I'm in love with Angelos. He's very serious and wants to be a nuclear physicist. We only see him in the morning when he wakes up and at night before he goes to bed. The whole rest of the day he's out roaming around with his friends. I've lost all interest in tanks and submarines. No more lies. Mom has gone to help Dad empty out the house in Ikeja. She left me behind, with Aunt Amalia.

Next fall Gwendolyn will be telling her proverbs to other kids.

I keep whistling the tune to "Please Tell Me, Dad," but Anna covers her ears when she hears it. Of course I don't tell her about the beauty pageants.

"Aegina ruined you," she says, raising an eyebrow, the one with the white streak.

"Why?"

"It made you dumb."

I look down at my shoes. She's right, after all.

"But maybe it's not your fault, it's those girls, what were their names again? Fotini and Martha."

Anna lectures me about how the Socialist Party in Sweden lost power after forty-four years and how the Workers' Party in Great Britain is weaker than ever before, as if I were to blame. She tells me that in Paris she made some important decisions, when she grows up she wants to be like Gisèle Halimi, Sartre, and de Beauvoir's lawyer who risked imprisonment for supporting the Algerian National Liberation Front. I understand barely half of what she says, but I keep nodding my head. She's determined to bring me back to the proper path, and tells me about Patty Hearst, who disowned her rich father and started robbing banks, and sixteen-year-old Nadia Comăneci, the human rubber band from the Montreal Olympics. We braid our hair to look like Comăneci, put on our gym clothes, roll aside the portable table in the living room and practice our splits. Next is modern dance. Anna always chooses the theme. Our choreographies have names like "Long Live the Revolution" or "The Students" or "A Carnation on the Polytechnic Memorial." The dances are full of *pas de chat* and when we start to sweat, we lie down on the rug and stare at the ceiling.

"A perfect score!" Anna tells me. "You're not dumb anymore."

I hug her and we roll like barrels into the hall, splitting our sides with laughter. That's where Antigone finds us when she opens the front door.

"You crazy girls, *on va manger quelque chose?*"

We eat backwards this year, too, main course first, then salad. Antigone shows me pictures from their summer in France. The whole family went to Deauville, to the house of some friends.

Anna's father has a blondish beard. In all of the photographs he's smoking a pipe and reading a newspaper. Anna is sitting in his lap, arms wrapped around his neck.

"Do you love your dad a lot?"

"What do you mean, don't you love yours?"

"Sure, I love him, only I've forgotten what he's like."

And yet that very same night, Mom and Dad come home from the airport. I cling to my father's neck, just like Anna, and burst into tears.

"Why are you crying, little grasshopper?" Dad says.

"Don't call her that, please!" Mom says, and she starts crying, too.

I'm afraid that now that he's come back to Athens Dad might start calling me Maria Papamavrou and saying that I'm a naughty girl, the way Mom does. I'm afraid that now that we live in Athens I might actually be turning into a naughty girl, not to mention a dumb one. That I might have left all my goodness and smarts in Africa.

This fall we have a man for a teacher, Kyrios Stavros. He's short and wears silk vests that barely contain his big belly. The fifth-grade reader is called *The High Mountains* and Kyrios Stavros says we're going to like it a lot because it's full of adventures. My biggest adventure, though, is the week when Anna stays home because she has the mumps. Angeliki keeps saying "teapot" over and over until it sounds like "potty," and Petros picks his nose, chases me down, and wipes his snot on my legs.

"When are you coming back to school?" I ask Anna over the phone.

"Not until my cheeks aren't swollen anymore."

"Anna, you have to come back. It's awful without you!"

I tell her about the things the other kids do to me during recess and Anna plots our revenge: we'll handcuff them to the fence and tickle them, we'll spit in their food.

Since she's been sick in bed, Anna finished the entire fifth-grade reader. She says it's almost as good as *Petros's War* or *Wildcat under Glass*.

"What are they?"

"You mean you've never heard of Alki Zei? Merde!"

I make Mom buy me all of Alki Zei's books and I read them at night in bed. Anna's right. They're wonderful, especially *Wildcat under Glass*, with the two sisters who say ve-ha, ve-sa when they want to show whether they're very happy or very sad.

"Ve-ha? Ve-sa?" I ask Anna over the phone, so she'll know I read *Wildcat under Glass*.

"Ve-sa, because I have the mumps."

I puff up my cheeks, trying to imagine what it would be like to have the mumps. Sometimes I'd like to be Anna, for better or for worse.

Kyrios Stavros tells us Savings Day is coming up and there are going to be two contests, for best essay and best drawing; the prize is a money-box from the postal bank. Anna and I both enter the drawing contest. Anna draws a bank all in pastel colors. The teller is giving money away to everyone. There's a cloud over his head with the words "*Liberté, Egalité, Fraternité!*" There are doves flying all around, and Patty Hearst is standing in one corner with her machine gun. Over her head it says, "*With so much justice in the world, who needs me?*"

"You didn't follow the theme," Kyrios Stavros tells her, and Anna sticks her tongue out at him when his back is turned.

My drawing is in colored pencil, of the storage room in Ikeja and a family living in there. I make the mother like Antigone, skinny, with a braid and fake eyebrows, only she's wearing Mom's dress with the yellow daisies. The dad has a beard, he's smoking a pipe and reading the newspaper *Acropolis*, which is the newspaper my father reads. The little girl has long blond hair, bangs, and a dimple in her chin. She's taking a can of milk down off the shelf and handing it to her little brother, a tiny baby who can't walk yet. The baby is hard to draw, it comes out looking like a caterpillar. I keep erasing it and trying again. When I finally get it right, my picture is beautiful. Up top I draw a rainbow that's raining drachmas, naira, and francs, which all turn into daisies as they fall to earth.

Kyrios Stavros comes into the classroom with the school superintendent.

"Will Maria Papamavrou please stand up?" the superintendent says.

What did I do now?

"Your drawing won first prize for our school. Come up front to accept your prize."

I walk toward the teacher's desk with bowed head. The superintendent congratulates me, kisses the top of my head, and hands me a blue money-box with a metal handle.

"Now applaud your classmate," Kyrios Stavros says.

Everyone claps, except for Angeliki and Anna.

"You're a thief!" Anna says. "You stole my family."

"But your family is better than mine, that's why."

She wants to split our desk down the middle again. I'm so happy about the prize that I don't object. When the bell rings at the end of the day Anna says, "I'll forgive you, but only if you give me your drawing."

"What if my parents want it?"

"Tell them you lost it."

Fortunately my drawing gets published in *Acropolis*. Dad clips it out carefully so he can have it framed.

"When I grow up, I'm going to be an artist," I tell him.

"That's not a job," Mom says. "You should choose a proper career, you can make art in your free time."

"But if I have some other job, where will I find free time?"

"You'll manage. Don't I find time to shop and to cook, and to take you to the park?"

"Yeah, but all you cook is biftekia and lentils, and you don't take me to the park all that much, either."

Mom gives me a threatening look, but she doesn't punish me. After I broke my arm she got rid of the key to the pantry. Now when she gets angry it's different: she just clenches her fists, lifts her eyes to the ceiling, and mutters under her breath.

Anna ruined my drawing!

"I didn't ruin it, I corrected it!" she shouts.

She drew doves all over the top of the page. She crossed out Dad's *Acropolis* with red poster paint and made it into an *Avgi*, the left-wing paper her parents read. She colored in the baby entirely, turned it into a coffee table and added Gauloises cigarettes and an ashtray on top.

"We're both only children, don't forget," she says.

I don't like being an only child. It's like saying lonely child. I'm jealous of Fotini and Martha, who share a room and can say ve-ha, ve-sa every night, like the sisters in *Wildcat under Glass*.

"I'd like to have a little brother or sister," I say.

"We're like sisters, aren't we?"

"Sure, but only on weekends."

And there's something else, too: when Fotini hid Martha's teacup in the yard, Kyria Pavlina sent her to her room. But who's going to punish Anna for destroying my drawing?

•

This year I'm sitting at the third desk from the front and I can't see the board very well. The letters are blurry and I have to squint to read our exercises.

"What's wrong, Maria?" Kyrios Stavros asks. "Do you think you need to see an eye doctor?"

Antigone gives Mom the name of a pediatric optometrist who studied in Paris. We go and sit in the waiting room. Mom is happy because there's a recent issue of *Woman* in the stack of magazines with an announcement for an embroidery and knitting contest. "I'll knit a blanket," she says. "Our family will sweep up every prize around!"

A man with a white coat and glasses shakes our hands.

"Come this way, miss."

He tells me to rest my forehead on a metal surface with little plastic bits for your eyes and use a knob to put a parrot in a cage. He jots something down in his notes. Then he tells me to read some numbers on a lighted board across the room. The numbers are kind of blurry so he puts these little lenses in front of my eyes and asks, "Is it better now? Or now?" With some of the lenses I can read even the tiniest numbers on the board. The doctor says I'm nearsighted, enough that I need glasses. I feel like crying.

"What's wrong, miss? Don't you know how stylish glasses can be?"

Yeah, sure.

"What do you want to be when you grow up?"

"I'm going to be a painter," I say, and then, looking at Mom, "and something else, too."

"How wonderful! All artists wear glasses, didn't you know?"

"All of them?"

"Anyone who thinks a lot, dear," the eye doctor says, tapping his own glasses.

Well, then. If I'm going to be a great painter, I guess I might as well wear glasses.

The next day Mom, Aunt Amalia, and I go to Metaxas Eyewear near Omonia Square. Mom insists on black tortoiseshell frames with wavy bits of red. The saleswoman says they look great on me, but I can't really see my face, I look blurry in the mirror.

"I really look good?"

"Miss Inner Beauty!" Aunt Amalia says.

These days inner beauty isn't enough. I want to be beautiful on the outside, too. We order the glasses. They'll be ready in a week.

"I'm so jealous that you get to wear glasses!" Anna says.

"Wait until you see them first."

"Glasses are *always* pretty," Anna says, and I sigh with relief.

"You're an owl, Teapot!" Angeliki says.

"An African owl," says Petros.

Anna and I pinch them as hard as we can so they'll stop, but they just put their hands over their mouths and dissolve into laughter.

"You're an ugly four-eyes!" Angeliki shouts.

"She has inner beauty!" Anna shouts back.

"Only inner?" I ask, but Anna is busy pinching the others and doesn't respond.

"I'm sure Angelos will fall for you," she says when the bell rings at the end of the day. "You look older, more mature. A ripe fruit!"

"And when a ripe fruit sees an honest person, it falls."

Anna loves it when I use Gwendolyn's proverbs. She gives me a sloppy kiss on the cheek.

"You're my best friend!"

"And you're mine!"

"Want to go pee?" she says.

When we're best best friends, like today, we go and pee in a parking lot on the next street over from our school. We slip between the cars, pull down our underwear and a little fountain of pee spurts onto the ground, splashing our socks and shoes. We never pee at the same time, so that whoever's not peeing can be the lookout. Anna wiggles her tush and sings Françoise Hardy. I don't move at all and only sing on the inside, *Well then, I'll say it, I love a boy* . . . I always take off my glasses, too, so they don't get splashed.

Only today there's a man in the car next to us. He slowly opens his door and says, "Girls, do you want to see my ice cream?" Anna vanishes, but I feel like it wouldn't be polite to run away. The man is holding his ice cream down low, between his legs, a reddish-brown rocket pop with a little cream at the top. Something isn't right. I take a few steps backward. When I'm far enough away, my heart starts beating loudly in my ears. Now is the time to use a phrase only good-for-nothings say. I make my hands into a megaphone and shout, "Fart on my balls!"

Anna holds out her hand. She's pale as a ghost. We wrap an arm around each other and run in no particular direction.

"All men are monsters," Anna says.

Merde, merde. All of them?

"He tricked you, Paraskevoula, the mayor's son . . ." We're dancing a kalamatiano in the schoolyard. We're still so upset about the perversion of men that we're not really paying attention to the words. The song gets stuck in our heads. The whole way home, all the way to Plaka, we dance the kalamatiano instead of walking. Our favorite bit is the little leap at the beginning when you lunge at the sidewalk and stomp your foot. At home, too, while Antigone is making us lunch, we're in the living room dancing. Suddenly she rushes into the room holding a half-peeled potato and a knife.

"What is this nonsense?"

We don't understand.

"Who taught you that?"

We shrug.

Antigone says that the kalamatiano was what people who supported the junta used to dance. And that the song we're singing is about a rich man taking advantage of a poor girl and if that's the kind of thing we like, we deserve whatever we get. Haven't we come into this world to fight hypocrisy? She'll take us to the Peroke Theater and give us something to think about: they're presenting two one-act plays, Chekov's *A Marriage Proposal* and Brecht's *A Respectable Wedding*.

We eat somberly, in silence. After lunch I go to the bathroom to wash my hands and through the open door I see Antigone sitting at the dressing table in her bedroom. Should I tell her I'm sorry for dancing the kalamatiano? She's fixing her hair, only her shiny braid is lying on the bed, and there's a little bun at the back of her head full of hairpins and clips. Antigone has short hair! The braid is a wig!

Then why did she tell us we've come into the world to fight hypocrisy?

Antigone takes us with her to the anniversary of the events at the Athens Polytechnic, when the dictators sent in tanks to kill the students who'd occupied the building. We bought red carnations to bring with us to the peace march. I told Mom I was going to Anna's house to do my homework, because she doesn't like demonstrations. She won't join the League of Democratic Women, either. She doesn't have time, she's too busy knitting her blanket for the contest in *Woman*. "Such a waste of time," Mom says. "Anna's mother has her head in the clouds." I still like Antigone, even if she's lying about her braid. She's skinny and she's fighting for justice, working to make the world a better place. Sometimes I dream that she's my real mother, and I always feel proud when strangers in the street say, "What lovely daughters you have."

"You should take off your glasses," Anna whispers. "There might be trouble."

Trouble? Like a state of emergency? Like with the Igbo and Hausa, people setting fires? What if someone grabs Antigone by the hair and her secret is revealed?

A man tells us that people are throwing stones over by the American embassy. But outside the Polytechnic things are calm. The huge bust in front of the building is festooned with carnations and the protesters are singing a Mikis Theodorakis song in unison: *"Life keeps climbing upward, life keeps climbing upward. With flags, with flags and drums."* Luckily Anna already taught me that song. I don't want to sing about boys and love anymore. I could care less! We sing ourselves hoarse, red in the face from trying to sing louder than anyone else. We're the biggest revolutionaries in all of Athens! That's the only way we'll get a scholarship from the Institut Français to go study painting in Paris for free. Anna doesn't want to be a lawyer like Gisèle Halimi anymore. She decided to study art, too. She wants us to be exactly alike.

We play our anti-junta skipping game all the way home. Then, at the house in Plaka, Anna puts on a Manos Loizos record while Antigone peels carrots.

"What would you like for your birthday?" Antigone asks me.

I'm happy that she remembered my birthday. "I don't know, whatever you think . . ."

"You don't want anything in particular? Come on, tell me."

Her knife flashes like lightning, she's barely scratching the peel, since that's where all the vitamins are. What I'd like most of all is to be able to peel carrots as gracefully as Antigone, then to toss them in water, boil them, and make a yummy sauce with lemon.

"Okay, then, I'd like a tea set, or dishes."

"A tea set? Oh, don't disappoint me, Maria. I'll get you *The Carousel*, okay?"

"What's *The Carousel*?"

"It's a record. The text is by Georges Sarri."

I'm ashamed of having disappointed her by wanting a tea set. It's easy to disappoint Antigone. She yells at us if she catches us reading *Patty's World*. But what does Patty do that's so terrible? She just loves Johnny Vowden, goes around town with her friend Sharon, and wants to be a nurse when she grows up. Antigone doesn't like women who become nurses and take care of men.

Sometimes I wish I were a boy.

I blow out all ten candles at once. Anna does a wolf whistle, Fotini and Martha clap. It's too bad Angelos didn't come. I wipe my sweaty palms on my velvet dress with the cherries. I'm more grown-up than ever now!

Dad takes pictures. Mom holds out a tray of bite-sized cheese pies to Kyria Pavlina. Mom is happy, the way she used to be, because she won second prize in the knitting contest. She hung a photograph from the awards ceremony in the hall, next to the coat rack.

Aunt Amalia doesn't want any cheese pies. Antigone doesn't, either. She puts on *The Carousel* and tells us to listen carefully to the lyrics: "*If all the children of the world held hands, boys and girls all in a row, and began to dance, the circle would grow and grow until it hugged the whole world.*" We girls form a circle and dance around the dining room table with all the other kids all over the world. When we're out of breath, we crawl under the table and play house. Anna is the dad, I'm the mom, and Martha and Fotini are our kids. We live in Africa, not in a house but in the jungle with the tigers. Then we live in Paris and drink coffee at Café de Flore. Martha starts whining because she wants us to live on Aegina, too, but Anna says, "Merde, we're not rednecks!"

We go into my room and play doctor. Anna is the doctor. She examines our behinds and pinches us with her nails when she has to give an injection. She writes us prescriptions for eye drops. Suddenly, as if she's just remembered something very important, she jumps to her feet and shouts, "Enough of this silly stuff! Let's go to the demonstration! We're the League of Democratic Women!"

"I'm not coming to the demonstration," says Fotini. "I don't like that game."

Anna's face clouds over. "It's not a game, merde. It's the struggle for a better life!"

"*No way* am I playing," Fotini says.

Anna goes over and pinches her. "I said, it's *not a game*."

Fotini doesn't cry, just opens her mouth wide.

Three

"Close your mouth, Daphne. A fly might get in."

I don't have to say it twice.

"Where do witches live?" she asks.

She's frozen in place, twirling a lock of her hair. That particular vanity seems to run in the family: Antigone's braid, Anna's barrettes.

"In caves."

"What do they eat?"

"Grasshoppers!"

She gasps in wonder. That must run in the family, too—Anna was always drawn to strange people, bizarre stories. The little girl scratches at her knee, takes a step backward, and stumbles.

"Watch where you're going! Why don't you walk normally, silly?"

"I'm scared you might turn me into a tiger, miss."

"As long as you behave, there's no reason to be afraid."

Daphne nods her head frantically, then runs out of the classroom, pulling the door shut behind her. I listen as her footsteps clatter down the stairs.

The room looks as if a bomb went off. Surprised by Daphne's sudden attack, the children left colored pencils, papers, markers, erasers lying everywhere. I pick it all up, leave everything in an ordered pile on the desk and go to find Saroglou.

"Have you ever seen such a child?" she exclaims.

"I know her mother. She used to be a friend of mine."

"She must be paying for some pretty juicy sins, to have a child like that."

"Oh, I don't know . . ."

"Why, was she a bookworm or something?"

"Not at all. She was captivating," I say.

"Well then, it's nature punishing her."

That's it. Daphne torments Anna the way Anna once tormented me. History repeats itself.

"Don't you dare switch on the light!" Kayo pulls a pillow over his face. Beside him, Anna-Maria does the same: she puts a leg over her eyes and starts to lick herself.

"But it's almost evening! You're still in bed?"

Kayo stretches and twists a few times under the sheet. I stroke his hair: thousands of tiny rasta braids, rough to the touch, like everything about Kayo. He's changed. New York brought him down, made him melancholy. His beauty dried up from within. Only his eyes still spark the way they used to.

"Get up! I've got news."

"Anna?"

"How did you know it's about Anna?"

"You've got this look on your face as if you were nineteen years old again."

In actuality, I'm almost thirty-five. But if we see life as a cycle, I'm still right where I was. I live in the same apartment in the blue building, not with my parents anymore, but with a depressed homosexual. The gap between the balcony rails has been there for nearly a quarter of a century, mocking my useless attempts at

escape. Nothing else from that era remains. The pantry is a darkroom, where we print our posters. The house hasn't smelled of lav-
ender or steam irons since my parents decided to move to Aegina
for good. Kayo brought an air of healthy living when he came: he
doesn't smoke and gets high off scentless little pills. The bathroom
smells of aftershave, the kitchen of cat food. I hate cats, but there
was nothing I could do: when he showed up with an angora that
was just skin and bones, as lost in life as he was, I had to either
take both of them in or send them both away. "Her name is Anna-
Maria," he'd said. "Why? She doesn't look much like a princess."
"Yes, but she's an odd mix of daring and timid," he answered slyly.
Apparently the cat had Anna's daring, but my timidity.

Kayo, Anna-Maria, and I have been living together since New
Year's, 1997. That day when he showed up, it had been roughly
twenty years since I swallowed my luck in the form of the coin
from a New Year's pie, and ten years since the show for graduates
of the School of Fine Arts, when I thought painting was the most
important thing in the world. Just five years since Aunt Amalia
died, and since we adopted the slogan "I bleed, therefore I am."
The socialists are still in charge of the country, they built a subway
and a few highways to placate the populace. But we didn't give in:
we made posters urging an occupation of the Attic Highway. We
painted the facades of a few banks with Day-Glo paint. Lots of people still think we're just pranksters. That a revolution based on colors, music, and demands for a better life is childish. And of course
those were difficult years to be launching protests in Greece: all of
a sudden the country was flooded with new money, fresh capital
that pulled the wool over people's eyes, tricked them into thinking
the prosperity was real. So we started to attend demonstrations in
more affluent countries, where people had a better sense of what it
meant for that flood of money to drown you, in the end. In 1998,
in Geneva, Kayo and some others overturned the Central Bank

director's Mercedes and we spent two nights in jail. In 1999 we sat on a crowded bus for days just to go back and shake the hands of the Zapatistas, members of the Indian KRRS, the landless of Bangladesh, people of all stripes who were protesting third world debt, genetically modified food, and the colonization of the global South. In June of that same year we flew to Nigeria to shout slogans against the oil companies, standing in a crowd of thousands to welcome Owens Wiwa as he returned to his homeland from exile. I was hesitant, but in the end I decided to go to Ikeja, where I located our old house. Kayo and I stood there for a while watching a couple of white kids playing in the yard. But that's another story.

Five months later was Seattle. Kayo and I vomited side by side at the barricades. It was the most tear gas we'd ever experienced. And yet it was a perfect moment: no central committees, no leaders, no dogma. *Look, Anna,* I kept thinking, *it's happening, it's actually happening.* It had proven impossible to follow her parting advice, to live like an amoeba.

In the breaks between protests we come home, take hot footbaths, look for work. This year I found the school, Kayo is doing some underwear modeling. At night he prints T-shirts with old situationist slogans: *In a society that has abolished any kind of adventure, the only adventure that remains is to abolish the society.* In the morning I find him curled up with Anna-Maria in my parents' old bedroom, a Kodachrome icon of the Virgin Mary that my mother left to protect me hanging on the wall above him. Kayo adores it. It's a bad habit he picked up in New York: he's always coming home with the cheapest, kitschiest junk. A mismatched family of characters, childish yet lurid, occupies his bedside table: a pink plastic Hello Kitty, a music box topped by a fake ballerina with gold pointe shoes, a plastic camera that squirts water, one of those flowers that bobs up and down on its stem when there's music playing, a Statue of Liberty made of hot pink foam.

I sleep in my childhood room. There's nothing angelic or little-girlish about it. "It's an absolute mess in here," Kayo mutters when he's in a bad mood. But I like it that way. Amid the newspaper clippings, posters, books, packs of anti-capitalist stickers, I'm somehow able to find myself. "*Lose* yourself, you mean," he says. To keep myself from hitting him I psychologize his own mania for cleanliness: he's biracial, the son of a white woman who washed him incessantly when he was a kid, and ironed a new shirt for him every day so that none of the other kids could say he smelled bad. Kayo smells wonderful, in fact, even when he's in a funk. I'm the one who always seems to need a shower.

"Where'd you see her?" he asks, tossing the sheet aside. He sleeps naked, but the sight has long since ceased to affect me. These days I just give him a cool once-over, as if he were soft porn on TV. Or an underwear ad.

"I haven't seen her. Yet." The thought of us meeting in person makes me shudder—the thought that she might come in to ask how Daphne is doing in class, or how I ended up there, an art teacher at a private school. She's presumably living a more note-worthy life than mine, doing more important things.

"Will you just tell me what happened?"

I tell him about Daphne.

"A miniature Anna? My lord, what a nightmare!" Kayo is one of the few men Anna never managed to charm. After all, he was always even more beautiful, more daring than she. Kayo stretches and yawns beneath the icon of the Virgin, a faded woman with a halo looking down on him from above, smiling a restrained smile. The way the icon artist painted her, she always seems to know more than we do.

A short while later, Irini and Kosmas show up with a Tupperware of warm potato salad. They hug us tightly, just like every night, as if we haven't seen one another in ages. It's nice: their young bodies give us a forgotten energy, a brief dose of electroshock that I otherwise only experience at protests. It must be how Kayo feels on those rare occasions when he approaches young men in bars.

Irini is nineteen, Kosmas twenty; they're both students in the Department of Mass Media. They're tall and skinny and have a healthy glow on their cheeks, though they're sworn vegetarians. Irini has a small mouth with full lips and teeth even whiter than Kayo's. Kosmas is like a happy alien. Now that he's cut his hair short, you can't help but admire his beautiful ears. The two of them aren't sleeping together yet, or with anyone else for that matter, and so they shriek and chase one another around the table. They dish out the potato salad, open a bottle of red wine, and wait for us to take a bite before they dig in.

"That's what I call respect for the aged," Kayo says. He'll be turning forty this year. Like all narcissists, he's got issues with his age.

Irini gives him a mournful look. She's probably a little bit in love with him; I certainly was at her age. When you're nineteen you fall for people like Kayo. All it tends to get you are some wrinkles around your eyes and a deep well of hopelessness in your gaze.

"Do you want to say grace today, old man?" she asks.

"I'm still sleeping," Kayo growls.

"Okay, then I will," Irini says. She clears her throat. Her eyelashes quiver in the light of the candles we always set out on the kitchen table. "We're not afraid of ruins. We're the ones who will inherit the earth. So they can go ahead and destroy their world before they walk off the stage set of history. We carry a new world in our hearts." Some of the words she uses hover midway between sentiment and sentimentality. The word "heart," for instance. Irini knows how to pronounce it properly, to give it meaning. At her age, if Anna and I ever said "heart" we surely would have burst out laughing.

She's less emotional in the texts she writes for *Exit*, though they come from the heart, too. In an article about the social ecology of Murray Bookchin, Irini dreamed of a society comprised of citizen groups that would take the place of multinational corporations in an attempt to *restore social desire in a world that revolves self-complacently around egos and profit margins. People want to reap without first cultivating the earth. They want rain without lightning, the ocean without the murmuring of its waves.*

Is that how Anna would speak if she were a teenager today? There's certainly no way she would end her text with an exclamation of this sort: *People say cities provide freedom of choice. Freedom means* doing *what you want, not* having *what you want. Today's cities are dominated by the logic of advertising. Our biggest source of anxiety isn't whether or not we'll have complete access to the sole object of our desire, but how we can consume lover after lover. Society makes sure to give you the distressing impression that, in choosing one person, you lose all others, as if people were coats to choose from, old or new.*

The coat Irini wears is a shiny, silvery old leather jacket, torn and covered with ink stains. Kosmas has a kind of retro air, too: he always has on a red scarf; you'd think it was attached to his neck, like the gold necklace in Gwendolyn's story. He's as jittery as a marionette, hands and feet in constant motion. He might leap out of his chair unexpectedly, for instance, and shout, "Why *can't* we sell the idea of revolution the same way they sell shoes? Why *can't* we make revolution irresistible, like a really stylish winter coat? Don't you want to bet that if we did, all those spoiled rich kids I went to school with would be falling all over themselves to get a revolution of their own?" Kosmas went to high school at the American College of Greece. He must've been one of those kids plagued by inner dilemmas: I may be rich, but I feel poor. It's more or less how I felt as the daughter of an oil company executive.

Kosmas and Irini are the digital brains of *Exit*, and of our activities more generally. They're the best hackers I've ever met. They can bring the Ministry of Finance to its knees in half an hour, though if you saw them waiting for the bus you'd think they were just two college kids like all the rest, headed to class with textbooks under their arms, whose biggest worry is whether they might get a pimple on their chin.

"Okay, we need to put our heads together here." I pull my glasses down to the tip of my nose, mostly because I know they get a kick out of my schoolmarm routine. "Speaking of ruins, Irini, we might want to think about the Attic Highway—we haven't done anything on that front."

"The Attic Highway can wait. We've got over a month for that. What we really need to talk about is the metro." Irini blinks her eyes a few times, and I can't help but admire her perfectly arched eyebrows, her jet-black lashes, which tremble so suggestively. Then again, perhaps it's just a matter of age. I see in Irini what Diana once saw in me: possibilities.

"What's wrong, Maria? Are you daydreaming?" It bothers Irini if my mind wanders even for a minute. Kids of her generation always want things to operate according to schedule: now it's time to space out, now it's time to work.

"I met the daughter of a childhood friend of mine this afternoon. I guess I'm feeling a little nostalgic . . ."

Anna-Maria leaps up into my lap. Cats can tell when humans have become cats, too, when they've slipped into a furry pouch of regression. She sinks her claws into my sweater; a single prick and I'm back to my normal self. I clap to get everyone's attention.

"Okay, people, let's get to work! Who has the final text for the metro?"

Irini clears her throat. It's her day. There are times when certain people shine, take the lead, while others would rather just disappear into their chairs, like me right now. Irini starts to read: "*They presented it to us immaculate, marble, smelling of disinfectant, like an airport bathroom. Cold white fluorescent lighting. Private security guards. The Athens Metro is a moving walkway that transports us home after hours of low-paying, back-breaking work. It feels like the inside of a bank, exudes an air of industriousness and order. Music and food are prohibited. Human activity of any sort is avoided. In Europe people at least make themselves at home in their metro, they sing, they sleep in its warmth—after all, no European government cares enough to actually solve the problem of homelessness. We take it a step further: we hide our homeless, we kick them out of the station at Omonia. They mar the Europeanized image of prosperity we're hoping might attract the business of multinational corporations. Sweep the dirt under the rug! Was the new metro designed for people so exhausted they've become zombies? Is this the new Athens we're so proud of? This imitation of Brussels? Say no to this asphyxiating state 'security'! Say no to the Olympic spirit being promoted by multinational corporations! Say no to the paternalistic aesthetic regulation of our city's working class! Bring your guitars and your sandwiches. Come help us give the Athens Metro the color and life we all deserve.*"

"Doesn't it sound a little too hippie at the end?"

"Maria, you're impossible! It's already been printed! You're always wanting to make changes!"

"What I certainly don't want, Kosmas, is for them to pass our movement off as just another wave of inveterate nostalgia. For them to dismiss it as utopian thinking and all that crap."

"You want our generation at the demonstration? You'll have it! I guarantee you, our whole department will be there."

"Kids whose most cherished dream is to get a job at a private television station are going to come down and occupy the metro?"

"Don't you want them to?"

"I want young people, not bearded hypocrites from the Communist Youth."

"Don't be prejudiced, Maria!" Kayo says, draining the last of his wine.

I throw him a disparaging glance and stand up from the table. Whatever claws I once had are gone.

I use the tongs to agitate the photograph of Irini in the basin of developer. Her features are fluid, our little phantom of liberty. Her eyes are shining, her long hair is braided into Princess Leia buns on either side of her head, which is at a slight tilt, neck bare, inviting a kiss or a bite. Underneath we'll print a line from Alice Walker, *Resistance is the secret of joy.*

All the darkroom equipment, the red light, the quiet swish of the liquid in the basin do nothing to alter the way that space echoes within me. The moment I open the door I experience a visceral sense of vertigo, a fear of falling and breaking my arm, even though there's no stool anymore, and no salt, and I no longer believe in proverbs. When I slip into this room and close the door, something African comes and colonizes Exarheia Square. Something that brings me back to the days of crickets and caves and dismembered dolls. "What on earth do you do in there for hours on end?" Kayo sometimes asks. "I breathe in chemicals," I answer. "I punish myself for being a racist."

Now he opens the door just a smidge.

"Close the door, Kayo, are you crazy? You'll ruin the photographs!"

He steals into the room and hugs me. His body is still warm from the sheets. Doesn't he ever tire of this game of incomplete conquest? A hug, a kiss or two on the neck, then each of us to our own bed. It only exacerbates the feeling that's been bothering me since afternoon, of having suddenly been thrown back into childhood. A six-year-old girl came and dusted off certain forgotten regions inside me: self-sacrifice, trust, admiration, disappointment, boundless love.

"Want to come and sleep in my bed tonight?"

I don't reply. Kayo goes out of the darkroom, and I follow.

"Don't you think it's time you found a place of your own?"

He's picking at the leftover potato salad, and freezes with the fork in midair. I stand on tiptoe and eat the bite off his fork.

"You really want me to leave? You're that upset?"

"You said our living together was a temporary solution. It's been three years."

I enjoy crushing his dignity from time to time. Maybe the cold potato in my mouth is to blame. Or the memory of Antigone's fake braid. Or of Anna's high-handedness: give me Apostolos, give me your drawing, pee here, smoke this cigarette, sing whatever song I tell you to. It seems fairly obvious that I'm trying to act as Anna would, to usurp her place. You just say whatever comes into your head and everyone else takes you at your word.

"I think you should leave, Kayo. Find a place to live already. Take your life into your own hands."

Merde. I'm a sadist.

I peek into his bedroom before leaving for school. He's cleared all the ballerinas and plastic flowers off the desk. His suitcase is out in plain sight. Is he staging his departure to make me feel bad? I grab my coat from the rack in the hall and run down the stairs. I'm afraid that if I stop for even a second at the mirror by the front door, I'll remember how I used to primp and preen in that exact same spot fifteen years ago, trying to be whatever it was I thought Kayo wanted. I wore men's suits and cut my hair short, shaved the nape of my neck. I lived on an apple a day.

These days the bones in my wrists still protrude, but at least my arms are the arms of a normal person, not a ghost. I've gained ten kilos since my Paris days. My hair is shoulder-length now, and I use a ballpoint pen to put it up in a bun, the way Anna did during the last phase of our friendship. The only thing Kayo still likes about my looks is the way I dress. I still shop at vintage stores—sometimes for elbow-length gloves, sometimes for men's suits. The gloves are straight out of *My Fair Lady*, but the suits are proof of his lingering influence. If I can survive without Kayo the way I survived without Anna, then I'll be truly free.

I take the metro to school. I scan the platforms for potential escape routes, passages that aren't being monitored. There are cameras everywhere. And our plan hangs by a thread: there's no central committee controlling things, just whatever collective telepathy steers us to a certain place, to this electrified now. I've got copies of our proclamation tied up in a tube and tucked into my scarf. I bend down as if to brush something off my shoe and shove the tube under the seat. Right before I get off at my stop, I slice the string with a knife and the proclamations roll all over the floor, a torrent of colored paper. I guess I did learn something after all, flying on magic carpets and playing Little Wizard.

"My mom says you should call her."

Daphne hands me a business card with both cell and land lines, of which there are four: home, work, a number in Paris, another that must be a summer house on some island. The card is warm from the girl's sweaty palm; it practically breathes.

"Thank you, Daphne. Now go and draw with the other kids."

"What should I draw?"

"Whatever you like."

She plops down on her stomach and sticks her tongue out at Natasha, who, terrified, quickly draws a rainbow at the top of her page, over the family she's been drawing, as if to protect her creation. Daphne turns her back on Natasha, hides her paper with one hand so the other girl can't see, and starts to draw, speaking all the while in a sing-song: "Look at the lightning, colored rain, the little kid cries, waaa, waaa . . ."

She's starting to pique my interest.

"Come on, little kid in the cave, pick a big leaf from the tree so you don't get wet, hmmm, hmmm . . ."

Natasha is straining her neck to see, even more curious than I am.

"Walk on the grass and mud in the big brown field, plaf, plaf. Hide, hide in the cave. The big witch finds you and says, Do you want to be a witch like me? Yes, yes, la la la . . . And the big witch says: eat these crickets and then we'll see. Mmmm, mmmm, yummy in my tummy, the little witch says. We'll take lightning and make the crickets turn blue, la la la. We'll sell them and make lots of money."

"That's stupid. Who would want to buy crickets?" Natasha asks.

Daphne looks at her imperiously. "All the vampires and ghosts will buy crickets and then at night they'll come to your bed and eat you, too! Mmmm!"

Natasha shrieks. My eyes, meanwhile, have filled with tears.

"What's that on the kitchen table?" Kayo asks. He's opened his suitcase back up and put his little plastic animals back where they belong. He even made onion soup to butter me up.

"A drawing Daphne did."

"I guess things are getting serious."

"I brought it home so I could look at it more carefully."

"What do you think you're going to learn from it?"

"What goes on in their house."

"Don't you think you're overestimating yourself, Maria?"

Not at all. If there's anything I know how to interpret, it's children's drawings. I've read a lot on the subject, but more importantly,

I remember. I remember the kind of need that drives you to draw caves and rain. Sure, I may have talked to her about caves and witches who eat crickets, but she was the one who thought up the lightning that slices across the page like tiny swastikas. And she added those reddish-brown splotches of mud—as if the landscape had come down with the chicken pox.

Daphne draws the way her mother did, with sweeping gestures, practically tearing the page as she goes. She's not afraid of the color gray. She made the witch enormous and the witchlet microscopically small, suggesting a certain balance of power. A strong female presence in the family—who else but Anna? And the cave, symbolizing protection. I imagine a house ruled by underground terror. Either there's no father at all or he's completely powerless, since there's no sign of him in the drawing. No siblings, either. The mother witch and the little daughter witchlet. They climb onto their magic carpet and head off to help the poor. Another witch, flying by, reaches out a hand and shakes the carpet. The witch and the witchlet grab hold of the tassels just in the nick of time. Come here, my pretty. You thought you could escape me, but you can't.

"What's wrong, child? Did a bakery burn down?"

That's how Mom scolds me for my long absences. It's a common enough idiom, but the subtext to her irony is that I only come to see them when something's gone wrong in my life. She's a busy woman now, fairly well-known as a children's writer, but she still plays the stereotypical Greek mother to perfection.

"I just missed you guys, that's all."

The house on Aegina, behind the fish market, was built in the '70s. The yard is like a faint memory of Nigeria: a well instead of a goldfish pond, pistachio trees instead of banana trees. On the veranda—rain or shine—a wrought-iron table with a marble top, just like the one we had in Ikeja. I have no idea how they managed it, but as soon as I set foot in the house, I'm half expecting Gwendolyn to appear, and I'm surprised to see Dad sitting there in his armchair. He was always at work. Now he folds his newspaper and gives me a thorough once-over, from my face down to my shoes.

"Did you wipe your feet on the way in?"

"Yes, old man." I kiss him on the top of his head, the way he used to kiss me once I'd reached the age when you're too big to be carried, but still too little for an adult to bend down as far as your cheek. It's as if he shrank. Of course he's sitting down, and curtseying isn't my thing.

The living room smells like incense and lentils. Mom is waving her censer in front of her icons and whispering something, as always, to the Holy Virgin and the saints.

"Mom made you lentils."

"What, no biftekia?"

"Are you mocking me?" Mom says, not turning to look at me, the censer dangling in midair.

It takes me half an hour to calm them down. When the complaints and the cross-examination are finally over and they pull out the old family albums from Africa, I know the moment has come for me to kick off my shoes and curl up on the sofa. Mom keeps it covered so that the upholstery doesn't get ruined, but I push the sofa cover away with my hand, just a tiny bit at the edge, then lean my cheek down and inhale the only bit of concentrated Africa I have left: Gwendolyn's sweat, spills from Mrs. Steedworthy's tea, the acrid metallic smell—drin! drin!—of my bicycle bell.

We pore over the photographs for the thousandth time. Mom in pointy heels with a striped kerchief on her head. "What a beautiful wife I had!" Dad brags.

"Compared to Mrs. Fatoba, you mean, or to poor Jane Steed-worthy?" Mom asks with a touch of coquetry in her voice.

"Could anyone compare with you, my dear?"

Mom bursts out laughing. "What about my little girl?" She points to a photograph in which I look absolutely pitiful—already Miss Inner Beauty even then. White shoes and hair in curls, a ridiculous Shirley Temple her parents dragged along to some tea party. Scabs on my knees beneath the white dress. My hair is nice, sure, but my smile shows a broken tooth.

"Dad, what a funny little colonist you were, with your socks up to your knees and your khaki shorts."

"If you only knew how long I spent ironing that crease," Mom says in a dreamy tone of voice. She's bending over my shoulder to admire us as if we were actors from the '60s, playing in her favorite soap opera.

"You? Not Gwendolyn?"

"Oh, please, Gwendolyn never ironed your father's pants. That was my job!"

"Your mother was an incredible woman," Dad says, as if referring to some prehistoric era.

Mom nods her head with a satisfaction tinged with sadness. These days she's written seven children's books and has a huge file of newspaper clippings and interviews—but she's never been as happy as she was back then.

After lunch the small family dramas begin. The table is strewn with crumbs; uneaten lentils are drying on our plates; after his first glass of wine Dad blows up at the least little thing; a note of exasperation creeps into Mom's voice. All signs point to the imminent eruption of the first argument of the afternoon. They bicker over the most ridiculous things: the telephone bill, who left the feta out on the counter, the motorbikes on Aegina.

"I'll slash their tires—then they'll think twice about making a racket during afternoon siesta!" Dad says.

"Enough already, you're always saying that and you never do a thing!"

I can't help but laugh as I picture my father sneaking around slashing tires, terrorist-style, Mom keeping watch to make sure no one is coming. They get mad at me for laughing and direct their irritation toward me instead. They insist that I go and lie down in the room they refer to as mine because they've put my old desk in there, and hung up an old poster of The Cure. A mausoleum for my childhood years. They've saved all kinds of appalling things: a box of dried-up pastels, the newspaper clipping of my Savings Day drawing, an old class picture with *A Souvenir from Grade Three* written on it.

I lie down on the bed, clutching the photograph. What else am I supposed to do on Aegina? Mom is busy writing her African stories or answering letters from kids, and Martha, two blocks down the road, is surely watching her afternoon soaps, so I might as well fix my eyes on something for a while, too: Anna, for instance, perched on a stool smack in the middle of the back row. You can't see the stools, so the kids in that row look like angels hovering in mid-air. Or, better, devils: Petros is picking his nose. Angeliki, with her satanic laugh, has her face in profile so the smushed turd won't show. I've been exiled to the very edge of the front row, in my cast and matching white tube socks, one pulled up to my knee, the other slouched around my ankle, the elastic apparently loose—what a mess. How young we were! What tiny fingers wrote that note to *"Dear Mrs. Anna's Mother"*! What non-existent hips emerged from our corduroy bell-bottoms during our peeing contests!

But why did they put me in the front row, so far from my best friend?

Of course—Anna's short! How could it never have occurred to me before? On the outside, at least, I've always been the stronger of the two.

"Surprise!" Anna is hovering in the doorway of my room, just as in our class picture. How does she do that? She's dressed as a hippie and before I can take cover, she lobs a Molotov cocktail in my direction. The sheets catch fire, I'm engulfed in flames.

Mom throws a blanket over me, trying to put out the fire.

"Where did she come from? How did she get into the house?"

"Who, honey? Calm down! You were having a nightmare. Haven't I told you not to sleep without a blanket? You'll catch cold."

I pull the blanket over my head, making a little cave. Mom shuffles out of the room, slippers flapping. She stops at the door, hesitates.

"Do you want a candy?"

She always carries candy in her pockets. On her visits to schools she treats the kids as if they were horses. She stuffs them full of candy, so you can't ever tell if she's actually their favorite writer or just a grandmother spoiling her grandchildren rotten. Personally I think her stories are atrocious, full of friendly colonists and cheeky little African kids, but then again she thinks I'm useless and don't even know how to draw. "What are those things you draw, honey? I could do that as well as you can!" She took my charcoals, copied a few of my oldest and worst sketches, and now passes herself off as an illustrator, too.

"Maria, I know you don't like it when I tell you this, but you still grind your teeth in your sleep."

"Okay, Mom, fine . . ."

"Honey, you have to be careful, that's how you broke your tooth when you were little."

I pull the blanket down off my head.

"What exactly do you want me to do about it?"

"Don't get annoyed. I'm just saying you should be careful."

I feel like telling her it's a sign of stress, something that stuck with me from the cave and the crickets. But I don't say anything. After all, I wasn't the only one who took years to recover.

"Turn around so we can see!"

Stella grabs the skirt of the dress I brought her and pulls it up just a smidge; her plump little legs do a girly spin in place. Then she starts to dance.

"Look at my little cabaret girl!" Martha says.

"Just yesterday she was learning to crawl, and now she's turning six!"

"You haven't seen the baby yet, either . . ."

"Oh, it's fine, let's not wake him up. I want to hear your news."

Martha is sitting in her favorite spot on the sofa—I can tell because it's where the cushion sags. Her belly is still swollen from her second pregnancy, and she has that lost, half-pleading expression on her face of a woman who's recently given birth.

"What news could I possibly have?"

"How's Fotini?"

"We've sort of lost touch. She and I are so different, Maria. She never even calls to talk to Stella, can you believe it? She's opposed to the nuclear family, she says. I mean, really, revolution? Who still cares about revolution these days? She's thirty-five years old! How stubborn can she be?"

Oh, Martha, if you only knew how I live. Writing proclamations in an apartment with bad plumbing. I come here bearing dresses with lace trim, like the ones they used to make me wear. I come for Stella, who was once the baby I knitted hats for and pushed in her stroller on the dock. But I also come in hopes of figuring out what on earth goes on in the head of a girl who's six, seven, eight years old. How she can shut out the whole world and just spin in circles around her own axis.

"What about your mother, how's she?" I ask, to change the subject.

"She's basically an invalid, just one illness after the next. If it's not some bug it's her back."

"I'm sorry, Martha. It's not serious, though, is it?"

Martha tells me about her mother's near mania for illnesses, her quiet depression, her constant hypoglycemia. Then she asks, "Who was it who gave my mother that name, anyhow?"

"My friend Anna, remember her?"

"Of course. Who could forget that girl? I always felt like punching her in the face."

"Why?"

"You really have to ask? I've never met a bigger, more frightening ego in my life."

Merde. Neither have I.

"Do you have to leave so soon?"

"I've got things to do, Mom."

"What things?"

Well, let's see, we're planning an event in the Athens Metro, it's been too long since we had a good, old-fashioned run-in with the police, with that absurd mediocrity that goes by the name of order. Every now and then we smash a shop window or two—a small, symbolic tear in the cloak of legitimacy that enfolds private property. But we're not nearly as active as we used to be. Kayo and I are the only ones with keys to the apartment, it's not all anything goes anymore. We don't just wreak havoc indiscriminately, either. And we've improved the fonts on our signs. We're revolutionaries with taste.

"I told you, Mom, things!"

"You live such a strange life, child. I just don't understand. The way I was raised, no matter how wrong life went, at age thirty-five a woman had a husband, kids, something to keep her busy."

"No matter how wrong things go, salt never gets worms, right, Mom?"

In my case, apparently, some inner worm has been eating away at the fear of God, at the desire for a family, at all the illusions that keep Mom alive.

"Let the girl do what she needs to," Dad calls from the living room. "Stop sticking your nose in all the time!"

They stand in the doorway, framed by flaking paint. To me they look older than ever, and as crazy as loons. Mom in her shawl, nails painted with peeling white polish. Dad in his prehistoric gym suit with the sagging knees. They're like little kids—like my kids.

"I should really paint the door jambs," Dad mutters.

"Just put newspaper on the ground if you do," Mom says. "I don't want you making a mess."

Perhaps I really did run away when I was nine years old, when I got out that checked suitcase and filled it with bananas, roller skates, colored pencils. I thought the stewardesses would have to take pity on me in order for me to get back to Africa. But perhaps you don't even need the airplane. Perhaps all it takes is a decision.

It's one of those days that makes you happy, though you couldn't say why. The Attic sky is that mysterious blue you see in tourist brochures: transparent, yet concealing something—whatever you want it to. Spring sneaks into your head, the sun numbs your temples. Athens glistens as if made of cheap glass. A quaver of heat and exhaust and spring sweetness spreads itself over everything, making the cement in the schoolyard shimmer. Today even Daphne drew a sun over her cave and grass all around. On days like this the kids are calm. They laugh at the drop of a hat, not in a hysterical way, but as if one of Mom's saints is watching over them. There's a kind of saintliness in the air—even if I don't believe in that sort of thing.

I'm alone in the classroom. When I was in grade school we always clambered up to the teacher's desk at the end of class. Clambered, because the desk was on a wooden riser that divided the classroom into two tiers: pupils on one, the teacher on the other. Anna and I would experiment with stolen moments of intoxicating power: "I'm going to sit in Kyria Aphrodite's chair!" Anna would shriek. "No, I am, merde!" We both could have fit, but Anna, the more stubborn, always won. From the first time she crossed my path, I learned to give way, to cede my place to her. Which is perhaps one reason why I now feel as if I don't belong anywhere. Though things have changed somewhat: there's a certain order to my life now, the squeak of markers on paper, the apartment in Exarheia, the demonstrations. There are regions that belong to each of us individually, while others are larger, broader, belonging to us all.

And into that broader realm now steps a thin woman in tall cowboy boots. I catch sight of her when she's still at the far end of the hall; as she approaches it becomes more and more obvious that she's one of those nutcase mothers who experience a rare and sudden flash of interest in their child and come in to pester us with questions. I can tell from the clothes: a sane person wouldn't show up to her child's school in sequin-studded jeans and a red leather jacket. Lord, she's headed my way. It's probably Natasha's mom, come to complain about Daphne picking fights.

Blond, skin and bones, medium height if you took off her boots. Straight hair, a wisp of bangs at her forehead. The hairclip is gone. And she dyed the white eyebrow.

It's Anna. Former radical leftist of France. My former best friend.

•

"*So, that circle we drew with the shard of a broken pitcher* . . . Did you ever wonder if that line by Titos Patrikios might be to blame?"

"For what?"

"For the fact that we ended up throwing stones . . ."

I've rehearsed this scene in my head thousands of times, imagined encounters from the most unlikely to the most banal: in the metro, at the post office, at a party, on a plane. On airplanes most of all, since there's nowhere to escape unless you open the emergency hatch. Never in all those imaginings did I picture Anna, so real and yet so fake, striding into my art room dressed like a rock star, without even a hello or a prologue of any sort. She just hops up onto my desk, crosses her legs under her, lights a cigarette and starts to recite that poem by Patrikios—one of the old anthems of our friendship.

"Why didn't you call me? Didn't Daphne give you my card?" Her voice is deep and husky from years of smoking. It's almost funny, such a gruff voice coming from such a tiny body—and if she weren't wearing makeup, she'd probably have circles under her eyes. Her lashes seem thicker, but her gaze itself is unchanged. There's something almost dramatic about her beauty, as if she's been through a lot since we lost touch. Her plum-colored lipstick leaves a mark on the filter of her cigarette.

"I was busy," I say.

"Busy?" She has an agitated look in her eye, the look of a person who wants to know everything.

"Who would've guessed we would meet again where we first met, in an elementary school classroom," I say.

"Can't you think of something a little more original, merde?"

"I leave the originality to you."

Anna laughs and coughs at the same time. She enjoys making me mad.

"How about I be the boring one, and give you time to think up something clever to say? I'll go back outside and come in again." She jumps down off the desk, goes out into the hall and closes the door behind her, then knocks theatrically.

"Come in!" I call. I snatch a cigarette from her pack and light it without thinking twice.

"Hello, Maria. I don't know if you remember me, but I'm your old friend, Anna. I heard you were my daughter's art teacher."

"Anna? Anna who?" I haven't smoked in years. The first lungful brings a sweet dizziness.

"Anna Horn, of course!"

"I'm sorry, you must be mistaken. I never had a friend by that name."

"Merde, globalization is so depressing." She wrinkles her nose for emphasis.

I shrug. We're sitting in a miserable coffee shop across the street from the school. It smells of plastic croissants. In those clothes, this attempt at solidarity doesn't suit her. She looks more like she should be easing into a matching sports car, the kind Kayo and I used to overturn, and driving down to Kolonaki for an espresso.

"Do you want to go somewhere else?" I ask.

"I don't care where we are, I care what we do there," she says. "Are you going to go first or should I?"

I shrug again.

"Fine, I'll start," she says. "After that thing with the Albanian . . ."

So she calls it "that thing," too. I never gave it a name, either.

After "that thing," she left for France. She packed her bags, went back to her father's place. She spent two months crying and staring at the ceiling. It took her half an hour to drag herself from the bed to the bathroom. First I'll stand up, she'd say, and then I'll lean against the wall. All with the utmost gravity, as if she were conducting a military operation. At some point she started psychoanalysis. According to Anna, psychoanalysis means admitting you've got holes in your heart and in your head, and then plugging them up with whatever you find, so you can live at peace with yourself. She discovered she wanted a child. She met Malouhos, a Greek architect living in Paris who was twenty years her senior, and within a year they had Daphne, while I was still holed up on Aegina knitting hats for Stella. She abandoned politics altogether. She lived an entirely private life, within the four walls of a two-story apartment on Champs-Élysées with double-glazed windows and shag carpet. For five years she didn't let the little girl out of her sight, except to go to her therapist, forty-five minutes three times a week. And after her appointment, straight home to the two-story apartment.

"A bourgeois life," I say.

"The bourgeois life came later. I'm getting there."

She would sit for hours at the window, Daphne in her arms. She looked out at the leaves on the trees, at the cars that slid soundlessly down the avenue, thanks to the double-glazed windows. At the passersby, bundled up in overcoats and scarves. She started to invent little stories for Daphne. "See that old man walking his dog? Well, the dog used to be the old man, but since he was always kicking his dog, a witch switched their places as punishment." Daphne believed so deeply in Anna's stories that she would bark at people and talk to dogs. And she wasn't alone: everyone believed Anna's stories. Everyone wanted to be like her. The little girl clung to her mother, taking shelter in a world of improvised fairytales. Hence the cave in her drawing: witch and witchlet joined forces in turning whatever they didn't like into a frog, whatever they did like into a prince. At some point things got out of hand. The world of elves and magic wands almost turned them, too, into unearthly creatures. Her therapist kept hinting that Anna's fairytales were turning reality into fantasy. That she had to sever the pathological umbilical cord that still tied her to her daughter. If he'd asked me, I could have told him that pathological umbilical cords are Anna's specialty: she was always attaching herself to someone or something, to me, to her father, to this boy or that, to Marx, to feminism. And finally, to Daphne.

"My mom became a professional storyteller," I say.

"Your mother? The same mother I know?"

Anna would never have thought my mother capable of anything more than knitting and filling the house with incense. So I exaggerate a bit as I describe her success, her *Stories from Africa* series, the prize for illustration she was awarded by some association of second-rate illustrators.

Anna nods as if bored, then returns to the period of her life when she finally let go of Daphne enough to entrust her to day care. She opened their two-story apartment to her architect husband's connections in the business world, came to terms with the thought that her father would be rolling over in his grave if he hadn't been cremated, started to accompany Malouhos to the apartments he was working on and to select works of art to match the interior design. In the end she decided to go and work at his firm.

She reacquainted herself with the social world, remembered the proper way to hold a champagne glass by its stem, got accustomed to entrusting her daughter to others' embraces. The girl was confused by this sudden passage from asphyxiating love to indifference. That's when the tantrums started, the shrieking and kicking. Anna decided it was time to make her peace with the past. The solution for Daphne's tantrums was the Greek sun: the Mediterranean lifestyle, a house with a yard in the swank northern suburbs of Athens. She convinced her husband that they should move back to Greece and make a fresh start. Though it wasn't actually all that fresh: for years Malouhos had been collaborating with major construction companies all over Europe, he has an iron in almost every fire around. He's a one-man multinational, responsible for some of those hideous glass monstrosities on Kifisias Avenue. We've even referred to him indirectly in *Exit*, in a piece about the new style of luxury office buildings: *The hothouses on Kifisias have constant climate control instead of windows you can open, the better to transform their workers into faithful reproductions of houseplants.*

"I want you to understand why I did it," she says. "Why I left, then."

"I do understand."

"No, you don't. You're still angry with me."

"I can understand and still be angry."

"What can I say, Maria, I was scared. It was like an earthquake for me. As if a house had fallen on top of me."

"You're still afraid of earthquakes?"

"It's fine, I've got it under control. But what about you? Tell me what you did."

Well, I returned to the favorite occupation of my teenage years: staring at the ceiling. After a while I convinced myself I could hide out on Aegina, at Martha's house, with Stella in my arms. It worked for a while, and then it stopped working. So I went to Paris, then to Berlin. I lived literally without anything, in squats in East Berlin. I ran into Michel after all those years. We shared a helping of pasta with spoiled tomato sauce that we found in a tin pot.

"Michel! How did you recognize him?" Anna asks.

"People have a way of sniffing one another out. He still had that same wreck of a bicycle."

"How was he? As sad as ever? Did he have a girlfriend? Tell me everything!"

"How should I know, Anna? Michel is a zombie, it's impossible to get him to open up. Anyhow, that situation had gone on too long. I went to New York, to Kayo. I couldn't stand it there, either. So I came back to Exarheia. Oh, and Kayo followed. We live together in the blue building."

"You live with Kayo?"

"Kayo has his life, I have mine."

"What about men?"

"Men? Rarely . . . I didn't go to therapy. I never learned how to plug up the holes."

It's not a complaint, it's a statement. But Anna reaches out both arms and literally falls onto me. Apparently she still has that same need for dramatic reconciliations. Her body is lighter than I had imagined. Lighter than she was when that thing happened. She strokes my hair, and I stroke hers. She probably dyes hers; it's brittle in the way hair is that's been damaged by dyes and hair dryers.

"Dirty lesbians!" a man hisses as he walks past our table.

"Ever since they started to feel like they're Europeans and stopped hitting on foreign women all the time, they've become so aggressive . . ." Anna says and sighs, without relaxing her hold on me. Her breath sends waves of warmth down the nape of my neck. Just like back when we would smoke to keep warm during recess, curled up in one another's arms. Or in the double bed in Aegina, when she would wrap herself around me and beg me to forgive her.

Odiosamato.

Four

We're smoking in the girls' room of the Varvakeio middle school, all in a tizzy. Our school is supposedly "experimental," but Anna calls it a "bastion of phallocentrism." And she's right. The boys can wear whatever they want, but we have to wear the same blue smock every day. "Stupid old magpies! They've blinded themselves willingly, they've scratched their own eyes out—and now they want to turn us into good little housewives, too!" Today she's got it in for Sartzekaki, our home economics teacher. Anna refused to make the little crocheted cap that keeps the dust off the extra roll of toilet paper, and she got what was coming to her. "I pity the man who marries you, Anna Horn," Sartzekaki said. "And I pity the one who married you," Anna replied, and got a slap on the face for her trouble. She ran out of the classroom, bright red with rage, and I ran after her to calm her down.

Anna is even more beautiful when she's flushed. She's sitting on the window ledge with her hands on her waist, giving me one of her looks, like lightning cracking. Will she get angry if I try to cheer her up by saying how smart we look in our uniforms with the Mao collar? "We're perfect little Maoists," Anna says when she's in a good mood, "full of contradictions." That's how she talks this

year. She reads Hegel and Marx and uses words like "alienation,"
"capital," "problematics." But before leaving school each day, we
always touch up our lip gloss in the girls' room and run a hand
through our bangs. At least this year we *have* a girls' room. In the
eighth grade we just had to hold it in until we got home. With
thirteen hundred boys and only sixty-five girls, it wasn't easy for us
to convince them that we have bodily needs, too.

"Come on, Anna, don't pay any attention to that woman, she's
just taking her own problems out on us . . ."

"Don't pay attention? People like her are going to decide our
future!"

As dramatic as always. I just bite my lip if someone insults me.
When they first sent us for gym class to the square by Agios Niko-
laos church—sit-ups on the sidewalk, between parked cars—I made
a face, and our harpy of a gym teacher saw me and said, "Are you
too high-class for us, Maria?" I just bit my lip and kept quiet. But
Anna is touchy, a fly landing on her sword is enough to set her off.

"I'm going to tell Antigone," she says.

"What do you think she can do?"

"She'll come to school and teach that fool how to behave. First
of all, she has no right to lay her paw on me."

Antigone comes to school at the drop of a hat—because the religion textbook says *The working wife fills the house with tension and
worry, as she is unable to fulfill all of her duties,* or *Many people, including young people, followed the illogical ideas of Sartre,* or *Foreign tourists
bring into our country the unbridled liberties of their own lands (morals and
customs, sexuality, the absence of public shame, styles of dress, etc.).* In
the end she asked for Anna to be excused from religion class altogether. I watch through the window as Anna walks around in the
schoolyard and am annoyed that I'm missing out on so many hours
of conversation with her, just so I can sit there and listen to crap
about Jesus. But what can I do? Mom turned religious. She spends

whole days going from church to church making offerings. She's even fatter now, and puts all her faith in God and Weight Watchers. As for Dad, he has no faith in anyone or anything. He opted for early retirement and spends his days in the coffee shop on the ground floor of our building, Sundays at the stadium. Fortunately I have school during the day, and afterward I have French lessons at the Institut Français, so I can forget for a while that my parents have become religious and weak, respectively. When I get home I call out a hello, then head straight for my room. I read whatever I can get my hands on, and listen nonstop to The Cure. The world could crumble around me and I still wouldn't leave my room.

No matter how wrong things go in the world, salt never gets worms.

Now why did I remember that again?

"Stop making faces! Don't be so squeamish," Anna says.

Over the summer we used pillows, or put our hands over our mouths. Now she insists on our kissing for real, with our tongues, so we'll know what it's like. Locked in the bathroom in Plaka, Anna is perched on the washing machine, and I'm standing in front of her.

"Close your eyes, merde! It's not the end of the world."

First her lips, like kissing a peach. And then a cool tongue, which gets warm and soft when it touches mine. Just when I'm starting to get used to it, Anna pulls back. She wipes her lips furiously with her hand.

"What's wrong?" I ask. "Why did you stop?"

"You liked it, huh?" she says, and laughs. "Aren't you the least bit ashamed?"

"Give me a break! It was your idea."

"Yeah, so we don't seem totally inexperienced. But we don't have to turn lesbian!"

She says we should place bets on who'll be the first to kiss a boy from the Varvakeio. "There are so many of them! We can experiment, a different one each day."

Anna starts her experiment the very next day, when school lets out. She's completely shameless, goes right up to a boy from the high school, Philippos, and asks if he'll take her home on his motorbike. Then she lingers there, straightening and unstraightening the mirror on his bike, laughing at nothing, stroking her elbow. I'm perched on a low wall across the way, biting my nails, because the bet is only good if the other person actually sees the kiss. Anna slides onto the seat of the motorbike, up on her knees with her legs crossed under her. Philippos is very tall, but that way they're more or less the same height. And of course they kiss. What else are a boy and girl supposed to do when their noses are practically touching? Anna makes the victory sign at me behind Philippos's back. She won, merde.

I hope I find someone before my birthday.

His name is Kostas! He's in my French class at the Institut Français.

"What a boring name," Anna says, sighing.

"Yeah, but he's a good kisser."

"Like how?"

First he holds your face between his hands. He concentrates, looks at you with a smile in his eyes, as if telling you not to be afraid. And he kisses slowly and gently: first with closed lips, then they part a little, then they're totally open, and finally there's his tongue. Then he does it all in reverse and ends with a gentle kiss on your lips. Then he puts his arm around you and you walk together down Sina Street with all of Athens glittering in the background.

"What kind of crap is that?" Anna says.

"He's so polite, Anna, like a real Frenchman. Maybe, you know, it's because he's learning French . . ."

"First of all, it doesn't count. We said a boy from the Varvakeio."

"But he's the one I found!"

"And you can lose him again just as easily. We're not going to turn into your mother. I mean, really! One man for your whole life?"

"But I like him!"

"He's already given you whatever he had to give. If you can't dump him now, when will you? After your third child?"

Kostas waves to me from his desk during our next French class. I see him in church, too, with the priest chanting, Mom wiping her eyes with her monogrammed handkerchief. But it's all ruined; kisses aren't just a game anymore. They lead to something else, something serious and scary.

"This is our last kiss," I tell him after the service, just at the point when he's kissing me gently on the lips, about to put his arm around me so we can walk together down the street. It's nearly winter, the days are getting shorter and a person naturally has a greater need of hugs and kisses. But even more than my ears, it's my heart that has frozen, at the idea of marriage. I'm not even fifteen!

"What's wrong?" Kostas asks. "Did I do something?"

"No, I just don't like you anymore."

It sounds harsher than I would have liked, but there's no way of taking it back.

It's February, a night like any other. I'm curled up in bed reading a novel by Albert Camus that I borrowed from the library of the Institut Français. Outside stray dogs are barking, the sky is faintly red. Suddenly our apartment starts to shake as if everyone had cranked the music up to full blast in every apartment in the building all at once. A few of the books fall from my shelf into a heap on the floor. Out in the living room, Mom's wooden elephants from Africa drop one by one from the cabinet. There's a humming sound and then all the lights go out. It's as if a wind picked up our apartment and set it down on a beach where huge gusts are whipping up enormous waves that threaten to engulf it. Mom lets out a cry—"My God!" Dad bursts into my room, shouts at me to hurry. I run barefoot down four flights of stairs. I'm clutching Camus to my chest as if the book were a living thing, like a kitten.

The whole neighborhood is out in the streets. Women in slips are looking around frantically. Men wrapped in sheets are deep in conversation, gesticulating, like Roman senators. So it wasn't just our apartment. Maybe it's the beginning of World War III? "An earthquake, an earthquake!" my mother cries as if she needs to repeat it to believe it. So that's what a real earthquake is like.

Maybe I should cross myself every now and then and try to believe in God. Maybe I shouldn't kiss just anyone.

Anna is in a terrible state. White as a ghost with fear, curled up into a ball in the garden. Our whole family has taken refuge at the house in Plaka because Mom is afraid the roof of our building will fall and crack open her skull. Wrapped in a blanket on a deck chair in their yard, Mom drinks the coffee Antigone brings her and repeats: "6.6 on the Richter! My Lord, how awful!" Dad and Antigone are the bravest of us all. They sit in front of the television, coming out every so often to relay the news: "The epicenter was the Halcyon islands." "So many dead!" "Devastating property damage."

I'm sitting on a stool beside Anna, trying to calm her down.

"It's over, Anna, it's over."

"But can anyone say for sure that it won't start up again?"

"Come on, would a real revolutionary be afraid?"

"Give me a break, Maria! Merde!"

She's sitting on the edge of her chair, ready to leap to her feet at any moment—to go where? There's an aftershock, practically

imperceptible; Anna screeches, Antigone brings her half a tranquil-
izer. We all sleep outside in the yard, in sleeping bags or on mat-
tresses we bring out from the house, except for Dad, who sleeps
in the car. Under normal circumstances Anna and I would be up
giggling until dawn, or would sneak off for a cigarette. But Anna
isn't Anna anymore. In the morning she wakes up with red eyes
and scans the yard as if the earthquake were a wild beast lurking in
some dark corner. I've forgotten my own fear, because I'm wrapped
up in Anna's. It's the first time I've ever seen Anna afraid. And her
fear makes me stronger.

"I'm going to go live in France, that's it."

"Are you crazy? What about me?"

Anna is hunched over on the toilet, a wad of toilet paper in her
hand. Even the way she pees is different: hesitant, not as noisy.
She's always prepared to jump up and race out of the house at the
slightest notice.

"There are no earthquake zones in France. I'll go live with my
dad. You can come, too, if you want."

I've never met Anna's father, because he never sets foot in Athens. He and Antigone are separated, something it took me ages
to figure out. They're supposedly all modern about it, and still go
out to eat together in France. "If I got a divorce from your father,
I wouldn't ever want to see him again, not even in a painting,"
Mom says. "But they're friends," I say. "Friends? How can they be
friends? It's completely unnatural, child."

This is one of the rare occasions on which Mom and I agree.
Anna and I never talk to our exes, we call them "stuffed shirts."
We'll go out with a boy from the Varvakeio for ten days, two
weeks at most, and let them kiss us and touch our chest. Next year
we'll see about more than that. We still like peeing together, but
not in parking lots anymore, in the bathroom. We shut ourselves in

for hours and talk about how this or that boy kisses, or how boys unbutton your shirt, with trembling fingers.

After the earthquake, though, Anna doesn't talk much about stuff like that. Actually she doesn't talk much about anything. She just sits on the toilet with a wad of paper wrapped around her hand looking as if she might cry at any moment.

"How am I supposed to come to France, Anna? My family is here."

"Aren't I your family?"

We hug and lean silently to this side and that, Anna with her underwear around her knees, I fully dressed and strong. She smells like fear.

"What about school?"

"We don't learn anything anyhow. Just crap about working women and how to make hats for toilet paper."

"You've got a point."

Anna looks at me pleadingly.

"Won't you come?"

"Could I ever let you go alone?"

And yet I do. I say goodbye to her at the airport with burning eyes. Our sweaty fingers slip through one another as we part. Who will I talk to during recess? Smoke with? Pee with? I sob inconsolably in Antigone's arms at the Hellenic Airport as my best friend's head vanishes on the other side of passport control.

She's leaving just for a month or two, on a trial basis. My mother says she'll cut off my legs if I even think about leaving, she'll have Interpol on my tail. It's a threat she invented when I ran off for Ikeja. I imagine the agents bringing me back home in handcuffs; all the newspapers print my photograph, as if I'm another Patty Hearst.

Anna and I exchange heartbreaking letters. She sends me poems by Verlaine, I send her poems by Titos Patrikios: *So, that circle we carved with a piece of a broken pitcher, is our circle. Let's hide the cricket's chirp in it, so we'll know we can find it again. So we'll be able to talk about whatever will happen in the great books of the future.* She writes: *Paris is so depressing without you, Maria. I go out with my father's friends, they talk about thousands of interesting things, but their voices are just an echo of my conversations with you. Our housekeeper's name is Roman and she's sort of like you in some ways. So I spend hours on end in the kitchen, and while she's cleaning the cupboards I eat an apple I'm not hungry for, drink some milk that I don't really want, just so I can be close to her and therefore also close to you. I miss you terribly. Will you come for Easter?* And I write back: *I miss you terribly, too. I don't go out with boys anymore. It's no fun if we don't pee together afterward and talk over all the details. My parents are always complaining, because of the long-distance calls, or because I'm always dragging myself around the house, not doing anything. On the weekends I almost always stay home, biting my nails and staring at the ceiling. At school, in religion class, I stare out the window, wishing you would appear in your uniform with the Mao collar and with a cigarette in your hand. Yesterday Antigone and I went to the movies. We saw* Doctor Dolittle. *She says it's no mistake they're playing it now, even though it's an old film—it makes her think right away of Andreas Papandreou! We laugh a lot when it's just the two of us, but something's missing: you! We miss you! Come home!*

I don't know if it's because Anna is gone or because our psychology textbook, by Evangelos Papanoutsos, the guy who also made demotic Greek the official language of education, makes no sense, but I understand pretty much nothing in that class: *When we observe our fellow human beings, or when we ask them to fill out questionnaires, we're asking them to delve deep into their emotional worlds and describe past or current experiences, while at the same time we're placing ourselves in their situation: we imagine ourselves doing what they do, so as better to understand what is happening in their inner world.* I don't understand our philosophy textbook, either: *Hermeneutic art, abstraction, and deliberate incomprehensibility in art provoke a rebellion in consciousness, by not allowing it to function aesthetically.* When I read stuff like that, it makes me want to really apply myself to art again, to make the most hermeneutic art I can, to be deliberately incomprehensible all over the pages of the textbook, over those stupid sentences. I want to correct that stupidity, the way Anna once corrected the *Acropolis* in my Savings Day drawing to an *Avgi*.

I spend my entire allowance on Da Vinci watercolors, on charcoals, sketch pads. It's been five whole years since I drew, since that fiasco with the Savings Day prize. But it's as if I've been drawing on the inside the whole time: where did these color combinations come from? The splashes of yellow, the animals, the women in long dresses, the urgent need for black? I paint like a construction worker pouring cement, thick layers of color on larger and larger sheets of paper. I want to paint the walls of my room black and then cover that black with pictures of snakes wearing crowns, leaky pirogues, female figures in long skirts whose hems blaze with flames. Indigent families warm themselves by that fire, children reach up to pluck fabric fruit off the skirts. The snakes with crowns are Anna's father. The pirogues are my parents. The women are Antigone, who this year has taken to wearing long, tasseled skirts. And the fire on the hem, of course, is Anna.

As for me, I'm the hungry child in the background, reaching for a piece of fruit.

"What kind of crap is this?"

I've unrolled my drawings on the table in the round room in the apartment in Paris, next to a pile of books by Deleuze, Lyotard, Baudrillard and Guy Debord, directly beneath a photograph of

Poulantzas and a poster that reads: *I take my desires for reality, because I believe in the reality of my desires.* It's Easter. I came to visit precisely because I believe in the reality of my desires. I had the cylindrical container between my legs for the entire flight and this is what I get for my trouble. Anna is back to making her familiar old faces. She's not afraid anymore.

"What don't you like about it?" I ask.

"Why don't you ask what I *do* like? It's easy, quick, ornamental. You're better than this."

"Do you want me to explain the symbolism?"

"Symbolism shouldn't be something you have to explain."

I have to admit, she has a point.

"Come on, I'll show you something that doesn't need explaining." She grabs me by the hand and literally pulls me up to her room, which for the next ten days will be our room. It's a tiny attic with a slanting ceiling and a double bed strewn with woven Moroccan pillows. She lifts the bedspread, revealing a wooden drawer in the base of the bed. She pulls open the drawer and hands me a photograph of a skinny boy with liquid eyes and short hair.

"Well? Does that need explaining?"

"You guys are a thing?"

"His name is Raoul. He's half French, half Algerian. Aren't those the most amazing eyes? I want you to meet him, Maria."

"Have you guys gone far?"

"Yes, I have to tell you about that, too . . . He touched me all over!"

"You didn't write to me about that!"

"There are some things you can't write about."

Anna confuses me the older we get. She's always telling me what to do—to kiss her, to break up with Kostas—and meanwhile she does whatever she likes. If I were the one who'd let a boy touch me everywhere, I'd have had her to reckon with.

"I think we're old enough now. It's so amazing, to be touched like that."

She explains in detail how a boy pushes aside your skirt, then your underwear, then slips his finger into your vagina. It sounds disgusting.

"And it doesn't hurt?" I ask.

"Just at first."

"What do you like about it?"

"It's a way of getting closer to someone."

Before we leave the house I shut myself in the bathroom for a little while. I lock the door and try to find my vagina, some depression that would admit a finger. If it brings you closer to someone else, maybe it could bring me closer to myself, too. But I can't find an opening. It's solid everywhere.

"What, you started locking the door?" Anna shouts, pounding on the door with her fists. "What kind of friends are we, anyhow? We don't pee together anymore?"

Raoul opens the door and kisses us the French way, three times, on alternating cheeks. He lives by Blanche station, in a tiny room with an unmade bed, posters for the band Bazooka, and books about Fassbinder, Godard, and Pasolini. His window looks onto the rooftops across the way and while the two of them kiss, I stare out at the depthless, tiled horizon. He's really very handsome and he's a university student, too, studying graphic design. From the very beginning, with Apostolos the plumber, I knew Anna would go for older guys. He's twenty years old, just imagine!

Raoul is very polite to me. "Anna talks about you all the time," he says, then opens a beer with his teeth and offers it to me. It's eleven in the morning and we're drinking beer; the day is off to a strange start. We go out into the freezing Parisian air, pull our hats down over our ears, and they take me to see Beaubourg. We wear ourselves out with walking, stop every few hours for coffee, mussels with pommes frites, or pear tarte, we climb Montmartre, Raoul and Anna kiss, I stare at my coffee spoon or the hem of my coat.

"We have to find you a boyfriend, too," Anna says slyly.

They decide to introduce me to Michel.

Michel dresses exactly the same way Raoul does—black shirt, a chain on his pants, a leather jacket with Sex Pistol patches—but his ears stick out and he has a sad look in his eyes. A similarity in dress says a lot about a friendship. Anna and I, meanwhile, are in our goth phase—romantic white blouses with lots of lace, white powder on our faces. It's not healthy, to consume such large doses of The Cure and Verlaine all at once.

"How did the two of you meet?" I ask.

Raoul tells me they went to the same boarding school. One day, during room check, when they were supposed to be cleaning their rooms, Michel picked up all his trash off the floor and pinned it to the wall, like butterflies. The monitor had no idea how to react. The rumor spread from mouth to mouth and Raoul was impressed. He learned everything about the Sex Pistols from Michel, about the situationists and the *Marche des Beurs* anti-racism movement, even formed ties with some people in squats in Berlin. I figure all that learning must have happened in sign language, because Michel barely ever opens his mouth. Could I fall for someone so silent? For now it's enough that he's active in the anti-racist movement and that he rides his bicycle all over Paris, and if he wants to tell me something he just draws it, as if he were mute. He wears glasses, too, like me. How do two people with glasses kiss, anyhow?

I find out that very same night. They take off their glasses, place them on the table by Raoul's bed and slowly sink into the pillows, half blind. If you're nearsighted, the other person always looks better when you're not wearing your glasses. His skin looks softer, his eyes sort of hazy, as if you're only dreaming them. Until the others come back bearing pizza, Michel and I kiss, just kiss. I try to unbutton his shirt. "Aren't we moving sort of fast?" he asks.

We sit on the floor eating pizza and Anna sings "*Avanti Popolo*" at the top of her lungs. Is that really a song that goes with pizza? Is it possible to say yes and no at the same time? I want and don't want? Can you curse your home economics class while touching up your lip gloss in the bathroom? Dream of freedom but be unable to find your own vagina? That night, when Anna and I crawl into bed in the attic room, I speak to her in a disjointed rush, still tipsy from the morning beers and the vodka we drank at Raoul's. Anna crosses her arms over the comforter and listens to me carefully. She's thinking.

"What do you say, Anna?"

She doesn't say anything. And it's not because she's still thinking. She's asleep.

I pad downstairs to the bathroom in bare feet. Anna is still sleeping, but her father is awake, sitting in his velvet armchair with the worn upholstery. It's as if he stepped right out of the photographs: he's smoking a pipe and reading *Liberation*.

"So here I am, finally meeting my daughter's alter ego," he says, and holds out a hand to me. His handshake is so warm it makes my knuckles crack.

"I propose we go out for breakfast. What do you say? It's a beautiful day today." He points out the window at a little café across the street. "That's my favorite place right there."

"What about Anna?"

"She's not a cripple. When she wakes up, she'll come find us."

We sit in the window and look out at the passersby, and they look back at us. I order hot chocolate and a croissant, Anna's father drinks a coffee but doesn't eat anything. I try to picture him with Antigone, in one of those moments that grown-up couples share. Him putting a finger in her vagina, for instance.

"What are you laughing about?" he asks.

"Nothing, I just thought of something funny."

"You're not going to tell me, are you? That's fine, I respect people who protect their thoughts."

Anna's father doesn't talk about leftist politics all the time, as I had imagined, about separatist movements and revolutionary tactics. He mostly just strokes his beard and tells me funny stories about when he first moved to France, how he got the metro stations confused, or would forget his keys and have to spend the night on the steps of his apartment building. He does tells me a political joke, though: "A leftist gets into a taxi. He tells the driver: turn left here, then left again, then the other way." At some point his face clouds over. He takes off his glasses, rubs his eyes and stares at me, deep in thought. A minute or two pass before he speaks.

"What's all this about the earthquake? What do you think, Maria?"

"I don't know. I've never seen Anna so scared."

"Scared? Just scared? Hopeless is how I'd describe it. Terrified. What did she say to you? Is she going back with you when you leave?"

"We haven't talked about it yet."

"It'll be a shame if she doesn't. She'll have to repeat a whole year of school."

Anna in middle school while I'm already in high school? Impossible!

"How about the two of us make a deal? Can you persuade her to go back? You're the only person Anna ever listens to—"

Me? Anna listens to me?

"—and when the two of you graduate, I'll bring you both here to Paris. The two of you can live here with me, all expenses paid. What did Anna say you two wanted to study? Psychology?"

"I haven't decided yet."

"Well? What do you say to our deal?"

He shakes my hand again, even more forcefully, and again my knuckles crack. Anna's father tells me to speak to him in the singular and call him by his first name, Stamatis. The world is suddenly simpler. Free studies in Paris. A warm croissant across the street from the house, Stamatis's treat. Art school. Boys like Raoul and Michel. A human shield in support of the Arabs. Pizza on the floor. Beer in the morning, as if we're characters in an avant-garde French film. And my best friend Anna by my side.

Speak of the devil—here she is, wild-eyed, pushing through the revolving door.

"If you ever do that again, I'll never speak to you!"

She's not talking to me, but to her father. She doesn't just love him, she adores him, and wants him all to herself.

Her anger at me, too, doesn't let up all day. We walk through Buttes-Chaumont Park as if we were racing, Anna deliberately keeping a few steps ahead.

"Anna, I would've woken you up if I thought it would matter so much."

"You should've known."

"But *why* does it matter?"

Anna can't explain it to me, she just shrugs her shoulders. She's perfectly willing to share her only sandwich during recess, but her dad is a different story.

"I'll forgive you, but only if we switch boys tonight."

"Are you crazy? You like Raoul."

"I like Michel more. I hadn't realized he was so smart."

"Take both of them if you want, I couldn't care less!"

"No, that's not how it works. Since you wanted to share my father, you have to share Raoul, too."

"How do you know Raoul won't mind?"

"Oh, he won't. We're in Paris, remember? People here aren't bourgeois."

The four of us meet at a café in Les Halles. Anna leans over and whispers in Raoul's ear, and he turns and winks at me. They're depraved. And in the name of liberation, or just in order to make a statement, they're making me do things I don't want to do. We go to the movies, it's something by Wim Wenders, I sit on the aisle, Raoul next to me, then Anna and then Michel. I'm worried that the poor guy has no idea what's going on, that he won't know what hit him. But soon enough, in the darkness of the theater, I see him and Anna kissing and feel Raoul's breath on my neck. I lean my head on his shoulder, try to relax and just let whatever's going to happen happen. I see Michel's hand on Anna's knees, pulling her skirt up and groping around. Now I'm the one who doesn't know what hit me.

I'm worried that Anna has a vagina and I don't.

I now avoid Stamatis systematically. Shielding myself from view behind Anna's back, I just throw him a quick hello or goodbye when we pass in the hall.

"Hold on, where are you going? Go and get Anna, I want to tell you guys a joke."

Anna comes down the stairs, sighing. "What do you want, Dad?"

"Don't get all worked up, I just heard this great joke I wanted to share."

Stamatis gets a tea bag from the kitchen. "Okay, so this is an American missile," he says. "When the Russians see it they want one just like it. They ask the Americans how much it costs. Ten million dollars, the Americans say." Stamatis tears off the tab where the brand name is. "What if we take off this piece? Then how much? the Russians ask. Seven million dollars, the Americans say, but without that piece the missile won't launch." Stamatis pulls off the little string, too. "And without that piece, how much is it then?" Finally he rips open the tea bag, dumping the leaves, which supposedly represent the fuel, onto a saucer. "Now the missile is dirt cheap, but what use is it without any fuel? the Americans ask." Stamatis stands the empty bag on the table, lights one edge with his lighter and starts a countdown, from ten to one, in Russian. The tea bag slowly rises toward the ceiling, then falls gently back down to the table—a soft pile of ash.

I clap enthusiastically.

Anna glares at him through slitted eyes. "It's insulting to the Russians, Dad!"

"Since when are you Russian?"

Anna heaves a sigh, takes the stairs two at a time and shuts herself in her room. I run after her.

"Leave me alone, merde!" she says, her head under a pillow.

"Anna, why don't you come home? Isn't it time we were both back in Athens?"

"I don't know."

"How about we go across the street for a hot chocolate and maybe you'll figure it out?" We wrap scarves around our necks and clomp down the stairs.

"I supposedly came here to bring you home," I say to her, stirring my hot chocolate.

"I don't know."

"You're completely impossible, but I can't live without you."

We're sitting in the window with the latest issue of *Actuel*, on Michel's recommendation. Anna shoots daggers at an old man reading *Le Figaro* across the way, then turns to me with a huge grin, as if what I said has just sunk in.

"Really? You really can't live without me?"

She adores hyperbole. She swings from one emotion to the next as if all flipping a switch in her brain: rage, tenderness, jealousy, love. Whereas I need time to collect my thoughts, to swallow my anger. This time Anna has gone too far. I don't like the way she tells me who to kiss and for how long. I wonder: do I really want her to come back to Athens? Or am I only doing it for the free studies Stamatis promised?

"Can you live without me?" I throw the question back at her.

"I don't think so."

"Well?"

"Okay, fine, I'll come."

We hug. But instead of relief, what I feel is unease.

Michel and Anna kiss. Raoul opens cans of beer with his teeth and flips through Bourdieu's *La Distinction*. I'm sitting in Stamatis's armchair, fingernails sunk into the worn velvet. I don't want to read, I don't want to be kissed. I don't want to drink beer, either. I want to cry. I jump to my feet, throw open the front door and slam it behind me.

The air outside is freezing and I've left the house with no coat. I need to find an Ikeja, whatever Ikeja still has room for me. By now I've learned how to pack a suitcase properly, I won't try to bring eggs or other breakables, I won't ask bus drivers irrelevant questions. I'll board a train, slide my suitcase onto the rack above my seat and watch as one landscape gives way to the next. As the trees whip past into the distance behind me, my thoughts, too, will fly out of my head one by one—*zzzmmm, zzzmmm*—until my mind is entirely empty—*sssssshhhh*—and I'll be nothing more than a girl on a train.

It's cold, absurdly cold. So I tweak the story slightly: a boy comes into the train car and wraps a blanket with red flowers on it around my shoulders. It's my baby blanket, and I'm sorry to have been defeated by my own limitations, but I needed someone to come and cover me with something. The boy's eyes are as liquid as Raoul's, he has Michel's bicycle with him, and he metes out attention with an eyedropper, like Angelos—just enough for me to fall in love without his lifting a finger—and because I don't like the story I've invented, I duck into the metro station and huddle in its relative warmth, shake my head so that every last thought will leave, curl into a ball on the tiled floor and start to cry. No one talks to me, no one asks me what's wrong. We're in Paris, after all, and—how did Anna put it?—people here aren't bourgeois.

"Where were you?" Anna asks. She's at the sink washing dishes and doesn't even turn to look at me.

"I wanted to be alone."

"You should say something first, so people don't worry."

"What's the sense in talking it over when the whole point is that you want to be alone?"

"You're a member of society, not a wolf. Besides, even wolves travel in packs."

"You're right, I'm not a wolf. *You're* the wolf."

"Excuse me?"

"You tear everyone else to pieces. You want everything for yourself!"

Anna turns off the tap and puts her hands on her waist. Her eyes are spitting fire, her one white eyebrow is raised. The dimple in her cheek deepens.

"What you're talking about is called communalism, it's called liberty. It's everything we've been fighting for, merde!" Right, like she's been out digging trenches. Like she only just put down the shovel this instant.

"You only say those things when it suits you, Anna."

"Try me. Ask for something, anything."

"I don't play those games."

But Anna does. She looks around frantically—for what? A rope to hang herself with, to show me how much she'll sacrifice for my sake? A weapon to use in the next revolution? She grabs a back issue of *Actuel* and holds it up to my face, pointing to a phrase by Foucault: *Our action, on the contrary, isn't concerned with the soul or the man behind the convict, but it seeks to obliterate the deep division that lies between innocence and guilt.*

"Fine. And?"

She sweeps all of Stamatis's books off the table onto the floor. They aren't even hers.

"Merde, merde! Look at you, lecturing me in ethics!"

"Me?"

"Are you trying to provoke a crisis of conscience? What do I have to do to convince you? Go out into the street and beg?" She grabs her coat and rushes for the stairs. I run after her. She dashes across the street without even checking for cars, takes the stairs down into the metro station two at a time, sits on the ground and starts to sing a song by Françoise Hardy: *"Que sont devenus tous mes amis, et la maison où j' ai vecu?"* Someone tosses her a half franc, someone else a handful of centimes. It's all on purpose, of course. She chose her song wisely, it's a sentimental one. Eventually she collects five francs. I'm standing across from her the whole time, leaning against the wall. What is she trying to prove?

"So you'll understand what communalism means, I'll treat you to *chocolat à l'ancienne,*" she says. She opens her arms and I fall into her embrace. Two poor little beggars of love.

Because at the end of the day, Anna loves me. She's willing to lay herself bare for me.

Roman cleans Stamatis's apartment twice a week. I watch her as she scrubs the toilet. She's a plump African woman of indeterminate age, and she doesn't look the least bit like me. But maybe the similarity lies in Africa, our mutual starting point, or in the deep sighs she's always heaving.

"Where are you from, Roman?"

"Kenya, Nairobi."

"Do you like it here?"

"It's fine, I have a job."

"Do you know the saying, when a ripe fruit sees an honest person, it falls?"

"No, mademoiselle."

"Don't call me mademoiselle, I'm not a mademoiselle."

"Of course you are," Anna calls, running down the stairs. "We're all ladies." It's something Antigone says.

"Do you know how to make puff puffs?"

Roman laughs. "How do you know about puff puffs?"

I tell her about Gwendolyn, Unto Punto, and the house in Ikeja. But it's like I'm talking about someone else, not myself. My memories have faded. They feel like an Antonioni film: devoid of realism, and devoid of emotion, too.

Anna grabs me by the hand, pulls me out of the apartment.

"I'm guessing you need something sweet."

We duck into a patisserie and she orders a dozen chouquettes, little hollow balls of warm dough sprinkled with crystallized sugar. We polish them off in five minutes.

"When we come back to Paris to study, I'll buy you chouquettes every day," she says, her mouth full.

"I decided to study art, did I tell you?"

"What, so you can paint nonsense on black backgrounds?"

"No, I'll improve, you'll see."

"What about me?"

"What about you? Aren't you going to study psychology?"

"The way I see it, you and I are working together toward the same goal. We support one another."

Merde, Anna, no. Please.

In order to discover your body, you'll need a fair bit of time, and privacy, reads the first issue of *Erotic Harmony.* Mom and Dad have gone to a wedding with Aunt Amalia. The house is all mine until evening. I shut myself up in the bathroom. It's now or never. *You'll need a mirror,* I read. *Spread the outer lips of your vagina and look at your body in the mirror. Love your body.* There's no way I can do all that at once, I can *either* spread the lips of my vagina *or* hold the mirror. *Your clitoris is concealed at the spot where the two inner lips meet. Massage it gently, patiently, and feel it grow more and more firm with each circular motion of your finger.*

It's kind of like drawing. Like spreading lines of charcoal again and again on a small surface until the tendons in your arm start to hurt. The repetition effects a change: the skin tightens, becomes electric. At some point, unexpectedly, your body opens up into a series of trembling slices, or ripples. My whole belly has turned inside out like a piece of clothing and I can see all the seams, what it's made of. I'm floating underneath my skin, in a deep, elastic space of darkness and nerve endings. The moment I realize what's happening, *tsaf!*, I'm back in my body. Only nothing is quite the same. It's sort of how I imagine absolute happiness would be. You fight for it, you achieve it for a few seconds, and then it slips from your grasp and you've got to start all over again from the beginning. Each time I try it takes longer and longer; my head swells and goes numb. Night falls and I'm still sitting there on the toilet. The bathroom is stuffy, my sweat is heavier than usual. My feet are pins and needles on the bathroom tiles; in the mirror a tiny wet cave reveals itself to me.

So that's my vagina. A half-open mussel. God, I'll never eat shellfish again.

I get up and wash my hands, exhausted. I use soap, but the mussel smell sticks to my fingers, like the smell from roasting meat on your clothes after a meal at a badly-ventilated taverna. The phone rings and I drag myself into the hall. The receiver smells like my vagina, too.

"What are you doing right now?" Anna says.

I shudder at that *right now*. "Nothing," I answer.

"Want to go for a walk?"

At last I have a secret. A new Ikeja, a chewed-up cricket in my mouth, a broken egg starting to smell in my suitcase.

"You're somewhere else today," Anna says when we meet.

"I'm tired."

We sit on a bench in Exarheia Square, her head on my knees.

"I decided to study art, too."

"Oh, nice."

"That's all you have to say?" Anna gives me a sideways glance. Since we got back she's touchier than ever, perpetually on edge. If a floorboard creaks, her whole body tightens and she asks, "Earthquake?" Fear makes her even prettier. Annoyance, too. Her eyes widen, she tosses her hair and bites her lip as if she's in the midst of an existential crisis.

"I think we could study different things and still be best friends."

"Oh, really?"

"We don't always need to do exactly the same thing, Anna."

"But then we'll grow apart, we won't be so close anymore, like your mother and Mrs. Steedworthy. Or Antigone and Françoise."

Françoise used to be Antigone's best friend. She was an activist, too, but then she got married and had three kids and ended up doing two loads of laundry a day. She didn't have time anymore to go out for coffee or talk about revolution.

"We'll always be together, Anna."

"What about this summer?"

"I'll take you with me to Aegina."

"Yeah, right. You'll be busy with Angelos all day."

I've been dreaming of him all year.

"You'll be the death of me, child!" Mom says.

She's standing in the doorway, gesturing toward the heaps of clothes and books on the floor of my room, at my drawings, at the records strewn around the stereo.

"Just look at this mess. Really, is this what a young lady's room looks like?"

Mom thinks that anyone female should dust and sew dresses and cook lentils all day.

"I told you, I'll clean it up. Stop being hysterical."

She takes off one of her slippers and throws it at my head. I push her out into the hallway, but she manages to stick her other slipper through the crack and so I slam the door on her foot by mistake. Mom shrieks. She stands there before me, an awful look on her face, sobbing. These days she's always crying. Because I don't pick up my clothes, because I stay out late and go around with good-for-nothings, because I never think about how she might feel. She wanders through the apartment in a plastic suit that's supposed to help her lose weight, though all it does is make her look like an overweight astronaut. The suit rustles like a trash bag. It's an incredibly annoying noise that only stops when Mom lies down on the sofa to read the latest installment of some romance story in *Woman*.

"I'm sorry," I whisper.

Mom isn't crying because of her foot, it's a different kind of crying. She's making this high-pitched, inarticulate noise, which sounds as if it were coming from the body she used to have, the thin one, trapped somewhere in the depths of that plastic suit.

"I can't take it anymore," she says.

I hug her, not because I want to, but because she wants me to.

"Where did I go wrong with you?"

I wish that for once she would ask where she went wrong with herself.

Mom has to go to the hospital for a thyroid operation. Before she goes, she fills the freezer with biftekia. Dad and I eat silently in front of the television, watching *Dallas*.

"How's school?" he asks.

"Fine," I say.

The rest is silence, except for our chewing and J.R.'s voice: "Don't think you'll get away with it. You'll pay for this!"

I spend my afternoons locked in the bathroom. I've got things to do. At night I read *Cosmopolitan* to learn tricks that Angelos might like, or Simone de Beauvoir's *The Second Sex* to learn other things, for myself. It's past midnight when I finally lie down and watch the reflection of headlights from cars in the street flitting across the ceiling and dream that I'm the perfect woman: a revolutionary, like de Beauvoir, but also just a normal person, like my mother, blond like Anna, and dressed like the models on the cover of *Cosmopolitan*. Only in real life a woman like that would be strange, almost a monster.

I'll have to choose.

"Okay, let's organize a plan of attack."

Anna is sitting on the bed Aunt Amalia and I used to share. This year it's Anna's and mine.

"Nothing works, I'm telling you. All he's interested in is rocks."

Angelos isn't going to be a nuclear physicist in the end. He's studying geology, since that's the department his exam scores were good enough for. He goes up hiking in the mountains with his friends from school and they dig up rocks all day. He has a 500cc motorbike and if you run into him on the beach, you can't take your eyes off him: his curly hair blows in the wind, his white jeans are perfectly ripped at the knee and the leather band on his wrist gives him a wild, romantic air. Angelos is the first right-wing guy I like. Okay, so he's not exactly right-wing, just apolitical. For him, politics is no match for digging up rocks. We grew up together in the summers. He barely speaks to his sisters, and only ever throws an occasional "Hey" in my direction, but he's a good guy. He has that stern kindness I admire in boys. He could never be a "stuffed shirt," like the boys at school. He's not full of himself the way they are.

When we got to Aegina, Anna gave him the once over. She says she finds him sort of boring, but she respects my choice. And now we're sitting on the bed making plans.

"I'll let you borrow my blue eye shadow," she says. "You're going to have to dress really carefully if you want to beguile him."

It always surprises me when Anna talks about clothes or makeup or uses words like "beguile." I'm still stuck on my old impression of her, totally sexless, still a child. I have to keep reminding myself of how irresistible she is in her khaki shorts and blue eye shadow.

"And stop biting your nails!" she shouts.

Anna's nails are painted with clear polish. Her hair smells heavenly. She's wearing a bracelet with green stones and half-moon earrings.

"Just show me what I have to do."

Anna laughs. She paints a layer of polish on my nonexistent nails. Then she gets her hairbrush from the other room and does my hair, parting it in the middle. Finally, she lends me a pair of earrings and her new denim skirt. No more white face powder, no more dark lipstick. We're girls again.

"Perfect," she says.

"What about my glasses?"

"Your glasses are the most beguiling thing about you, Maria!"

She grabs my shoulders, turns me toward the full-length mirror on the closet door. I see her reflection first: that angelic face, her dimple, her eyes, two deep pools. For a second I imagine I'm her. But Anna shakes me back to reality: I'm completely colorless, my eyes and hair are the color of a smushed turd—who was I to make fun of Angeliki? And why does Anna have to be so beautiful? Why couldn't there be a communist God?

"Say something, merde! Talk to him!"

Angelos comes up to us on his motorbike, rests one high-top on the sidewalk and revs the engine for no reason.

"You girls having fun?" he asks.

"Sure," I say.

I feel like I might faint. Ever since I discovered those strange reactions my body has I'm shy around boys, I'm afraid they might somehow guess what I do in the bathroom. With Angelos it's the worst.

Anna comes to my rescue. "Want to give us a ride home?" she says.

She gives me one of her famous pinches so that I'll get on first and be the one to hug him around the waist. She hops up behind me, and it's the most wonderful moment of the whole summer: Anna protecting me, Angelos driving me, guiding my way. I dream that we're flying, that I'm weightless, that I've shed all thoughts, even my vagina. We're bodiless. Angels crossing the sky.

When we pull up in front of the house, Angelos kills the engine and I plummet back to earth. I get off on the wrong side and my leg brushes up against the red-hot exhaust pipe. I refuse to scream, because Angelos is watching. I just bite my lips. There's a perfectly round red mark on my skin. *Angelos's imprint*, I think. Even the pain makes my love grow.

They put burn cream on my leg and wrap it up. I'm an invalid and everyone pampers me. They bring me a sketch pad. Anna reads me some incomprehensible passages from *A Lover's Discourse* by Roland Barthes: *an ancient sign which . . . in the remote days of my earliest childhood . . . afflicted me with a compulsion to speak which leads me to say "I love you" in one port of call after another, until some other receives this phrase and gives it back to me*. Angelos buys me the latest issue of *Mickey Mouse*. Martha and Fotini make me chocolate mousse out of a box, then sit at the foot of my bed and chatter about this and that. I like to have them all buzzing around me. They're my new family. We'll move to Paris together, Anna and I will study psychology and art, Angelos can do a masters in geology. Martha and Fotini will cook for us.

Maybe God is a communist after all.

"Can I come in?"

Angelos pokes his head in the door.

"Of course," I say.

He sits on the floor, directly opposite my bed. We start in on one of those philosophical conversations that never go anywhere. Education, people, death, that sort of thing.

"Are you thinking of doing a masters?" I ask.

"It depends. There's this girl here . . ." he says, smiling.

"Do I know her?"

"What do you think?" he crawls on his knees over to the bed, rests his chin on my pillow. "What I'm wondering is if she, you know . . ."

"You could ask," I say, and swallow hard.

"So I'm asking. What do you think?"

"I think she does. I'm sure she does."

Angelos hugs me tightly, but doesn't kiss me yet. He's shy, bright red, and my heart is about to burst.

"So she told you?" he asks, sighing into my hair.

"What?"

"Anna told you she likes me?"

My temperature spikes. Aunt Amalia says I should have dressed more warmly. Kyria Pavlina thinks it's psychological, the shock of my accident. I've found my explanation in the book by Barthes: *Sometimes, hysterically, my own body produces the incident: an evening I was looking forward to with delight, a heartfelt declaration whose effect, I felt, would be highly beneficial—these I obstruct by a stomach ache, an attack of grippe: all the possible substitutes of hysterical aphonia.* That's the name for what I've got: hysterical aphonia.

Martha and Fotini bring me romance novels from the kiosk, which are always written by some Rachel or Betty or Nerina and have dramatic titles: *The Misunderstanding*, or *The Price of Love*, or *Fleeting Time*. They read them in a single day, bawling their eyes out, then have to wait until the next one is released the following Thursday. It's the picture on the cover that interests me: a woman, almost always blond, gazing over her shoulder, hand on her heart, at the man walking up to her from behind, a glass of champagne in each hand. Or the woman is walking off, suitcase in hand, and the man is running after her, his tie loosened and flapping in the breeze. Or they're dancing in the moonlight. Anna is nowhere to be found. I picture her with her hand on her heart, or packing a suitcase for a vacation with Angelos, or the two of them dancing in the moonlight. Barthes writes, as if he knew: *Countless episodes in which I fall in love with someone loved by my best friend: every rival has first been a master, a guide, a barker, a mediator.*

Aunt Amalia puts it more simply: "Your friend is a spoiled brat," she says as she puts curlers in her hair.

Spoiled is right.

"She can't just stay out until all hours without ever telling me where she's going or where she's been. What am I supposed to say to her parents?" Aunt Amalia can't comprehend that there are parents in the world like Antigone and Stamatis, who you can call by their first name, or smoke in front of, or go to demonstrations with.

I roll over and pretend I'm asleep. Whereas actually I'm picking at the stuccoed wall, scratching into it with my nails. I, too, need to leave my mark somewhere.

A gentle breeze picks up, stirring the bougainvillea outside the window. Its shadow falls on the sheet, shaping human figures that kiss and part, kiss and part. Anna undresses in the dark and crawls into bed next to me. She wraps herself around me and starts to cry. Her tears trickle down my back, tickling me. With her arms around my waist it's as if the two of us are speeding along on a motionless motorcycle. As if we're headed at breakneck speed toward some interior spot, deep inside ourselves. Barthes writes, *Jealousy is an equation involving three permutable (indeterminate) terms: one is always jealous of two persons at once: I am jealous of the one I love and of the one who loves the one I love. The odiosamato (as the Italians call the "rival") is also loved by me: he interests me, intrigues me, appeals to me.*

"Can you ever forgive me, Maria?"

I pretend I'm asleep. Anna sinks her face into my hair, sighs on the nape of my neck. Her body has an acrid smell, like the silver spoons my mother is always polishing.

"Please, Maria, talk to me . . ."

She sticks her knees in the hollows of mine and we're like two of those spoons in my mother's drawer—some of that metallic smell

rubs off on me, too. She doesn't relax her grip all night, I keep
waking and drifting off again in her asphyxiating embrace. Only in
the morning, when she gets up to pee, do I realize that what I was
smelling was the smell of sex, her sex. The mussel.

Odiosamato.

I throw off the sheets and hurriedly get dressed. I don't want to
be pitied. I throw a swimsuit, towel, my sketch pad and charcoals
in a bag, and *A Lover's Discourse*. I sneak out of the house on tiptoe,
borrow Fotini's bicycle and ride off, upright on the pedals all the
way to Perdika. I've got a certain rock formation in mind. That's
where I'll stay. I spread my towel in the cave, open the pad and start
to sketch. I'm still there at sunset, drawing people with tiger tails,
portraits of Medusa with snakes for hair, strange animals that don't
exist in nature. When it starts to get dark, I lie down with Barthes:
*The lover's anxiety: it is the fear of a mourning which has already occurred,
at the very origin of love, from the moment when I was first "ravished."
Someone would have to be able to tell me: "Don't be anxious any more—
you've already lost him/her."*

Him, her. Him, her, himherhimherhim. My teeth are chattering.

I'm not hungry, or thirsty, or tired. My gaze is trained on a little
spotted insect slowly creeping up my towel. I've lived this scene
before. I know what comes next. I reach out my hand, grab it, and
put it in my mouth.

A helpless insect. Cold, crunchy. African.

Anna and I have decided on a major change: we're going to cut our
hair. September is hot this year, and besides, we can't very well start
high school with braids and ponytails. Aunt Amalia takes us to a
fancy salon in Kolonaki. The hairdresser's name is Gino. He looks
like a rooster, with a coxcomb of dyed orange hair. A red-haired
girl hands us a book with pictures of different hairstyles to flip

through. There's a bob we both like, with bangs and wisps framing the face.

"No," says Gino. "It's not right for you girls. You're young, do something daring for once!"

He rests his scissors high up on my neck, and with one fell swoop my hair lands in a heap on the floor. I look like one of the convicts Foucault wrote about in the latest issue of *Actuel*—the ones who try to obliterate the deep division between innocence and guilt. Anna looks like one of Genet's prisoners. Her face looks naked, almost debased; her enormous, questioning eyes are more prominent than ever.

"What did he do to us?" she whispers, throwing me a sideways glance in the mirror.

The red-haired girl finishes us off with an assortment of gels and sprays. We leave the salon looking like aliens, hair stiff with hairspray. Aunt Amalia takes us to her apartment, which Anna and I call "the antique store," because it's full of old furniture and taxidermied birds. She makes us spaghetti with meat sauce, but neither of us can eat a thing. We lock ourselves in the bathroom and cry.

"Girls, for goodness' sake, don't make such a fuss!" Aunt Amalia shouts from the other side of the door. "Just wash it a few times and it'll be longer."

We wash it, we pull on the ends, but our hair doesn't get any longer.

"How are we going to show our faces at school?" I ask.

"What's Angelos going to say?" she says.

That's not my problem. From the morning they found me at the far end of the beach at Perdika, shaking with cold, feverish and delirious, I swore I'd never give the two of them another thought. Angelos was dead to me. Anna is still alive, of course, of necessity. She's my best friend. Odiosamato.

And as always, she finds a way: she manages to do her hair in a way that looks good. A few wisps tucked behind her ears and she actually looks cute. I don't. I push my hair back, it falls forward. I brush it forward, it goes wherever it wants. Then one Sunday when we're hanging out in Monastiraki, by the flea market, my gaze falls on a pair of army pants in a shop window on Adrianou Street.

"Aren't they a little too punk?" Anna says, making a face.

All of a sudden I flash back to Raoul and Michel, the anti-racist movement, the Sex Pistols, the squatters in Berlin.

Why not?

In the army pants I feel stronger. I put three pins on my leather jacket, all of Siouxsie and the Banshees. I walk around singing "Christine" under my breath, as if it were my own personal anthem: *She tries not to shatter, kaleidoscope style, personality changes behind her red smile, now she's in purple now she's the turtle, disintegrating* . . . What exactly is kaleidoscope style? Or purple disintegration? The weirdest boys in school come up to me during break and want to talk to me, all because I'm wearing my leather jacket over my uniform.

Anna, in contrast, is going through an annoyingly pink phase. She says sex is allowed now, since it'll help us mature. If I push her on it, she quotes Barthes: "In no love story I have ever read is a character ever tired," she says proudly, as if she thought it up herself. And yet she herself seems tired, tranquil, predictable: she waits for Angelos after school, sits with her legs to one side of his motorbike seat, folded just so, as if we were back in the '50s and she were Grace Kelly riding off with her prince. They have sex every weekend. As for me, I'm there in the bathroom, alone. I'm dating a guy named Pavlos, we're still at the hand-on-the-chest stage, but I tell Anna all kinds of stories that I lift straight from the pages of

Erotic Harmony. Pavlos has a motorbike, too. But he understands my fear of exhaust pipes and never offers me a ride. He just pushes his bike in the street as we walk side by side, and the whole school makes fun of us for it.

Pavlos is an active member of the socialist party's youth movement. Ever since the Rallis administration resigned, he's been slapping PASOK stickers on parked cars. He wants to convert me.

"There's no way I'm turning PASOK," I tell him.

"But it's totally obvious, don't you see? Papandreou is the only solution."

I call Papandreou "Dr. Dolittle," Pavlos calls him "a charismatic leader." We usually part ways having fought. On October 15th, during the run-up to the elections, PASOK holds a rally in Syntagma Square and Pavlos climbs a utility pole. I see him on television, waving his plastic flag as if it were a banner for the revolution.

"How'd he manage to muster such a crowd?" my father shouts, slapping his palm against the table.

"Do you think he'll get elected?" I ask.

"Absolutely not, I'd see the world end first." Dad remains unrepentantly right-wing.

And yet the world does end. A hundred and seventy-two seats in parliament, 48.6% of the popular vote. How could I forget that moment? The day PASOK wins the elections, I lose my virginity.

Now that's what I call a "rendezvous with history."

We can see everything from the roof of our apartment building. We can hear the honking of horns, the rhythmic chanting—"PA-SOK, PA-SOK"—and the slogan, "With you, Andreas, we'll make Greece new." Dad is seething, Mom just shrugs.

These are dark days, they're agreed on that. My parents are a couple, and exhibit the fundamental weakness of all grown-up couples: they respond to things nearly identically. If Anna and Angelos stay together, which will pull the other toward his or her way of thinking? Will Anna move toward the right, drink coffee, and swap cheap romances with Martha and Fotini? Or will Angelos become an activist and follow her to France? Both scenarios seem equally unlikely.

The downstairs buzzer rings twice.

"Who could that be, at this hour?" Dad says.

"It's Anna! I'm going out."

"Two girls, out on their own in this chaos?" Mom's shrill voice follows me out the door, fading as I run down the stairs.

It's Pavlos, and the double ring on the buzzer is our signal for emergency situations. He grabs me and twirls me in the air. "We won, baby!" he shouts. I'm not a baby, I've got on my leather jacket with the punk pins, but I like the way his eyes are shining. He wants to go down to Syntagma to be in the thick of the celebrating crowds. I climb onto his motorbike for the first time—today I'm not scared, the atmosphere is electric. Other drivers call out to us, make the victory sign, all because Pavlos has a flag in one hand. Everyone is shouting, "The *pe*-ople *won't* forget—*what* the *right* has *done*," and honking their horns to the rhythm. That's something I can shout, too, it's a leftist slogan. My heart is pounding; I finally feel as if I belong somewhere.

The rhythmic chanting of "PA-SOK, PA-SOK" imprints itself on me, working its way inside as we drive down to Syntagma, like a refrain by Siouxsie and the Banshees, or the jingle from a Coca-Cola ad on TV. It's as if the word "PASOK" has come to mean love, or peace, or justice, simply because there are so many of us, and we're pounding together on the horns of our cars, and we all want for something to change. As if I'm not myself, no longer the same old Maria, I feel my mouth open and that same cry pouring out: "PA-*SOK!*" A shock indeed! Pavlos drives the motorbike up onto the sidewalk, turns around on the seat and takes hold of me in an entirely different way, pulls up my shirt and bites me low on my belly. His eyes shine in the dark.

"Let's get out of here," he says.

He spreads a sleeping bag on the roof of his building, behind the water heater. It's warm here, the cars down below are still blasting their horns, and we've put it all on pause. We've switched gears from a major revolution to a minor one, though actually I couldn't say anymore which is which. It hurts, a lot. I feel like my vagina isn't there, doesn't exist, or that Pavlos is excavating it as he goes, digging blindly and insistently with his gyrations. A narrow space, all membrane, fights back. I clench my teeth and tell myself that millions of women all over the world do this all the time. To make the torture end, I wrap my legs around his waist and pull him closer, willingly abolishing the slight distance between us. There's no sound, no pop of a champagne cork. But I know: I'm not a virgin anymore.

It's nothing like my experiments in the bathroom, the circular motions, the absolute happiness. *Erotic Harmony* is perfectly clear about this: *It can take a little while, even a long while, for a young woman to learn to enjoy lovemaking.* It says nothing about the breaking of the hymen, the relief of that moment. The passage from humiliation to freedom.

It says nothing, either, about how Aunt Amalia must feel.

"Why do you girls never button your coats? You'll catch cold!" Aunt Amalia greets us at the door. I smile. Ever since I stopped being a virgin, I feel like I'm the aunt and she's the niece.

"We have to find her a man," Anna says.

"Are you kidding? She's fifty years old."

Anna insists that we need to sit her down, do her makeup, buy her a new suit with a slitted skirt, and take her for a walk in the Field of Ares.

"She's not a dog, Anna! She's a person!"

Anna pays no heed. She whirls into the living room like a tornado and pinches Aunt Amalia on the cheek.

"Okay, get dressed!" she cries. "You're coming with us."

Aunt Amalia calls her a handful and a spoiled brat behind her back, but to her face it's as if Amalia is a schoolgirl and Anna her teacher.

"Where could you girls possibly take me? I'd spoil your fun."

"Don't be ridiculous. We're going to find you a husband!"

Aunt Amalia laughs.

"See? She likes the idea!" Anna says, winking at me. We make Aunt Amalia put on some lipstick, take her by the arm, one on each side, and pull her out into the street. Anna is in a fabulous mood. She points to this man or that and says, "Do you like that one? What about him? On a scale of one to ten? A six? Come on, Amalia, you're too harsh. How about eight?"

Aunt Amalia is wearing a woolen dress with little black doodads sewn onto it. All her clothes are made from dark fabrics. She toys with her corsage and gives a nervous laugh. It's the first time I've ever seen her so happy. She looks the men up and down as if they were vegetables at the farmer's market, just as Anna wants her to. Then again, isn't that how she looked at them her whole life long? The king was a perfect ten, an enormous, ripe hothouse tomato, and beside him the poor, scrawny bunches of parsley could only hope for a five at best. For some inexplicable reason I've got tears in my eyes. I whisper to Anna to stop the game.

"What's wrong with you?" she says. "It's never too late."

But it is. If you don't discover your vagina at fifteen, you just keep putting it off. You grow old before your time, with your taxidermied birds and your creaky, worm-eaten chairs.

·

It's November, we're wearing turtlenecks and are opening a bottle of Veuve Clicquot on the grass. We cry *"Santé, amour, fraternité!"* and sip from Antigone's best glasses, the ones hordes of famous Greek and French revolutionaries have drunk from. The Field of Ares has never known such luxury. Today I'm turning sixteen, and Anna organized a surprise picnic: chèvre sandwiches, champagne and a cake from the Metropolitan Bakery. I blow out the red candle and some crazy guy passing by laughs and claps his hands maniacally.

"Great, now get lost," Anna calls to him. "Beat it!"

He doesn't budge. Anna shouts, "I'm coming for you!" and gives him a threatening look, and the man runs off, emitting a series of inarticulate cries. Perhaps in his madness he understood something I haven't yet? She's my best friend, but I don't trust her anymore. She spent her entire allowance on my birthday, and today she hugs me and shouts, "Happy birthday to my best friend!" But tomorrow she might give me the cold shoulder. That's just how Anna is. Odiosamato.

The burn from Angelos's exhaust pipe has faded into a scar. But it's still there.

"Any perversion associated with the reproductive system will affect an individual's psyche, social standing, intellectual development and general progress. Perversions of this sort can cost us dearly in our lives. For that reason, we have to be very careful about what kind of people we choose to spend time with . . ."

Kyria Kontomina is at her desk, leaning on one elbow, reading the next chapter of our anthropology textbook out loud with somewhat more interest than usual. She must not have done any class prep before coming to school, and didn't know what would turn up in today's lesson.

"Look how she's sitting," Anna says. "Like a lounge singer on a piano."

Poor Kyria Kontomina. She's pudgy, with a bright red face, and puts her hair back in clips as if she were in elementary school. She always wears black, with a colored scarf around her neck to match that day's clips. Her glasses hang from a chain around her neck and she's always fidgeting with them during class: she peers at us over the top of her glasses, or through them, or lifts them up and peers at us from *under* them. It's probably because there's no smoking allowed in the classroom, and outside of class Kontomina smokes like a chimney. Just like us.

Quickie for a fag? Anna writes on my desk, then winks at me. Ever since I had sex with Pavlos I haven't had a moment's peace. Cigarettes are *fags*, every loose sidewalk tile is a *hump*, and if I go out with Pavlos she's concerned the next day about how *bushed* I look, and can we *snatch* a moment to talk. She's always punning on his name, too: she calls him Kavlos instead of Pavlos, from "*kavla*," which means having the hots for someone. In psychology class she never misses an opportunity to whisper to me about "Kavlov's dogs." Not even Angelos's mother can escape her wit: Kyria Pavlina is Kyria Kavlina to her now.

We tell Kyria Kontomina that we have a student council meeting. Anna is our class president and I'm treasurer. We not infrequently abuse the power of our positions to sneak off and smoke in the girls' room.

"What's up?" I ask.

"Angelos and I had a fight."

It doesn't even occur to her that this news might make me happy, that he actually meant something to me.

"Again?"

"Merde! We're just so different. He says white, I say black."

"What happened this time?"

"He wants me to go to a wedding with him next Sunday."

"Blech!"

"His cousin is getting married."

"Don't go, Anna. Marriage is the greatest social hypocrisy there is."

I'm parroting her own words back at her. Ever since Antigone took us to see those one-act plays at the Peroke, we've always sworn that we'd never go to a wedding, no matter what, because it's like silently accepting the history of the oppression of women. Anna bows her head and crosses her arms. In that position she looks like a good little Christian, even a bride. I take a drag on my cigarette, inhaling her image along with the smoke. Anna a bride? Impossible!

"I promised I would go in a moment of weakness and now I want to take it back."

"Weakness?"

"Yeah, we were in bed, you know how it is . . . but it was so stupid of me!"

I try to mimic the tone Anna takes when she's rebuffing me. "Really stupid," I say.

"Do you think it matters, just this once?"

"It's not the frequency that counts."

"What about what Nietzsche said, *Einmal ist keinmal?*"

This year Anna started taking German lessons so that she can read philosophy in the original. But if she keeps going the way she is, she won't need German at all, or philosophy, for that matter. The most she'll be reading is wedding magazines and cheap romances. I tell her that—admittedly with a dose of glee. Anna takes a deep drag and blows the smoke in my face. Then she crushes the butt of her cigarette under her shoe with such rage that you'd think she was crushing me.

•

"Was the bride pretty?" I whisper, mimicking my mother's tone of voice, from her days of drinking tea with Mrs. Steedworthy. They were always chattering about weddings, babies, and dress patterns. Anna gives me a look like a wounded dog. Her silence only encourages me. "And the wedding dress? Oh, tell me about the wedding dress, please!"

She slaps her palm against the desk. "Shut up, Maria!" The whole class turns to look. We're in essay-writing class and she and I always finish first. I mean, how much is there to say about something like: *In the context of our nation's entry into the European Economic Community, certain historical changes are unquestionably taking place. Greeks themselves, no less than other Europeans, are being called upon to protect our cultural heritage and to proceed with the modernization of Greek society. Please present your views on this subject.* The topics are always as demagogic as PASOK proclamations: context, unquestionably, modernization. Anna and I react by writing as formally as we can, and Kyria Zapa, our writing teacher, scrawls at the bottom of our papers: *Mediocre. Try to express your ideas more simply.* Or: *Don't forget, there's only one accent mark now!* The government recently abolished the polytonic system of accent marks, but we still use graves and circumflexes out of habit.

"If you're finished, you can go out to the yard and work out your differences there," Kyria Zapa says.

She doesn't need to say it twice. We run to the girls' room, hop up on the windowsill and light cigarettes. Anna gives me a pinch to end all pinches. Then she changes tack, droops on the sill, pale as a sheet.

"What's wrong? Was there an earthquake and I didn't notice?"

"Don't be so hard on me," she says.

"Don't be such an idiot," I say.

"I'm not an idiot, I'm pregnant."

I swallow hard, the smoke trapped in my lungs.

"Will you come with me for the abortion?" she asks.

Merde, an earthquake all right. Off the Richter scale.

What our religion textbook has to say about abortion: *An individual's sense of self-importance leads to an arbitrary intervention in the progress and preservation of the world.* Anna ostentatiously burns that page over the cinders we've heaped up over our potatoes. We're sitting by the fireplace at the house in Plaka, pretending to be brave. Tomorrow is the big day. Angelos doesn't know a thing. Anna broke up with him for good and doesn't ever want to see him again. Anything having to do with children and marriage makes her sick.

"But he needs to accept his responsibility," Antigone says.

"I don't want him to!" Anna shouts, so loudly and hysterically that the conversation ends there.

I get kind of hysterical, too, with Pavlos. I check all our condoms to make sure they didn't break, I wash myself obsessively after sex and keep having this recurring nightmare. There's a store that sells sperm in little plastic containers. If you buy just the right amount you don't have to worry about an unwanted pregnancy. So women come to shop there, only they go all gaga over the sperm, buy too much and end up getting into trouble. Among them is a girl who looks like Anna. I watch all this unfold and decide I can live without sperm, it's not the end of the world.

"Be careful," says the girl who looks like Anna. "All men are monsters."

I haven't heard that phrase since we were nine years old.

Digenis struggles for his life and the earth terrifies him. I don't know why that line from a folk song in our Greek literature textbook comes to my mind as Anna opens her eyes on the stretcher and whispers, "Antigone? Maria?" We stand over her, each of us holding one of her hands, until the nurses push us aside and lift her swiftly and surely from the gurney onto the bed. In the other bed is a forty-year-old woman from the provinces. She has five kids already and doesn't want a sixth. She's watching *The Bold and the Beautiful* with the sound off. Fortunately Anna is completely out of it from the drugs. She hates soap operas. Still, I stand over her in such a way as to block her view of the television. Anna doesn't open her eyes. When she speaks, she just mouths the words, as soundless as the actors on the show.

"Water . . ."

Antigone dabs some water on her lips. I'm afraid I might faint. It's only the second time I've been inside a hospital, the first was after Mom's thyroid operation. Hospitals terrify me, and back then I swore to myself that if anyone ever tried to make me visit a sick person again I would emigrate to Africa. But this isn't just any sick person. It's Anna. She needs me. She's not strong anymore.

"I'll never forget . . ." Anna says, still without sound.

"Shhh," I say.

". . . you're the best friend in the world."

I hug her tightly. Outside the rain is falling hard. The woman in the other bed turns up the volume with the remote control. The music from the show envelops the room but we don't make fun, don't pinch one another, don't make faces.

Tomorrow this might strike us as funny, we might say, "*Einmal ist keinmal.*" But what if we actually get into trouble for real? What if we start to watch soap operas, to cry, to not have abortions? What if we get tired of being kids and want to be women?

I can't even think about it.

Antigone gives me Yiorgos Ioannou's latest book for my birthday, *Of Adolescents and Others.* Adults just love to remind you that you're not one of them yet. "From now on we get to celebrate your birthday and the Greek National Resistance together!" she says, popping a bottle of champagne. There's no picnic this year. These days nature disgusts Anna, and she doesn't like to walk, either. She's gotten listless and lethargic.

"Yeah, except that I was actually born in November, whereas they just chose the 25th as a symbolic date for the resistance."

This year the government has declared November 25th an official holiday in honor of armed resistance against the Axis occupation, because on that day in 1942 a group of Greek partisans blew up a bridge in the village of Gorgopotamos. I worry that Antigone is happier about that anniversary than about my birthday. Anna, meanwhile, isn't happy about anything anymore. She pokes at the fire like a modern-day Cinderella weighed down with worries. She broke up with Angelos, she quit smoking, started again, quit again, then finally started up for good and is reading a book of poetry by Yiannis Patilis called *Non-smoker in a Land of Smokers*. She has a deep need for symbolic gestures and symbolic speech.

"Did you hear that Evangelos Papanoutsos died?" she says to me.

"And?"

"I thought you might give it some more thought, about studying psychology."

"Anna, I've made up my mind. I want to study art."

"Fine, I get it."

"We'll still go to campus together every morning. And spend our evenings together. We'll eat our chouquettes. What more do you want?"

"I want to not be alone for even a second."

Antigone folds Anna in her arms and strokes her hair, which is long enough now to be pulled back into a short ponytail. Antigone calls her "my little girl."

You'd think it was Anna's birthday, not mine.

Five

"Where are we going?"

"You'll see."

She's driving an old Porsche. The seats are deep, our bodies reclined at an unusual angle. The smell of the fake croissants from that café is still clinging to our clothes. When we reach Kifisias Avenue, she points out the buildings her husband designed. Precisely what I expected: tinted glass and marble columns, with hideous public art outside.

"Did you choose those sculptures?"

"Yeah, aren't they awful?"

"The worst I've ever seen. Why did you pick them?"

"It's my only way of fighting the system, Maria."

"Are you kidding? By throwing money and opportunities at talentless artists?"

"You want to know exactly what I do?" She shifts into fifth and the Porsche darts down the avenue, passing on the left and right, weaving between cars. We're flying. Her face hardens and I get a glimpse of the old Anna. The wind musses her hair and she laughs a guttural laugh—laughs, then coughs. "I shape the image of our company's taste. A bronze statue holding a cell phone—can you think of anything more kitsch than that?"

"Did you ever think of the people who have to see that shitty sculpture every day on their way to work?"

"That's why I put it there. To make them furious. When they get mad enough, when they can't stand the idiocy and the terrible taste a second longer, when they're sunk up to their chins in shit, they'll finally go and smash that statue with crowbars. All you can do is push things to the limit, cross your arms and wait."

"And build office complexes out of glass? Greenhouses for the workers?"

"As Malouhos says, glass buildings are the easiest to break."

"Wait, you mean your husband's in on it, too? He builds and sells for the good of the revolution?"

"Malouhos is a genius!"

She's lost it. She still wants to save the world, but in a way only a crazy person could think up. We're back on our magic carpet, flying at a thousand kilometers an hour. Instead of a table on wheels, it's a Porsche. Instead of the songs of Françoise Hardy, the wedding march for the marriage of two lunatics.

The house in Ekali looks as if it hasn't been touched since the '70s, though of course that's the style now. It's full of shag rugs and shiny leather couches without a single scratch on them—the opposite of Irini's jacket. Orange stools with dull metal legs, straight from the junk shop. Futuristic white floor lamps. In the kitchen, stainless steel cabinets and recessed lighting. In a heavy gold frame with a red velvet border, the poster from the house in Plaka: the kid peeing on the crown. They've hung it in the dining room.

"We take that down whenever we have royalist investors to dinner," Anna says with restrained pride.

The table is completely white, with leather stools.

"What happens if you spill sauce on it?"

"We don't eat sauces, remember? We eat healthy, lots of salads. Old habits die hard."

"How is Antigone these days?"

She lights a cigarette. She blows the smoke as far from her as she can, squinting her eyes. There's no white eyebrow anymore to give that old dramatic effect. But her face is white, an expressionless mask.

"Antigone died."

"What? I hadn't heard! When? How?"

"I don't want to talk about it. Can I fix you a drink?"

"Anna, what's wrong with you? I'm asking because I loved her!"

"You loved her! Everyone loved her. But did *she* love anyone? Now *there's* the rub."

She tosses her boots onto one of the rugs. The shag is thick, but the thud still echoes through the minimalist house.

The sun is setting and Anna is fixing a second round of martinis when we hear a key fumbling in the lock. Daphne bursts into the house, raising a ruckus with her roller skates. After her comes a pregnant woman with beads of sweat on her forehead.

"Daphne, didn't I tell you not to tire Svetlana out? She has a baby in her tummy!"

Daphne keeps on skating as if she hasn't heard, until she practically runs right into me. "Oh, it's my teacher! Are you friends with my mother again? Come here, I want to show you something!"

The little girl pulls me by the hand. We clamber upstairs and she takes me straight to her room. She's even messier than I am, there are things scattered everywhere: pieces from board games, stuffed animals, clothes, hair bands, broken pastels, lumps of plasticine.

"This is my cave!" she says, pulling me down to peer into the space between her bed and her desk. She's padded it with a blanket and put her teddy bears in there, and a tea set in one corner. Directly opposite is a heap of sweaters, piled into a woolen barricade.

"With all this thunder and lighting, we have to keep warm, see?"

"I see."

"Do you want some tea?"

Anna finds us in her daughter's cave. We're sitting cross-legged, sipping non-existent tea from cups the size of thimbles.

"Come on out," she says to me. "You're a grown-up now."

Well, not so grown up. Not too big for a child's cave.

Anna insists on my staying to meet Malouhos.

"Yes, yes!" Daphne says, hanging from my forearm.

"Another time."

"How about another martini?"

"Anna, really! We've already had two."

"You mean you can't count to three?"

She's giving me the evil eye. I remember that look well. All those years of psychoanalysis didn't do a thing for her. When Anna wants something, there's no messing with her.

"Okay, fine, one for the road."

Their refrigerator has an ice maker. From across the room, with the shaker in her hand, Anna looks like some carefree housewife from a commercial. Self-sufficient, charming, a barefoot woman in jeans who's discovered the meaning of life in the circular movement of a cocktail shaker. And the olive, too: it sinks and rises back to the surface, hovering there in a region of transparent meaning. That's it, I'm drunk.

Anna goes upstairs to put Daphne to bed and for a little while I'm enveloped in the solitude of their vast living room. The space throbs around me like a huge, white, sanitized heart. I rest my cheeks in my palms, start to make plans: I'll go away, I'll disappear and cover my tracks so she won't ever find me. I'll quit my job. I'll go to live in some other country, as far from here as possible. Anna was always a harmful presence in my life, I have to free myself from her influence. She can't come and go whenever she pleases, completely destroy me, shake me up the way she shook up our drinks.

She comes down the stairs like a Hollywood star, hips swaying, cigarette clinging to her lips. She has an incredible mouth, there's no doubt about that. But it borders on brazen, too, as if she's constantly offering herself to anyone and everyone who comes along. She's changed into a robe. She points at the logo of a horse embroidered on the chest.

"See? That makes all the difference."

My plan to run away makes me more tolerant than I might otherwise be. "If you say so," I respond. But that just annoys her. She wants me to disagree so she can convince me bit by bit.

"You think I've lost it, don't you?"

"You're eccentric, you always were."

"I'm exploiting capital, Maria. It's what I always do. It's what I know how to do best. I can live without any money at all. Do you doubt me on that?"

She picks up an empty crystal vase from the coffee table.

"Look at this. Such a simple design, yet so expensive! Just look what money can buy. Where did the materials come from? How was it made? By whom? How different are those people's lives from your own?"

She opens her hands in a theatrical gesture, and the vase drops to the floor and breaks into a thousand pieces. A shard of glass sticks into her calf. She picks it out, licks a finger and wipes away the blood, casting an uneasy glance my way. She apparently still remembers my fear of blood. Though ever since I figured out the reason behind that fear, it's not so bad. Just a brief spike in my pulse, that's all.

I drain the last of my martini, sink my teeth into the olive. "I don't understand."

"What's to understand? I enjoyed that. It's been too long since I broke something."

"So you married him?" We're on our fourth martini and by now I can say whatever comes into my head.

"Stop it, Maria!"

"I mean, in a church?"

She curses theatrically and brings over a photograph album. "Here, if you really need proof. We got married at city hall in the sixth arrondissement. What kind of question is that, if we got married in a church?" As she bends to show me, her robe falls open. She's got on a matching nightgown underneath.

The album opens to a page that sends shivers down my spine. Is that her father? No, but it looks like him. The same blondish beard and untamed hair. He's younger than Stamatis and there's a kind of Olympian calm in his gaze. A compass of a man—you could use him to guide your way.

"What do you think?"

"Malouhos? I've got to admit, he's attractive . . ."

Anna at his side, equally attractive, with a fake white fur and pregnant belly. If I'm calculating correctly, the photograph must have been taken just seven or eight months after that thing happened to us, after we parted ways for good. She's beautifully made up for the ceremony, but if you know her well, you can see the fear in her eyes. The lack of confidence. Perhaps the lack of options, too.

"What about his life before you?"

"Two marriages. Three children. He'll never leave me, though."

Of course he'll never leave. If anyone leaves, it'll be her.

•

A warm handshake. A bow. Thick, wild eyebrows. And a funny first name: Aristomenis. He's part ancient Greek, part tired architect in designer jeans. Usually I abhor guys like him. But he has something about him, something to do with his not trying at all: he's just himself, and lets you be yourself, too. He seems modest, quiet. And he smokes a pipe, like Stamatis. He and Anna give one another a quick kiss, he musses her hair, asks after Daphne. They're a real couple, like my parents. Bound together by so many things.

"I've heard so much about you, Maria. Anna has worn my ear out with stories. I'll tell you over dinner. You'll stay and eat with us, right?"

"I was just getting ready to leave." My head is spinning from the martinis, my mind aching with memories. You can't just dig a hole, Aunt Amalia. It turns out it's not that easy.

"Where are you going to go, out here in the middle of nowhere? Stay and eat, I made stuffed tomatoes this weekend, with the first tomatoes from our garden. And they're better as leftovers. Afterward I'll drop you wherever you need to go."

"No, I don't want to put you out . . ."

"I've got a business drink later, I'll be going downtown anyhow."

I ask where the bathroom is. They point to a door under the stairs. I pee for hours, wash my hands. As I'm drying them on the hand towel I catch sight of something familiar in the mirror. A spattering of yellow. Lots of black. Snakes with crowns on their heads, pirogues, women in long skirts with flaming hems. She's framed my painting, my very first painting!

"Anna, can I talk to you for a second?"

"What is it?"

"Why did you hang this here? You always hated it."

"I don't hate it. It's grown on me over time."

"Then why did you put it in the bathroom? To humiliate me?"

"Oh, that's right, works of art belong in the living room, over the sofa. Maria, I don't even recognize you anymore! The bathroom was always our favorite room."

Yes, it was, back before you betrayed me. When I could still undress in front of you. Literally and metaphorically.

We chew discretely, silverware barely clinking. Aristomenis— Menis, Anna calls him—laughs loudly and deeply, as if he were gargling. I'd like to be able to call him a stuffed shirt with no personality, I'd like to find some flaw. But I can't, apart from all the wealth he's accumulated, and Anna has cast even that in a revolutionary light. As for his stuffed tomatoes, they're excellent, with parsley and raisins in the stuffing.

"I soaked them in wine first. Are they too soft?"

"They're perfect."

"Well, then, eat up. Why are you two looking at me like that?"

Probably because you're a rare bird, as men go. You're the man Anna always dreamed of, since grade school, though deep down she always thought you didn't exist. You cook, you garden, you fill the house with the smell of pipe smoke, a smell she adores. As an architect you support her and shelter her, literally: you've built a sturdy house, one that has quelled her fear of earthquakes. I'm sure you could care less about soccer, don't tell cheap jokes, don't look down on minorities, don't ask her why she's late, where she's been. You don't have a beer belly, and you seem to take no pride in your wealth. You're considerate to her friends. You were once very handsome, but your looks have faded a bit, just enough for her to feel safe with you. You're distinguished but unconventional. You don't puff yourself up, but you do believe in yourself. You also believe in a theory—an entirely irrational one, in my opinion. What matters, though, is that you believe, and that you've swept her up in that belief, so that she's finally able to reinvent herself. In short, you're a man made for Anna.

At night, Kifisias Avenue looks like an amusement park under construction. Mountains of cement, detours, floodlights illuminating the road works. Bulldozers parked on the shoulder, enormous billboards advertising the performances of pop singers at clubs on the coast—and in the background, Malouhos's glass buildings. A surreal landscape. Like a Dali painting.

"You find our theory perverse, don't you?"

"What can I say? It's a theory," I answer. Over dinner we locked horns a few times, though politely. I told them their ideas struck me as a patchwork of beliefs adopted by two people who were deeply bored.

"Molotov cocktails, marches, human shields—I've done all that, Maria. I'm too old for that now. Besides, we're living in the heart of the capitalist system. If we want to see results, we have to fight from the inside. We have to fight as actors on the stage of reality."

"What does that mean?"

"It means that human relationships are now based on inequality, on competition and work. Communication is bought and sold. The city has become a factory."

"And you're the factory boss, the industrialist par excellence."

"Isn't it important for the industrialist to have an awareness of the situation? To not get mad when some group of anarchists smashes his car?"

"First of all, anarchists don't smash cars. What you're saying sounds like Bakunin to me, with a sprinkling of the nightly news. Anarchists have contributed a lot less to the violence of this world than nationalists, socialists, monarchists, fascists, and conservatives, not to mention organized crime. Anarchists never had a Robespierre, or a Stalin, or a Pol Pot." I smile to myself in the dark. It's like one of our Direct Action meetings from years ago; I sound like Camus.

"But they did have a poetics of destruction. They had Nechayev. Do you remember what Kropotkin said? 'I hate these explosions, but I cannot condemn the hopeless.'"

"At any rate, we're not going to rewrite history on Kifisias Avenue."

"Let me put it another way: if you build nice, human offices, it means you believe in the value of labor. If you put people in a space where they'll feel and act like sheep, you've got greater chances of provoking some kind of response."

"Of course, self-destructing capitalism! Just what the Marxists said, after the war."

"What I'm talking about isn't Marxist. It's straight out of Proudhon: 'Destruam ut aedificabo.'"

"Can you explain that for us commoners who don't know Latin?"

"'I destroy in order to build.'"

"You know what I see in what you're saying? The people of Athens as guinea pigs. It's not enough that there isn't a decent sidewalk in the whole city, you go and shut them up in aquariums, too. You turn them into fish. And then you expect those fish to sing the anthem of a new revolution!"

"They've been promised Europe, right? And Europe has been brought to their doorstep. A semblance, of course, no one's actually importing the Eiffel Tower. French cheeses, clothes, ethnic restaurants, a false tolerance. At first it's all well and good. You take a number at the bank, you don't have to push and shove anymore. You conserve energy. And why? So that you can work even harder. You buy a car on monthly installments. Then a second car, again on monthly installments. You buy a television with Dolby surround sound, the whole house quakes as you watch the war in Yugoslavia, or a dozen people with handkerchiefs over their faces overturning cars and setting them on fire. You curse them. You're afraid they might set your car on fire, too. You keep working like a slave, buy a weekend home. You pile the whole family into your new car. You're looking for some kind of asylum, a pseudo-retreat, far from wars and banks. But there's so much traffic that you can't just zip down the highway to get there. You curse, pass, weave, practically get yourself killed. You're with me so far?"

We've gotten stuck, too, in the nighttime traffic on Kifisias, directly across from one of his buildings. A line of turtles, impatient turtles with turn signals and horns.

"I don't see where you're headed with this," I say.

Aristomenis combs his eyebrows with his fingers, as if it were actual hair.

"If you live that way for ten, fifteen years, what do you think will happen?"

"You'll have a few accidents? They'll raise your insurance premium? You'll start to have panic attacks. Get a divorce. Retire. Fly into a rage if someone dents your car. Have you ever seen an old man cursing to high heaven over a scratch on his car? He's got one foot in the grave and he's hoping against hope that he'll die first, so he won't have to witness the demise of his beloved car."

"I'm not talking about my generation, Maria. I'm talking about kids in their twenties. Where will they be in ten years?"

"Up there." I point to the top floor of his building. "I know those kids well. Most of them dream whatever dreams their parents told them to. A masters degree, a good job working for the European Union, lots of money. They're just kids, and you know what they're most afraid of? Unemployment."

"No, they'll get tired of being afraid. They've got brains, and they're already bored. Sooner or later they'll reach the limits of that situation. And the situation is already starting to reach its own limits. In five, ten years at the most, everything's going to burn."

"That's what you want? For everything to burn? Who are you, Nero?"

"What interests me is rage. Resistance. I want people to understand deep in their bones precisely how this system of exploitation functions. Only then will they go out and start to smash things. You know what really sets our era apart? The utter delegitimization of the state."

"Education isn't going to set people free, it's freedom that will educate them. You're going about it backwards. Revolution isn't something to be organized by the chosen few."

"Who said anything about the chosen few?"

"You did! You're talking as if you were the secretary general of the executive committee for the coming revolution."

"I won't try to convince you."

"No, convince me. Try. Convince me!"

Aristomenis sighs. He drums his fingers on the leather steering wheel.

"Where should I begin?"

"From the beginning."

In the beginning, then, were the mountains of Epirus, blanketed in untouched snow. In the beginning was a simple, honest life. A barter economy, spontaneous regional cooperatives, an anarchic utopia regulated by human need: I'll trade you my eggs for your wine, that sort of thing. When he was fifteen he left for Athens, went to live with his bookseller uncle. He was happy to have traded the open horizon for a top-floor apartment in Pangrati. School during the day, afternoons at the bookstore. In the evenings he would go up onto the roof and look down at Athens unfolding beneath him in a sheet of grayish white, like snow that's melted under the wheels of a truck. The apartment buildings that had sprung up all over the city seemed to him like so many bumps on a person's head. He wanted to make bumps, too. He was fascinated by how a life can take shape around a lighted window, a window constructed to embody that life and to project it out toward the horizon. In a book about architecture he came across some strange houses with low concrete roofs. The architect's name was Frank Lloyd Wright.

The first things you read that really influence you can create a kind of metaphysical obstinacy: you keep trying to prove that your life has something in common with the life of a person you admire. So what did Aristomenis and Frank Lloyd Wright have in common? Their love of nature, of harmony, of simplicity—their admiration of a snail's shell. The daydreaming, the shared ideal of a decentralized city. Their indifference to money and material things. Their persistence, their single-mindedness, their ability to commit landscapes to memory. The idea that decoration is simply emphasized form, and that form and function are one. And also, as it later turned out, their chaotic, tragic personal lives. Of course if you begin with this notion of convergence, sometimes you actually shape your life, even unconsciously, to accord with that of your idol: in response to Wright's religious beliefs, Aristomenis developed a confused metaphysics of the natural order of things. In response to Wright's undisguised arrogance, he developed an equally undisguised imitation of arrogance.

He got his undergraduate degree from the architecture department at the University of Athens, then went to Paris on a scholarship from the Institut Français. At the height of May 1968 he got involved with the situationists and abandoned his master's thesis in the middle—"work" was practically a curse word, a blight brought by consumer culture. He got used to committing acts of vandalism and sabotage, the only legitimate responses to the society of the spectacle. He took the slogan "free your passions" literally and discovered the joys of sex. At the end of that amazing period he felt poor and deeply alone. He spent his days drinking and drawing his own versions of Piranesi's fantastic prisons. A phrase from the committee for the occupation of the Sorbonne—*Humanity won't be happy till the last bureaucrat is hung with the guts of the last capitalist*—sent him back once more to the source. How had Frank Lloyd Wright put it? *Bureaucrats: they are dead at 30 and buried at 60.* And how else? *Democracy is the opposite of totalitarianism, communism, fascism, or mobocracy.* How else, again? *Maybe we can show government how to operate better as a result of better architecture.* That was it, the idea of architecture as a saving grace, as ideology and political essence. Aristomenis set to work, struggling to balance his romantic nature with concrete action. On the one hand was Pamela Reed's theory of self-transcendence and the Goodman brothers' "communitas"— an intellectual return to the villages of Epirus, to a society in which production isn't divorced from consumption. On the other was the slanted drafting table where buildings took shape at a feverish pace, combining form and function.

His personal life was chaos. His first wife left him for a right-wing French politician. His second was an eccentric, final-stage anorexic who might as well have used their fridge as an umbrella stand. He was so wrapped up in his work that he didn't realize how bad things were until a few weeks before her death. He fell into a deep depression. Then he started to work even harder than before. The only kind of woman he wouldn't drive insane was one with whom he could share his ideas. At the house of a friend of his, a professor, he sometimes ran into the professor's daughter: a young woman who spoke in quotes, who slammed doors and went bright red with rage. Startlingly beautiful, with a dimple in her chin and one half-white eyebrow. The professor died and the daughter fell apart, revealing in the process her inner beauty, another landscape for Aristomenis to commit to memory. After all, that was where his talent lay: after a visit or two to a site he could imagine the ultimate result, the building that didn't yet exist, the building he would create.

The young woman, of course, was Anna. When she came back to Greece for what would turn out to be our final summer together, Aristomenis had already taken things a step further: tired, disappointed by the utter stupidity of society, he had begun to overturn some of Wright's theories. A positive is the sum of two negatives. So if form and function are one, then function can also destroy form, which can in turn destroy the original function. Architecture as the destruction of the system that nourished it.

He started to take on big projects, office buildings, in an attempt to solve that awful equation: how can you influence people's lives through form, materials, function? How do you mobilize workers whose lives are a senseless cycle of daily needs, daily exploitation and tedium? How do you fight a rotten system that transforms creativity into mere labor? One way is to reverse function and use: you give a bank the form of an ancient temple. You build a sky-scraper whose windows don't open, thus creating the illusion of a world that both belongs and doesn't belong to the worker. You design an enormous, open-plan office that's also a cell of sorts: no walls anywhere, yet the very openness of that space comes to oppress the people who work there. They can't pick their nose or eat garlic or make a personal phone call without the person at the next desk knowing. Life becomes harsh, unbearable. It takes on an outward sheen of luxury that only heightens the sadness, the lack of freedom. People cease to think. The rage within them builds.

Rage—now there's a word that must have charmed Anna back then, when her inner world was a battlefield of unbridled rage and contradictions. They ran into one another at some reception, Aristomenis talked to her about Stamatis, about situationism and his theory of what he had started to call inorganic architecture. His method of exploiting the system captivated Anna from the start. I can imagine what happened next. They joined forces, joined their lives.

"How does she seem to you?" he asks, downshifting smoothly. We're almost at my place now. We pull up at the corner of Ippocratous Street and he turns on his right blinker. The downward slope of Kallidromiou always brings an inner warmth.

"She seems fine. Happy, I mean."

"It's a fragile happiness," Aristomenis says, combing his eyebrows again. "I feel more secure when I know she has people around. I'm so glad she has you now."

You're just like Stamatis, aren't you? You want me to look after her.

"She doesn't take care of herself. Have you heard that cough? She's always running a fever, and gets sick at the drop of a hat," he says.

Then she shouldn't smoke so much. What am I, her nurse? I'm tired of dealing with Anna's problems. "Spring can be tricky," I say. "It's so easy to catch cold when the weather changes."

Aristomenis shuts off the engine and looks at me with big, sad eyes. "I'm worried it might be something more than just spring. I'm worried she might be self-destructing."

Everyone's always worried about Anna. Something about her still shouts, *Look out, merde! I'm not like other people!*

"Look out!" Kayo shouts in the darkness. He's lying on the sofa and I almost sit down on him. I don't turn on the light. I take off my shoes the way Anna did, trying to toss them onto the rug with a similar flair. I light a cigarette.

"What's wrong with you? You're smoking now?"

"I saw Anna and her husband today."

Kayo, me, and the glowing tip of my cigarette. A silent agreement: he doesn't ask any questions, just waits for me to start.

"They have a nice house."

"I had no doubt."

"And they've planned a bourgeois revolution."

"I wouldn't put anything past Anna. What's he like?"

"Strange, smart. Sort of paranoid."

I tell him the whole story, more or less.

"Just don't get sucked in again," Kayo says.

"I don't have time for any of that. I've wasted too many years of my life that way."

"So what exactly are you doing?"

"I'm curious, that's all."

"Curiosity killed the cat," he says in English. Usually Kayo and I speak French to one another. Like all French people, he sounds funny when he speaks in English.

"Where is the cat, anyhow?"

"She had another freak-out. She scratched me on the arm."

I turn on the light. There's a long line of dried blood on his arm. I bring cotton balls and hydrogen peroxide from the bathroom.

"I don't understand. We've had our heads bashed in by the police more times than I can count and you still can't take care of a wound?"

"I was waiting for you to come home," he says.

All things considered, it seems sort of unlikely that he'll actually move out. I lean my head on his shoulder, rest my palm on the scratch on his arm, and the loneliness fades.

I'm wearing jeans and sneakers so I can move quickly. My shoulder bag is stuffed with bright green wigs, goggles and confetti. Kayo has the proclamations. Irini and the group with the yellow wigs will be waiting for us on the platform in Syntagma. The plan is to have three in each car, so there are enough of us to fill the whole train. Music right away so that people don't get scared. We don't have instruments, we'll just hand out whistles. We also brought rain sticks, which in a pinch can serve as batons to fight the police. The Bears will give the rhythm with lids from pots and pans. At Syntagma we'll all head toward the exit, to meet Kosmas and the Reds. From there we'll see how things go.

Kayo winks at me as he steps into his car, with two of Irini and Kosmas's classmates. I board my car, too, with two kids from *Exit*. As soon as the doors close, we pass out our proclamations and whistles. With our goggles and wigs on, suddenly we're the Greens. Kind of ironic, if you consider that green is the color of the socialist party, and I used to be in love with a PASOK youth organizer.

The first few seconds are crucial. There are always more young people out in the afternoon, but that's no guarantee of success. Things could go either way. "Are you a theater troupe?" asks one woman who looks like Aunt Amalia toward the end of her life. The lining of her coat is torn, like Amalia's was. "It's not theater," I reply, gently squeezing her wrist, "it's life!"

"The metro is ours!" the kids shout. "It belongs to us all. Athens belongs to us! Say no to a dry life!"

It was Kayo's idea, he's crazy about rain. Dry life on the one hand, rain sticks on the other. "A cataclysm of joy," is what he called it. The idea for the wigs came to us in a kind of free association from that—it seemed important to have color involved, since people always associate anarchists with black.

The rhythm works its magic. We shake our rain sticks and impromptu sambas break out all over the train. From neighboring cars, the Bears accompany us with spoons and pot lids. The sound is deafening, pleasantly primitive. We keep passing out whistles. A few girls in office attire start laughing; the mood is contagious. A window breaks somewhere nearby and a woman cries, "My God!" but her voice is drowned out by rhythmic clapping from the rest of the crowd.

Most people are on our side, I can now say with certainty. Of course some are pale with fear, mouths hanging open. I never understood why people freak out when a window breaks. As if it were the most precious, irreplaceable thing.

The train doors don't open at the next station. The people waiting on the platform stare at us through the windows as if we were aliens. "We're for *real!* We're for *real!*" shout the kids in the next car, and the new slogan makes its way from car to car until the whole train is shuddering with the noise. A few terrified older passengers are reading the proclamation. The train is moving now, and doesn't stop at the next station, either. It's clear: they're bringing us straight to our destination, the last stop, just a little bit faster. By now the platforms in the stations we're passing through are completely empty. At the fifth station we bypass there are policemen lining the platform. We open the windows and douse them in confetti.

One woman pounds on the windows with her fists, gesticulating at the policemen in despair. "Don't expect them to do anything," I say to her. "We're not doing anything wrong. Here, read this!" I hand her Irini's text about the homeless. My favorite part is this: *A girl was walking absentmindedly through Syntagma Square, probably headed home after work, loaded down with grocery bags. She almost walked straight into a group of homeless people. She jumped back with an expression of disgust on her face. Our greatest fear is absolute poverty. Today people with no jobs and no homes are suddenly appearing in front of us: they're not hidden anymore, they're not ghosts, and they're not creatures out of our worst nightmares. They're real people. And since they continue to exist, they can free us from our greatest fear: that we'll cease to exist if we ever lose our jobs. The state actively contributes to the creation of that illusion. It hides the homeless, pushes them away, considers them a miasma. Restaurant owners chase beggars away, just as people used to chase away lepers. Let the homeless sleep in the metro. Or else give them a home.* The woman is tugging at my sleeve, waving the proclamation in my face. She's trying to tell me something, but I can't hear her over the din.

"What?" I ask, cocking an ear.

"What I said, love—I don't know how to read."

She speaks with an accent. Ten to one she's Albanian.

I'm gliding along on a magic carpet. The crowd is pushing me. Even if I refused to walk, all these elbows and hands would get me to the escalator somehow. The whistles are blasting, teenagers are jumping up and down in place as if it were a concert. It must be nice, but I can't tell, can't judge. I'm gripping the woman's hand, the same hand that just now tugged at my sleeve. I can hardly breathe.

"Where are we going, love?"

Maybe it's the word she uses: *love*. Her difficulty pronouncing the "l." The simplicity of the phrase, "I don't know how to read." It's getting harder and harder for me to breathe. The stairs quiver before me. People's faces, too. The sound of the whistles is distorted now, almost demonic in my ears. I feel hemmed in, claustrophobic. I have to take care of this woman and then get out of here. But where will I go?

Anna, the Albanian's face still haunts me. I see it behind the reflective guards the riot police wear over their eyes. I see it in the bathroom sink when I'm washing my face. On the proclamations we write about equality and justice. In pots of boiling water. Even in the toilet bowl. I flush twice, three times to make it disappear. How did Camus put it in our charter? *Direct Action means having the passion necessary to embody your emotions, to dramatize your political thought.* Well, I've embodied my emotions completely: I'm trembling all over. My heart doesn't fit in its usual place. There's no one here to bring me back to myself. Only this woman, a stranger. She reaches into her purse to take something out and cuts her hand on a slip of paper; a drop of blood springs from her fingertip. That's all it takes. I faint.

"What happened?" asks a girl with bright green eyes and a yellow wig. A giant cricket. She shakes me, undoes the top button of my shirt. It's all over, she's going to eat me.

"Maria, can you hear me?" She slaps my face once, twice. "Can you hear me? Maria? It's Irini!"

I'm falling into Daphne's drawing. Running across brown fields, plashing through mud, headed for the cave. My feet sink deeper and deeper into the mud. I can't breathe at all. I'm not a witch, not even an apprentice witch. I'm swimming in slow motion through a bog, my head the only part of me that's above water, and I can barely keep it up. I'm beginning to understand: my head is the mouth of the cave. My body isn't just numb, it's made of stone.

The cave is me.

Six

I keep having this recurring nightmare: university qualification exams, essay question. Topic: *In our contemporary era, interpersonal relationships are complex. Evaluate the importance of true friendship in this context.* Everyone else has turned in their papers; the room is empty except for me, still sitting before a blank page. My left arm is completely paralyzed, as if it were back in the cast from the third grade. I attempt to scribble something with my right hand. Kyria Fotaki, our literature teacher, is standing over me, looking at her watch. "Your time is up, Papamavrou." She's right, it is.

Ever since Anna left for the École des Beaux Arts in Paris I kill entire days watching television—sitcoms, MTV, commercials. I don't read, don't draw, barely leave the house. I just smoke and change channels manically, leaving nail-marks on the plastic buttons of the remote control. I scarf down chips and chocolate bars, get fat, start to resemble my mother. I'm hoping not to enter the next phase, when you give yourself over to God's care, cross yourself all the time and hang incense over your bed. Deep down, I actually do believe that someone, something, will come to my rescue.

And once again, that someone is Andreas Papandreou. He comes into the apartment, grabs me by the hair and gives me the push

I need to reenter the world. By all rights I should have joined
PASOK out of gratitude for that alone.

It's March and the news bursts like a bomb: Papandreou is propos-
ing Christos Sartzetakis for president. Sartzetakis is still a house-
hold name, two decades after he served as prosecutor in the case
of Grigoris Lambropoulos's assassination, and Papandreou's decision
creates an unlikely coalition of anti-Karamanlis forces. Two birds
with one stone: Papandreou diffuses President Karamanlis's power
while also challenging the excessive power exercised by the office
of the president itself. The political media have a field day. I start to
actually follow the news again, to take an interest in current affairs.
I may be ideologically opposed to what Papandreou is doing, but
it's still brilliant. The issue is power. Who will have the upper
hand.

Antigone calls me to curse him up and down over the phone.
It's the first time we've spoken since Anna left. Antigone is back in
the trenches: committees for the abolition of the death penalty, for
political prisoners in Cuba and Zaire, for human rights. She doesn't
ask how I am, just vents her anger at Papandreou, calling him a
cynical utopianist. I hold the receiver away from my ear—she's
taken it to heart and is shouting with rage. I'm pretending to listen, but I'm actually thinking my own thoughts. Such as: if I were
an administration in need of internal change and Anna were the
chief executive, how would I get her out of the way? By finding a
Sartzetakis of my own, of course. I wouldn't give her any warning,
I'd let her think she's still in charge. I'd just dig a hole and watch
with satisfaction and joy as she fell right in. After all, she deserves
it. The whole family has been lying to me all these years. Studies
in Paris, sure. She packed her bags, told Stamatis to get the attic
room ready, and at the last minute told me, "Don't come to the airport. It'll be too painful, merde!" In my head I had imagined it all:

art school, chouquettes, boys, rallies, Les Rita Mitsouko concerts. Anna destroyed it all with a single kick. *We should both go to art school so we'll be together all day . . .* And where is she now? As far away as she could get. She writes me heartfelt letters plastered with stickers that say *Touche pas á mon pote*, to prove what a good activist she is. She comes home for Christmas with a grab bag of phony presents under her arm: Anaïs Anaïs perfume, Milan Kundera's new novel, a de Kooning poster from the Pompidou, stale chouquettes from the neighborhood bakery. She's wearing '50s black-framed glasses, though she's not the least bit nearsighted, a Les Négresses Vertes pin on her jacket, and pointy second-hand shoes, which must be all the rage over there. And, of course, dried paint on her hands: she's the very image of an art student. I, meanwhile, didn't get high enough scores on my exams to enter any department. I really did turn in a blank sheet for my essay question.

I start to hang out at Brutus, a taverna near Alexandras Avenue where I meet writers, students from the law department, and a depressed young theater director with awful teeth. That's my university: impromptu lectures on philosophy and aesthetics over a bottle of wine. Shortly before the parliamentary elections in June, I meet Diana, a painter who teaches in the School of Fine Arts. She's around forty, skinny, with beautiful almond eyes. From her warm handshake and the look of encouragement in her eye, I know I've hit the jackpot.

I've found my Sartzetakis.

"Come and audit my class starting in September," Diana says. "You can take your exams again next year."

"I'll think about it."

"There's nothing to think about."

She takes me with her to the home of the new rector of the art

school. I bring my portfolio, all of my old drawings, starting with
the era of burning dresses. One of two things happens: either the
rector and his wife actually like my work, or they can't bear to tell
me how terrible it is, out of a French sense of courtesy. Their family just moved back from Paris, and they eat backwards, like Anna's
family—main course first, then salad. The rector looks like a cross
between Modigliani and one of his sculptures: curly hair falling
into his face, but thin and very tall; he stoops instinctively to pass
through doorways. His wife is an architect, or used to be. Now
she mostly seems wrapped up in her husband's career, though she
doesn't want to admit it, even to herself. Their kids are teenagers,
at an age when they could care less about anyone who's already
graduated from high school. They all throw in French words without even meaning to, creating a little colony of Parisian sentiment
around the dinner table. I've drunk a fair bit and at some point I
start to cry. The rector's wife puts an arm around me. "You're a
true artist, crying at the drop of a hat!" Well, not at the drop of a
hat. A backwards meal with leftists who lived in exile in France,
with works by the *nouveaux réalistes* on the walls, is more or less a
compendium of everything I've repressed.

Diana drives me home that night. My parents are on Aegina for
the weekend—this year they're renting the Room of Sighs, as I call
it after Angelos and my big disappointment in love. Aegina reminds
them of Ikeja, they dream of buying property there. Diana wants
to come up and see the big monochromes I've been painting. She
examines them eagerly, then examines my chest even more eagerly.
"Maria, they're wonderful!" Is she referring to my paintings or my
breasts? I couldn't care less. By now I've started to put up a con-
scious fight "for even better days," as Papandreou's slogan would
have it. I guess I'm a cynical utopianist, too.

If any members of the administration saw me slathering paint on
my monochromes like an overzealous housepainter, they'd surely

use me as a negative example in their austerity slogans. Look at Papamavrou, consuming more than she produces, gobbling up five kilos of paint at a single sitting, then letting the water run for hours, supposedly to clean her brushes. The epitome of the thoughtless and unscrupulous Greek citizen.

But there's good and bad waste. Instead of destroying the remote control with my nails, I let my hands guide my way to more creative acts—sometimes on paper, sometimes on Diana's body.

"Just don't tell me you're a lesbian now!" She's shrieking straight into my ear and looks as if she might start crying at any moment. We're sitting at the bar at Pieros's, shouting over the music. It's fitting, really: Depeche Mode, "Don't You Want Me."

"I'm not a lesbian, Anna. Stop making generalizations, please."

"Are you crazy? Completely crazy? Do you want to destroy your life?"

"Are you implying that anyone with sexual preferences different from yours is destroying her life? You've been forming some really progressive ideas in Paris, haven't you? So much for your *Touche pas á mon pote.*"

Both of us are pretty drunk, and we've taken some of those pills that are doing the rounds. We more or less let loose on one another. The others rush to pull us apart, though we manage to get some nasty scratching in first. Anna pinches me hard on the forearm and I slap her with the back of my hand.

"I'll have to put you two in handcuffs," Diana tries to joke.

"Wouldn't you like that, you filthy, second-rate artist!" Anna shouts.

"Look who's talking! All you are is a spoiled, vulgar little girl who lives to exploit her friends. That's exactly what you are!"

Anna takes a step back. She's sobbing, spittle dribbling down her chin. For the first time in her life she's ugly, frightening.

"You have no idea what you're talking about. Maria is my best friend! She's . . . she's . . ."

I'm shaking all over.

Anna turns on her heel and leaves the bar at a run.

"If you go after her, we're through," Diana says.

But I'm already headed for the door.

"You deserve whatever you get!" Diana shouts at my back as I go.

We're nineteen, but you'd think we were nine. Lying on our backs on the beach, Anna and I are digging holes in the sand with our heels, chattering away, moving from one topic to the next as if we'd never been apart, as if our friendship had never wavered. She tells me about Urlich, a German of Iranian descent, and then about some bass player who's always high and pays absolutely no attention to her. I tell her about the rector and his wife.

"Oh, Maria, will you introduce me to them?" she asks.

"Maybe, we'll see."

I'm afraid she'll charm them, like she charms everyone. But I can't just live in fear, can I? Besides, Anna doesn't just take, she gives, too. Thanks to her irrepressible sociability, we strike up a conversation with Christophoros one night on the stairs outside Pieros's bar. Christophoros is a bit older than us, he just finished his masters in chemistry. He talks about practical things, and uses verbs that indicate action and energy: I went, I pulled, I carried. He has a biting sense of humor and a slight hunch that makes you think his embrace must be warm and capacious. Up until now I've treated my relationships like stairs, one leading to the next. I wonder if Christophoros might be a landing, a place where I can at last pause and look out at the world.

•

Diana won't speak to me anymore, so I unlearn my role as audience member. But she did plant her seed: the rector and his wife invite me to dinner one warm evening in September. "Bring a few friends," they say. I bring Christophoros and Anna. Anna doesn't waste any time: before they serve the coq au vin and salad with chèvre, she's got her drawings spread out on the dining room table. Abstract expressionism, intense experimentation with color. Now I understand why she brought me that de Kooning poster.

"Well, if a painting isn't showing a story from the Bible, or some familiar scene, we all might as well be Australian aboriginals," Christophoros says, scratching his head.

Anna makes a face.

The rector opens a bottle of wine. "I like people who admit their ignorance," he says.

"Who accept the relativity of knowledge, you mean," Christophoros corrects him, and the two of them laugh. Our hosts have taken a shine to Christophoros. He doesn't know anything about contemporary art, but he has a kind of natural charm. Anna has something to offer them, too: memories of their beloved France. They talk about Guy Debord and Nicos Poulantzas, about Cornelius Castoriades, about her father, Stamatis. Anna still hasn't quite figured out whose side she's on, whose ideas she believes in. Names and theories get mixed up together in her speech like a huge salad, with so many flavors that you can't be quite sure what you're eating. Is she an orthodox Communist? Is she with the situationists and against party politics? Would she align herself with Orgapolis, a new branch of the Marxist-Leninist UCFML?

"What do you think of all this?" the rector asks me.

"All I want is to keep my distance from the logic of parties and power." I might have added: *I've had more encounters and run-ins with power than I'd like, I've lived it in my skin, with Anna's pinches.*

"You can't do that—you'll end up an apolitical being," Anna says. For the time being I cross the situationists and Orgapolis off the list.

"Watch out, Anna," I reply, "you sound like any other cog in the party machine."

"You have to critique the system, to not give it a moment's peace."

"But you're speaking the language of the system itself! It's as if you're conceding that there is no other language." I attack the coq au vin with my knife and a piece of skin slips off my plate.

Perhaps I'm a romantic anarchist after all.

The rector's wife and I are clearing the table.

"What you guys were saying earlier," she murmurs, "it doesn't really hold anymore."

"What doesn't hold?"

"Politics is dead. I don't say that with any sense of nostalgia. Everyone just goes to work, comes home exhausted at night, doesn't want to know anything."

"Not everyone."

"Everyone!"

"What did you think of Anna's work?" I ask her, to change the subject. It makes me sad when people reject the possibility of a revolution in our day.

"Her technique is good, but she has no vision of her own. You, on the other hand, have vision, but could care less about technique."

"Should I take that as a compliment?"

"It's the truth, Maria. Take some art lessons, don't let yourself get lazy. And take the entrance exams for the school."

"I don't believe in art school."

"Neither do I. But it'll give you a technical foundation that you can throw out later on if you want to. Right now you need it, the same way you need the illusion of a political vision. If you get too old, you'll build up your defenses, maybe go for some psychoanalysis, and it'll all be over. At that point no one will be able to teach you anything."

Merde. She's taken it personally.

Under the influence of Christophoros and the rector's wife, I become a good girl again. I stop watching television entirely, cut down on cigarettes, and start taking art lessons from a guy named Terzis, a painter who drinks so much that he's destroyed his liver. He's an odd bird who cancels classes whenever there are anti-government workers' strikes downtown. I can't imagine him marching in his combat boots, with his expressionless rat's eyes and his freakish hair.

"I don't march," he says. "Not all problems can be solved through peaceful means." That makes more sense—I can certainly imagine him throwing Molotov cocktails. But Terzis clams up and won't say more. "Okay, time to work."

During the summer of 1986 I take placement exams for the School of Fine Arts, and Christophoros starts his military service. He's used up all of his deferments. Our parting is dramatic; I make him five mix tapes full of songs about breakups and reunions. Could we possibly live together forever? Could a year of monogamy turn into a lifetime of monogamy? They send him to basic training at a camp by the Evros River, near the border with Turkey, and he calls me, nerves totally shot, after waiting in line with a hundred other conscripts to use the phone. His voice on the other end of the line keeps breaking up. I go out for beers with Terzis. The froth in the glass is unbearably sad. One thing leads to another and before I know it I'm lying naked beside him on his disgusting mattress on the floor. All I remember is his long, yellowed fingers on my body.

"What's his name?" Anna asks the next day on the phone.

"I call him Terzis. That's his last name, though, I don't actually know his first name. Someone called him Camus."

"Camus? Like the writer?"

"I have no idea. You can't imagine how ashamed of myself I am! How can I be in love with Christophoros but sleep with Terzis?"

"You're ashamed of yourself because that's how you've been taught to feel. You've been taught that a woman who sleeps with lots of men is easy, while a man who sleeps with lots of women is experienced. You can't enjoy sex as a purely physical experience, you have to get emotionally involved, otherwise you're a bad girl. Am I wrong?"

"No, you're right."

"And all those men who go out to clubs every night and screw whoever they can find aren't whores? Besides, at the end of the day, what's wrong with being a whore? Your body is yours to do what you want with, right?"

"Right."

"So stop feeling guilty and get yourself over here so we can screw all of Paris!" She holds nothing sacred. I'll have to cross orthodox Communist off the list, too.

Then what's left?

Paris glistens in the sunlight. Anna and I are sitting on her big Indian scarf in our favorite spot at Buttes-Chaumont, eating chèvre sandwiches, just like at our picnic on my sixteenth birthday. Anna can't stop talking about men, she's become a sex fiend. She tells me about her one-night stand with one of Basquiat's lovers, and how sex with bisexuals is amazing because they've got such serious identification issues that they practically screw you with their mind.

"It doesn't sound like much of a turn-on . . ."

"Oh, Maria! You have no idea what you're missing!"

"Me? Have you forgotten what you put me through back then with Diana?"

Their place in Paris hasn't changed a bit. Roman still scrubs the stove as manically as ever. Stamatis still reads in his velvet armchair, a pipe dangling from his mouth. It's as if not a day has passed since I left. The only difference is that as Anna and I get older, her father starts to behave toward us in an old-fashioned way, as if we were young ladies from another era. "Oh, mademoiselle, welcome," he says, and kisses my hand. I pull it away; I'm still angry at him. If he'd brought me to Paris as he'd promised, I wouldn't feel like such a failure.

That night Anna drags me to a bar where all hell's broken loose: there are women undressing on barstools, men kissing. Anna elbows her way between two total strangers and signals for me to follow. I'm in no mood for planned debauchery. I head downstairs to the bathroom and literally run right into a tall, dark boy with dreadlocks. We both lose our balance and fall in a heap on the stairs, where we start to laugh uncontrollably.

"What's your name?" I ask.

"Kayo," he answers.

"Kayo, you smell like Africa."

He shoves me away.

"No, you don't understand! I was *born* in Nigeria." I hug him, sink my nose into his neck and breathe in the smell of Gwendolyn, grilled suya, soil after a tropical rain. Kayo's eyes tear up—he must be pretty drunk, too. Then he bends down and kisses my hand.

"Maria!" Anna is standing over me, shouting in Greek: "He's a complete fag. What's wrong with you? Can't you see?"

Kayo and I, out walking, caught in a sudden August rainstorm. We don't run for cover, just keep strolling along at the same pace. He likes to open his arms wide, lift his face to the sky and spin around with eyes closed in the middle of the Place de la Bastille. "It's the only way to really feel the rain," he says. He's so beautiful that sometimes I pretend my shoe is untied so I can drop back and admire him for a minute. Heads turn when he passes by. Young people, old people, men, women, children, see in his height, in his velvet eyes, in his full lips an embodiment of pride. It's not just about beauty: Kayo is a real prince, straight out of a fairytale. He can grant you any three wishes, with one exception—that he sleep with you.

Like a true gentleman, whenever we cross to the other side of the street he makes sure I'm still walking on the inside. "It's how my mother taught me," he says. With him I forget about feminism and equal rights, because he makes me feel not just equal but better. My own obligations, in return, are to let him lean on my shoulder, to talk to him about Africa, about human rights, about Foucault, and to give him backrubs. Sometimes I can't stand it and give him a kiss on the neck, and Kayo sighs and says, "Oh, my little African," which only makes the moment more tender, but when I open my lips in search of something more, Kayo says, "Oh, sweetheart, get it into your head." Get what into my head? His body responds, it's warm, he's always touching me. Why doesn't he at least try, why won't he take that risk? "There's no way," he says. Anna asks around and finds out it's the first time Kayo is going around with a girl. She tries to analyze it: "Maybe because you're tall and skinny, and wear pants and have short hair. Forget him, Maria. He wants to turn you into a boy."

I cut my hair even shorter and buy a man's suit. Kayo tells me I look wonderful, asks if I want to submit a portfolio to the modeling agency he works for from time to time.

"Kayo, I hate fashion, advertising, consumer culture. I'm not doing it for the sake of style, don't you get it? I'm doing it so I can be with you."

I look at myself in the mirror, trying to see what he sees: my cheekbones protrude, you can see all of my ribs individually, like Antigone's. There are black circles under my eyes. All I eat is fruit, my stomach has closed up entirely. In the space of a month I've become a ghost of myself. I found my prince, only he won't let me up on the horse.

Kayo is like one of those old-school reporters with connections in every social sphere, from the underworld to upper-echelon government. He finds out when the next Orgapolis meeting is and we go together to a seventh-floor apartment in Ivry. The room has high ceilings and tiny plaster cherubs in the molding. About forty men and women are passing around photocopies. Our connection is Joel, an ex of Kayo's with eyesight so bad you can barely see his eyes through his coke-bottle glasses. Instead of thinking about politics, I find myself thinking about sex: why him and not me, that sort of thing.

I glance down at the photocopy in my hand: *A political space is the material manifestation of a particular politics. When that politics is exercised by the people, the resulting space lies outside the institutions and operations of the state. It is a free space. State-exercised politics, on the contrary, mutilates and destroys the multiplicity of spaces in order to project a single space, the space of power, of the ruling class. In Stalinist politics the only existing space is the Party. In a parliamentary system it is the state itself. Even the smallest splinter group of the opposition inevitably organizes itself around elections and appearances in the mass media. Its influence is thus limited to whatever crumbs the state throws to those marginalized by the great parliamentary machine. Orgapolis takes its own politics as a starting point; it attempts to foster conditions under which people can think and act in ways that enable us to imagine a true democracy.*

So my hope wasn't entirely unfounded: there is a space where you can escape power relations. You carve a circle, within which you are free to think as you please, though in a manner no less political. You don't engage in dialogue with power on its terms, in its space; rather, you cultivate your own. Power still slaps, still pinches—but if you carve that circle, it doesn't hurt quite as much.

"Just tell me," Mom says. Her shrill voice says it all.

"I got in!" I hold the receiver away from my ear so that Anna can hear too.

"I lit a candle, I'll have you know!"

"Oh, Mom, prayer isn't enough with a thing like this."

"It's more than enough, young lady. God can do all things."

"I really wonder how you came out of a mother like that," Anna says, after hugging me and saying a few merdes. "Does she know you take to the streets with Molotovs?"

What about you, Anna? Do you have any idea how it feels to believe in the colonial enterprise and to have to leave Africa because a group of poor blacks, led by a schizophrenic white man, breaks into your house? Because, along with your grandmother's jewels, not to mention your daughter, they rob you of the thing that's most important to you in the world—your illusions? Do you have any idea how it feels to be forced to go back to a place you'd hoped never to set foot in again, thousands of kilometers away from fairytales, toga parties, afternoon tea with Mrs. Steedworthy? It's one thing to pretend you're English in Ikeja, another to return to Greece in 1976. You don't speak, just stuff your mouth with food; your storage room is gone, so you pile things up in your mind. At some point you start to overflow; your thyroid goes out of whack. Your life, too.

Anna and Kayo come to Orly to see me off. Even in this final moment, Kayo won't kiss me for real, he just squeezes my hand and whispers in my ear, "Oh, my little African." He promises to keep attending Orgapolis meetings and to send me their proclamations. Did someone there catch his eye? He's not exactly the type of person to be overcome with passion for political collectives. He's too self-absorbed to get involved in the lives of others. Anna gives me a packet of chouquettes for the plane. I stare at my shoes to keep from crying. As I walk through passport control I'm afraid I'm saying goodbye to real life, going off into the unknown. I've forgotten all about my family back home, forgotten about Christophoros, forgotten that I'm now a student in the School of Fine Arts.

"Oh, child, what happened to you?" Mom lets out one of her customary little cries.

"What do you mean?"

"You're skin and bones, I hardly recognize you. And what kind of clothes are those? You look like a tomboy."

I shut myself up in my room to escape her complaints. Christophoros asks over the phone: "Don't you love me anymore?" I hear myself answering woodenly: "There are lots of different kinds of love." At night in bed, I'm restless. I try to re-discover my vagina— I don't need a partner; the memory of Kayo, my prince, is enough. The phone rings in the night but by the time I get to it, there's no one on the line. My mother treats me just as she should, as if I were an unhappy princess out of a fairytale: each morning she brings me my breakfast on a tray, each afternoon she takes it back, untouched. And just as in a fairytale, I only start to eat again, if only bread and jam, when a letter arrives from my prince: *My little African, Paris is empty without you. Joel told me at the very last minute about an Orgapolis meeting. I called Anna. We got there late, and when we walked in someone was saying, 'A real political gathering is intellect in action. Before the gathering, we don't know what might happen, what will be decided. And we leave a true political gathering stronger and more capable.' I thought you'd like that. Joel invited some of us back to his house and we dropped LSD. I suddenly saw you, as if in one of those drawings you showed me, wearing clothes that were on fire, with snakes all around, and I was so worried that I called you in the middle of the night, but no one answered. Where are you? When are you coming back?*

I leap out of bed, leave a message on his answering machine: "Kayo, Athens is empty without you, too. I heard the phone ringing. I was in bed under the sheet, thinking of you at that exact moment—do you think we've met in a previous life?"

I slowly ease back into my everyday reality. I'm exhausted. School, my classmates—it all seems so petty to me, somehow lacking. All that's different is my art. I start to use party materials: stickers, flyers. I cut them up and paste them back together so that New Democracy politicians appear on PASOK flyers and vice versa. I hesitate to do the same for the left, thinking primarily of Antigone and the rector's wife. But in the end, my hands have lives of their own.

And as it turns out, my hands know what they're doing. In the general elections that October the conservatives clean up, thanks to the convenient neutrality of the Communist Party.

"If it were up to me, I'd shave all their heads and send them in for life," Dad says, pounding his fist on the coffee table. It's the anniversary of the events at the Polytechnic, Athens is burning and Dad is trying to restore order from his spot in the living room.

Oh, Dad, if you only knew how badly I want to be out there with them right now, throwing rocks, smashing storefronts! If only I could talk to you about my view of activism, my way of understanding revolutionary initiative. They cram us all into the chicken coop of parlimentarianism, feeding us crumbs, while outside are vast fields, thousands of untouched acres of free thought.

We sit here side by side on the couch, taking turns with the remote control, and yet we're living on different planets. You still belong to Africa, to the oil companies that exploit people who look like Kayo. Meanwhile, I dream up posters, dream of marching against them—against you. I dream of violence, too. Sometimes a little violence is just what's needed. But if I go down into the streets with a stick, I won't be your daughter anymore.

I'm twenty years old. Anna sends me a vibrator for my birthday—she's completely out of control. Kayo sends me a plane ticket to Paris.

"Where will I stay?" I ask over the phone. "Anna's place is a total bachelorette pad these days."

There's a brief silence. "You'll stay with me," Kayo says.

With him.

Kayo's apartment is on the outskirts of the Marais. A large, sunny studio with a double bed and a fold-out couch. The first night we sleep together in the bed, in an asphyxiating embrace, fully dressed. In the morning he kisses me gently on the face, all over, everywhere but on the mouth, and in my despair I bite his shoulder, hard. We stay in bed all day, suspended between sleep and waking. Like a couple. Almost. Kayo tells me about his mother. I've heard about her before, of course. He says he'll make me croque monsieur the way she used to, and then a dessert she used to make, too. Why do women do that to their sons? Unconsciously, perhaps, but they still do it: they create a romantic idyll that will take the place of each failed love story in their lives.

Kayo's mother was white, his father was black; they were together only briefly, and weren't married. And yet Kayo was a miniature of the man his mother had loved, with bits of herself grafted on: dark skin, but her light eyes. Large hands, but her delicate fingers.

Robust features, but a girlish melancholy in his gaze. She bathed him every day, dressed him in white shirts that smelled nice, did her best to make sure no one ever spoke badly of her son. If he had been white, would she have scrubbed quite so obsessively? Kayo says yes. His mother was a clean freak, he says. A germaphobe. She was always scrubbing the bathtub and the kitchen floor; she had a remarkable collection of cleaning products, room fresheners, floor polishes. She washed her hands every time she touched money.

"That's romantic," I say when he gets to that part of the story. "A distrust of money." Kayo nods his head in satisfaction. He scrubs his mother's memory the same way she used to scrub their house. He remembers her frozen in postures of generosity: shining his shoes; ironing the collars of his shirts; dusting his bedside table. She died young, of a heart attack, in the act of mopping the floor. Kayo found her fallen on all fours, a monument to cleanliness.

Anna calls us in mid-afternoon, while we're eating our croque monsieur. "Maria, did you hear? A Turkish patrol entered Greek territory. They've opened fire on one another up near the Evros. A Greek soldier was killed."

I spit out the bite of food I just took, hang up and call Christophoros's house. His mother is in hysterics. "They won't tell us anything, they've got them all on alert. Oh, child, the Turks are going to get him!" I can hear his father blustering in the background, "It's all Papandreou's fault. You can cut off my hands if I ever vote for him again!" I sit on the floor and cover my face with my hands because I no longer know who I am, where I belong, who I want.

Anna comes whirling in like a tornado. "But you dumped Christophoros! What use is there in feeling guilty now? There's an entire value system in play here, Maria. You can't feel guilty, you're not responsible for anyone's fate."

"But what if something's happened to him?"

"Nothing's happened to him. It's just the exaggerations of the mass media. They say all this stuff on purpose, to make us afraid, to control us. Haven't you learned anything at all from Orgapolis?"

Kayo hugs me from behind. My whole body is suddenly on alert, just like the Greek troops. I forget Christophoros, the Turks, Orgapolis. At Kayo's side, I exist in the only space I can properly call political: the space of desire.

I travel back and forth. Athens, Paris. School of Fine Arts, Orgapolis. Christophoros, Kayo. I'm not sleeping with either of them, of course, since one is in the army, the other in a world of his own. Besides, the AIDS epidemic has broken out, and sex is seeming more and more like a germ, an ordeal, a wound. Kayo is earning tons of money from underwear ads and he pays for my plane tickets. He says it makes him feel calm to lie beside me, though there are plenty of nights when he doesn't come home. I'm not only jealous, I'm scared of AIDS, too.

"We'll shrivel up into sexless old ladies if we have to ask every person we sleep with for a résumé first," Anna says. She's sitting on Kayo's sofa with her shoes on the cushion. That's her idea of making herself at home. If Kayo saw, he'd have a fit.

"You don't think we should go get tested, just to be on the safe side?" I say.

"And if it turns out we're positive, we'll stop having sex, is that what you think?"

She squints at me. She's adopted an ostensibly free-wheeling air. When she looks at me like that, I feel like slapping her. Instead, I just stare at my knees.

"Well, I'm going to," I say, and the issue ends there.

As soon as I get back to Greece, Antigone takes me to get tested. She's gotten involved with a committee that deals with AIDS and she knows where to go. "It's such bad luck for you girls," Antigone sighs as we walk under the harsh lights of a hospital corridor. "It's going to rob you of all your spontaneity."

Mom thinks that God sent AIDS. She's almost happy about it, because it means she won't have to keep tabs on me herself. She's putting me in trustworthy hands—patriarchal, punishing hands that grip me by the neck as the needle enters my vein to draw its blood. Another Maria, sick and ailing, shuffles down hospital corridors with sunken cheeks, missing teeth, lesions from Kaposi's sarcoma all over her body, pushing a pole with a bag of fluid hanging from it. That other Maria says to me, "You've done nothing with your life, you're useless. You faint at the sight of blood. All day long you cut up pieces of paper and stick them back together again. The only way you'll ever get out of this rut is if you find some idea to fight for, if you start to think about other people's problems."

The test comes back negative, but I decide it's time for me to get involved on a personal level. I start to design posters about AIDS. A pair of tigers tear one another to shreds inside a pink condom; the end result is too pop for words. I photograph a condom centered on a placemat, fork on one side, knife on the other, with "Bed and Breakfast" as a caption—but it looks too much like an advertisement. Finally I come up with a decent idea: dozens of I.D. photos of couples kissing. We'll go into photo booths in pairs and everyone can kiss everyone else, boys kissing girls, girls kissing girls, boys kissing boys, to fight back against the conservatism that's been spreading as fast as the virus.

On my next trip to Paris, I tell Anna about my idea. She makes a face.

"It sounds like a Benetton ad."

But when we pull the little curtain closed in the metro station at Saint Michel and the flash goes off, Anna parts her lips and our tongues touch. She's learned a thing or two since the last time we kissed.

My legs are trembling when Kayo and I shut ourselves in the booth.

"Like it or not, you've got to kiss me for real."

There are all kinds of tongues, square ones, round ones, wet, dry, warm, cold, lively and lethargic ones—but none as ethereal and inventive as Kayo's. He's on the rotating stool, I'm in his lap, the flash goes off four times and our tongues touch, chase one another, rest, rush at one another again. He starts to pull back and I bite his tongue, hard.

"Why'd you bite me, Maria?"

Because I didn't want you to leave. I want you to know how it feels for your whole body to ache with desire. I worry that art and activism always have an ulterior motive. In this particular case, it's Kayo's kiss.

We print as many copies as our meager funds will allow in a cheap print shop where Orgapolis prints its materials, too. We go out that night and put the posters up in the metro; we take turns standing guard; we're quick and methodical. It makes me sad that I don't have any real friends in Athens so we could put them up there, too.

"We'll come and help," Kayo says.

They don't, of course. I always go to them, they never come to me. It makes me feel that Athens is small and lacking, as if everything is happening elsewhere. And that reminds me again of how Anna tricked me, left me behind.

"Mom, I decided to move out after all. I found a two-bedroom place on Stournari Street."

She turns toward me, her hands covered in soap suds.

"Where on Stournari?"

"Just on the other side of the square, Mom. Right around the corner."

Whenever we talk about it, something always drops from her hands—a knife, a glass. The way she sees things, if a child wants to move out, it means the parents have failed.

"I was thinking we could buy a bigger place, so you could have a little more space, a studio to work in . . ."

"Mom, it's done. I signed a lease."

She turns her back on me.

"I've already made it clear to you, we can't afford to pay your rent."

"Don't worry, I found a job."

"What kind of job?"

"I'm going to wait tables at Brutus."

That's when she drops the plate. "My daughter, a waitress?"

A waitress with a tough shift. Nine at night to two in the morning, every day, in a closed space full of smoke and loud music. My clothes stink of tomato sauce and garlic, my mouth tastes like an ashtray. I feel sort of like a character from an old movie, with a white apron and a cigarette dangling from my lips, accidentally blowing smoke into my own eyes as I serve plates of pasta. The fatigue I feel on the way home after my shift is incredible—as if I've been out marching all day, at a demonstration whose goal is simply to save myself.

My social conscience has shriveled up again. I should really be thinking more about others. We're supposedly on the verge of war with Turkey again, this time over the Sismik, a Turkish geophysical survey ship exploring the area between Limnos and Mytilini. Antigone has put all her trust in Leonidas Kirkos and his new leftist party. Anna, meanwhile, has entered a new phase. Just as I had anticipated, the fear of AIDS found its way to her, too: she found out that Basquiat's lover, the one she slept with, was HIV positive. She goes to get tested in a state of hysteria. The results come back negative, but she replaces sex with communist ideals, just to be on the safe side. And we're talking hard-core communism. Near the very end of the spring semester she decides to drop out of art school, because "art isn't interested in the needs of the working class."

"Come on, Anna, really?" I say over the phone. "There *is* no working class anymore, there are only working conditions." Anna heaves an angry sigh on the other end of the line. Our mobilizations, she says, should serve the greatest number, and our creativity should be poured into the production of awareness-raising materials that people can take with them—flyers, posters, newspapers— rather than isolated works of art intended to be hung on the wall.

Anna disappears off the face of the earth. Kayo tells me she's spending all her time at factories, with the workers—she calls him at some point to say that union leaders have set up tents for striking workers outside the factory where she's spending most of her time, but they haven't yet taken over the building. How on earth, she says, can you call for strikes and passive resistance all day long and then go quietly home to your nice, warm bed at night? What kind of armchair revolution is that?

Around the same time I wake from my lethargy, too. When the PASOK wiretapping scandal breaks, I start to record conversations with people I know and edit them at a studio in the suburbs. I dream of setting up two megaphones in Syntagma where I could play these conversations between six and seven every morning, when people are on their way to work. At that time of day you're still half-asleep, but the things you hear get recorded in your subconscious. Returning home at the end of the day, shop clerks and civil servants would start to think again about the recordings, and thus about the wiretaps, would wonder just how much the state apparatus is hiding from them, how much it knows. I'm hoping that Anna might finally be proud of me. I've done the closest thing to political art that a person can do in 1987, in an atmosphere of mass complacency that even these continual political scandals can't seem to disturb.

"That's not political art, it's narcissism. The only truly political art is when you take to the streets, when you stop believing that the problems of an artist are different from those of a blacksmith," she says over the phone.

"Anna, just let me send you one of the cassettes—"

"I don't have time for stuff like that, Maria. When people get all dressed up to go to some gallery opening, they're missing the whole point."

"It's not a gallery piece. I don't believe in galleries, you know that."

But she sighs at the idea of Syntagma, too. "The only sound we should be hearing in public squares is the shouting of slogans."

I record that conversation, too. She'll be furious if she ever finds out, but for me art is as important as politics. As important as Anna.

"I hope it's just a phase." As always, Antigone isn't eating her salad so much as playing with it. It's my day off and we're having dinner at a taverna in Exarheia.

"She hasn't set foot in the university in ages," I say.

Antigone wrinkles her brow, and her face fills with tiny little lines.

"Why didn't you tell me earlier?"

"I thought you knew." I'm sick of her treating me like Anna's keeper, like a detective agency with only one client.

She pushes her plate away. "I don't know where I went wrong. We were democratic parents, we never deprived her of anything, she was always free to voice her opinion. These days she's just part of the herd—she asks permission from the party just to go to the bathroom!"

People at nearby tables turn to look at us. Antigone's voice has grown louder and louder, until now she's practically shouting. She hates the Communist Party even more than she hates the right. Her leftist politics are nostalgic, with a tinge of elitism. That may be what Anna is reacting against, just as I'm reacting against my mother's political agnosticism.

"How is your family doing these days? Your mother?" Antigone asks, as if she read my mind.

"She's fine, same as always, with her soap operas and her icons."

"Part of the herd, just like Anna. Sometimes I wonder if you two girls were switched at birth."

If she'd said that to me ten years earlier, tears of pride would have sprung to my eyes. Now I just take another bite of my food.

I drag my bed over to the window so the light falls on it, position a chair in the middle of the room like a statue. I haven't put anything on the walls since I rented the apartment, but now I hang some of my paintings. Kayo is coming! The Athenian sun, the arrangement of the furniture, the male nudes from my first year of art school—it all screams out how badly I want him. He's not HIV positive, it's not too late for him to change, to think seriously about bisexuality, and to pass from there into heterosexuality, into incurable love for me.

I keep breaking glasses at Brutus. I'm dreaming with open eyes: Kayo embraces me at the airport, we come back to the apartment, the light falls through the grates over the windows, we make love on the chair in the middle of the room, Kayo gives up modeling and helps me design posters about racism, minorities, AIDS. We go out at night to put up the posters, get caught in a downpour,

Kayo opens his arms wide and shouts, "This is how to really feel the rain!"

In actuality, though, there's an early heat wave, Kayo sleeps on the edge of the bed with one leg on the tile floor to keep cool, and when I try to get close to him, he says, "I'm hot, little one." He breaks the news on the third day, as he's stirring a pot of pasta sauce on the stove.

"I've had an offer to go and work in New York."

In a sudden flash, I see him on magazine covers, in karaoke bars, strolling down wide avenues, always with his arms spread wide, just in case it rains.

"What about Orgapolis?"

"I only do that for your sake. Collective action isn't really my thing, you know that."

"What about me, then?"

"You'll come for visits."

Kayo's princely temperament is out in full force on our evening walks to the Herod Atticus theater. He makes me look up at the moon. He tells me romantic tales about ghostly spirits and gods with animal forms. He recites poems by Kofi Anyidoho: *Because because I do not scream / You do not know how bad I hurt / Because because I do not kiss / on public squares / You may not know how much I love / Because because I do not swear / again and again and again / You wouldn't know how deep I care.* I should be the one speaking those words.

The people in my life are always going somewhere. First Anna, now Kayo. And I'm forever in the background, waving a handkerchief as they leave.

Anna is the first to taste the strawberries with whipped cream, and spits the bite out onto her plate.

"Merde, it's mayonnaise!"

Aunt Amalia wanted to welcome Anna home to Athens with a nice meal. She made us pasta, only she left it on the burner until it was a pile of mush. And now this: strawberries topped with mayonnaise for dessert. She's getting worse. She forgets things, puts her clothes on inside out, rings strangers' doorbells.

"Amalia, I'll have my strawberries plain," I call to her in the kitchen.

"You girls are skin and bones with all your dieting!" she calls back.

Anna laughs until tears come to her eyes. I, meanwhile, am crying on the inside.

"What's going to become of Amalia? Of all of us, for that matter?"

"This thing with Kayo has made you too sensitive," Anna says, wiping the mayonnaise off her strawberries with a paper napkin.

"So you're allowed to believe in your utopia but I'm not allowed to believe in mine?"

"Not all utopias are made equal."

"Yours, as always, is better."

"Don't be a baby, Maria. You take offense at the least little criticism. The only way to pose a danger to the system is to join a collective utopia. A utopia of the possible."

I feel like we're back in grade school, sitting in our uniforms waiting for the bell to ring. We're bored of school, bored of life. We're anxious for something to happen, but we don't know what, and until it appears we chew on sharp, dangerous words.

"What a stupid island."

Anna doesn't enjoy summer in Greece the way she used to. She sits in the shade in a long Indian tasseled skirt reading Alain Badiou's *Peut-on penser la politique?* Every so often she lifts her head from the page and makes a face—at a woman in a gaudy bathing suit diving into the sea, or a man walking by, checking his Rolex. She doesn't wear makeup anymore, puts her hair up in a bun with a ball-point pen, lives like a monk on an apple and a bar of dark chocolate a day. I stopped eating for Kayo, she stopped eating to fight the system. I barely recognize our reflections when we walk past a shop window. Our elongated figures look like shadows, or characters out of a comic book. As always, Anna pulls it off brilliantly. The whole island of Paros is in love with her. The other day a boy turned to look at her and almost fell off his moped. Whenever she puts down her book, pulls out the pen, shakes out her hair and dives into the water, every single pair of eyes on the beach turns her way. On top of everything else, she's an amazing swimmer. Her body, still pale from the Parisian winter and our rented umbrella, is beautifully toned. Even if she spends most of the day lying down, reading.

"It's not the island's fault, Anna. It's your mood."

"How about we put it to the test? Can we go to Donousa? Or Amorgos?"

So we change islands. We go to Amorgos, set up shop on an outcropping of rocks, surround ourselves in nature and solitude. Anna scrambles around with the help of a stick she found. She sits and reads in a wide-brimmed straw hat, feet dangling in the water. I, meanwhile, sweat and peel peaches with my penknife. Pairs of boys keep wandering over our way, and either whistle at us or ask what time it is, depending on how they've been brought up. They all assume that two girls on their own must be looking for company. They don't know Anna.

"Beat it!" she shouts.

And they do—sometimes baffled, sometimes cursing. Anna slides towards me on her behind, stretches out on her towel and whispers in my ear, "Boys are monsters. You, you're my best friend."

To seal the deal, she pinches me on the shoulder.

"Merde, Maria!" Anna looks me up and down as I button my pants, hunched over in our tent. I've done something wrong again.

"What's wrong?"

"Is that another new pair of pants?"

"You want me to make a list of all my purchases and submit it for your approval?"

"I'm afraid you're turning into your parents."

"What did my parents ever do to you?"

"To me, nothing. The question is what they've done to themselves, and to you. Their only dream was the accumulation of wealth. And when they had to give up that wealth, they stopped being happy, too. Why do you think you won first prize in the drawing contest on Savings Day in the third grade?"

"Because the judges liked my drawing?"

"Your drawing was an encapsulation of bourgeois stereotypes. Just imagine, money falling from the sky! It's like an ad for the lottery!"

"And bank robberies and doves are better?"

"I don't claim to be better. But I try."

"Whereas I don't try hard enough, is that it?"

She makes me feel useless. Unimportant. Stupid. She doesn't listen when I describe my sound installation. She says that capitalism is what's driving Aunt Amalia crazy. That my new pants are a symbol of the created desire for material possessions. That the storage room in Ikeja was the site of a traumatic experience, and ever since that day I've had a need to acquire. Me? A need to acquire? I always give her half of what's mine, I just don't make a big fuss over it the way she does. Take half my sandwich, give me the man of your dreams.

"I can't be like you. I don't want to be. I don't like the way you are!"

Anna's eyes open wide, enormous. "You don't like the way I am?"

Merde, it slipped out.

"Have you seen a blond girl, my age, very skinny, with a dimple in her chin and one eyebrow that's half white? Wearing a red t-shirt and a black skirt with tassels?"

I've been scouring the island for her since yesterday. In bathrooms. Behind tamarisk trees. In restaurant kitchens. In hotels. What has she eaten? Where did she sleep? She ran off yesterday without her wallet. I open her backpack, rummage through her clothes, but what am I expecting to learn? Whether she's been honest with me? Whether she bought anything new, too? I go into all the bars, stores, and coffee shops on the island; I've become a regular private eye.

"You still haven't found your friend?" one waiter asks. "Maybe someone swept her off her feet?"

All that swept her off her feet was her inflated opinion of herself.

"What's wrong?" the waiter asks.

A sudden flash of understanding: Anna is putting my friendship to yet another test, just like when she ruined my drawing, or wanted to swap Raoul for Michel, or stole Angelos. She's following me, measuring the extent of my devotion. She'll appear again as soon as she finds my display of concern sufficiently moving. Or if I stop looking for her altogether.

I leave her backpack in the tent, gathering only my things. I write her a note: *Anna, you've been using me my whole life. You may be more beautiful, more intelligent, more committed to your ideas (though that much I doubt), but I'm tired of running after you. I want you to accept me, the same way you accept your workers at the factory. You work hard to make them feel proud of themselves. Did you ever think about my pride? Maria.*

I tear the note up. There are no words to express my pride.

I thought you were something more than my friend: you were the sister I never had. Your behavior is making me re-evaluate my whole life, my priorities, my entire emotional world. You just left me there and went off. I could have fallen from a cliff. Were you always so selfish, or are you improving with age?

That's the kind of letter Anna has been writing to me this fall. Every two weeks or so I get an envelope with a French stamp and know exactly what's waiting for me: a tirade. She doesn't call, and doesn't pick up when I call. It's our era of vicious correspondence. I have no choice but to write back: *Anna, be serious. When I said I didn't like the way you are, I meant that I didn't like the way you act toward me. You pressure me. You want to have your own way. You can call that the utopia of the possible, if you want, but it's the utopia of your possible. You need to leave a little room for mine, too.*

She responds with something irrelevant: *You know how the work of philosophers falls into different periods? I like early Nietzsche, but not late Nietzsche. Well, I have fond memories of Maria One, but not of Maria Two.* I don't know what to say to that. I'm starting to think I have issues with Anna One *and* Anna Two.

I've forgotten what her voice sounds like. Sometimes I imagine her leaping out of bed with that tremendous energy of hers, rushing downstairs, running over to the café across the street and writing me a letter. Bitter, confused, with a pile of crumpled sheets of paper on the table before her—but those are just my fantasies. I'm sure she's fine. She'll have found a new group of friends, the hard-core kind she wants now, and they'll all eat together in their collective and discuss the utopia of the possible in a smoky, high-ceilinged room. I'm sure they're all overflowing with revolutionary fervor, and have nothing but disdain for anyone who would buy a new pair of pants without absolutely needing them.

"Don't waste your time on her," Kayo says. His voice sounds strange, coming to me with a time delay. I have to wait until he finishes each sentence before I respond, otherwise neither one of us can hear what the other is saying. If Anna were to hear his stories from the fashion world, she'd throw containers of yogurt at him the way they do at politicians. But he's Kayo, my Kayo. It's impossible for me to judge him. Of course I preferred how he was when we used to go to Orgapolis meetings together, but you can't have your friends cut and sewn to order. That's something Anna has never understood.

"I miss you," I say, and hear my own voice on the line, doubled, carrying a double despair.

"I miss you too," he answers. In New York it's morning, Kayo is just waking up, and I really have no idea who's sleeping at his side.

Papandreou is dovetailing me again: he too has a secret correspondence, with Turgut Özal, prime minister of Turkey, over Cyprus. They meet at the World Economic Forum in Davos, Switzerland and come up with an impressive agreement, largely because they avoid talking about the Cyprus problem. Anna and I meet at my place on Stournari, when she comes to Athens for New Year's. There's been nothing diplomatic about our own correspondence these past few months. So now we sit facing one another, on opposite sides of the coffee table. Anna is wearing jeans and sneakers, her eternal ball-point pen in her hair. I made sure to dress in my painting clothes, a gray long-sleeved t-shirt full of holes and covered in dried paint that I'm hoping she'll like. I show her the catalogue from a group show I was in. She doesn't throw it in my face. She just says, "So that's what you've been up to." We talk about how expensive things have gotten in Paris, whether we liked Alki Zei's new novel, *Achilles' Fiancée*, and then on an impulse I turn to her and ask, "Ve-ha? Ve-sa?"

"Ve-ha-sa," Anna says. That much we can agree on. We're twenty-three, too old for unmixed emotions.

Just like Papandreou and Özal, we too avoid discussing our equivalent of the Cyprus problem. We admit that our friendship is in crisis, but what can we do, these things happen. We open a bottle of wine she brought from Paris and clink glasses without meeting one another's eye. The wine is terrible, practically vinegar, but neither of us says a thing.

"Don't tell me you don't remember me?" She's my age, short, plump, with green eye shadow and gold earrings shaped like daisies. She's carrying a plastic bag full of strawberries and looks like a classic working girl headed home at the end of the day.

"I do remember you, but from where?"

"I'm Angeliki, we were in grade school together."

Merde! Angeliki, the smushed turd! She's had the mole removed from her eyebrow. How on earth was I supposed to recognize her?

"I'm exhausted, it's been a long day at work," she says, rubbing one ankle against the other. She's dying to tell me about how far she's climbed up the social ladder. She works at *24 Hours*, a newspaper owned by financier George Koskotas, who was recently charged with sending bribes to members of Papandreou's administration, hidden in boxes of Pampers. Angeliki just got engaged to a co-worker at the paper, too. If Anna were here now she would tell Angeliki off to her face, letting rip about how deep in PASOK filth she is, about the bourgeois institution of marriage, about all the diapers that'll soon be coming her way.

"What about you?" she asks.

I tell her I'll be graduating from the School of Fine Arts this year.

"That makes sense . . ." She looks me up and down. When I'm working, I wear my painting clothes out in the street. I must look like a bum with my shirt full of holes and paint on my hands. She's dressed for office work, in a suit and pumps.

"Do you still see Anna?" she asks.

Tough question. We talk on the phone every so often. We keep one another up to date about what's happening in our lives as if giving interviews to a reporter—always holding back, never telling the whole truth. She tells me about her activist friends in Paris, about the group *Ne pas plier* and a writer named Natacha Michel who writes Maoist novels. I describe the preparations for the exhibit that the art school's graduating class puts on each year.

"Anna lives in Paris," I answer.

"So you've finally got some peace and quiet," Angeliki says, flaring her nostrils. She's one of those people who flare their nostrils instead of laughing.

"What do you mean?"

"She's not dragging you around by the nose anymore."

Any minute now she'll stick out her tongue and start chasing me around the square, shouting "teapot, teapot, teapot."

The student exhibit is a big hit. The rector gives a speech telling us not to sell out entirely to the system. The rector's wife gets drunk and takes off her shoes. One of my fellow students, Loukas, douses me with champagne. Diana tells me I ruined my piece by turning it into an installation with actual phones and wires, that the real strength of the work was the idea of the wiretaps, of the voices layered over one another. All the rest is mere decoration.

"You have to choose." She's not just talking about art, she's talking about relationships, too.

Perhaps she's expecting me to choose her. But I choose Loukas. He's small, always smiling, with hands weathered by paint. He comes back to my apartment and immediately starts playing with my things—what's this, what's that. I have no patience for something that has to pass through all the usual stages—first a drink, then a kiss, then a hand on the chest. I pull him toward me, onto the chair in the middle of the room, and my mind strays to Kayo and all that never happened. I close my eyes, conjure him up, bite his tongue all over again.

"Slow down, little animal," says Loukas.

My desire evaporates.

"Did Anna call you?" As usual, Antigone is practically shrieking. I hold the receiver away from my ear.

"No. What happened?"

Stamatis. A heart attack. He was lying in bed, working on his notes for his book, and died on the spot.

"Was Anna with him?"

"She's the one who found him. She's completely lost it."

For the first time in my life I rush to the airport without a suitcase, without even a change of clothes. It's something Anna and I used to dream of when we were kids: flying off to Paris for a coffee. But what we had in mind wasn't the coffee they serve at funerals, and certainly not at the funeral of her father.

She's a mess, nothing but a pile of bones. She's wearing a long nightgown that's the exact same shade of pink as the liquid antibiotic they give to kids. She won't budge from Stamatis's armchair, where she sits absentmindedly stroking the worn velvet. I haven't seen her like this since the earthquake, or at least since the abortion. I make her tea, I bring her chouquettes from across the street, she doesn't touch any of it. The house has been overrun by friends and colleagues of Stamatis who wander around in hysterics. My gaze falls on the old, familiar poster on the wall: *I treat my desires as realities, because I believe in the reality of my desires.* I'd like for us to leave, to escape all this. That's the reality of my desires.

"Should we go to the park?" I say.

Anna puts on a pair of sneakers and pulls a long orange hooded raincoat over her nightgown. She looks like a patient just let out for her first walk in the hospital grounds after an operation. She lies down on the grass in Buttes-Chaumont and crosses her hands over her stomach. The ball-point pen falls from her hair. I grab it and draw a heart on her hand.

"What's that?" she asks.

"A confession of love."

I lie down beside her, grab her and hold her tight.

"I'm here for you, whenever you need me."

"And you'll make all my wishes come true?"

"Every single one."

"Then help me die. I want to die." Anna clings to me and starts to sob, heartrending sobs that sweep me along with them. At first I'm crying for Stamatis, who will never call me mademoiselle again, never take me for coffee at the café across the street, never make false promises to anyone. And then I'm crying for Kayo, and for Angelos. For my butchered hair, my butchered finger, my vagina. For the uniforms that made us look like Maoist schoolgirls, for all the ridiculous things we learned in home economics and in religion class. For Aunt Amalia, serving strawberries with mayonnaise. For my father, who can't tell the good guys from the bad. For my mother, for Gwendolyn, for all of Ikeja. And finally for Anna, my best friend.

We scatter his ashes in Trouville, off a pier where Anna used to count boats as a little girl. He hadn't specified a place in his will, just "in the sea." For some reason I remember the joke he once told using a tea bag. The missile that takes off by a miracle, out of sheer poetry, without any fuel, and flutters back down to our hands as ash. I close my eyes so as not to see Stamatis vanishing. I'm still not sure whether or not I believe in a God. When Anna and I used to talk about the power organized religion exercises over the masses, we were never holding an urn full of ashes that a short while before were an actual human being, with a beard, glasses, and boisterous laugh—ashes that a short while before were her father.

"Listen, we need slogans that reflect *our* era. That whole 'Bread, education, freedom' thing is old news: we've seen for ourselves how public education can destroy a perfectly healthy mind. As for the association of freedom with bread, these days we have all the freedom we want to die of starvation."

It's been a month since Stamatis died and Anna won't let me go home to Athens. This whole time I've been wearing her clothes, which are all too small for me; I struggle each morning to fit my breats into one of her bras. At first it was because she wanted help with various bureaucratic, practical matters. Now she wants for the two of us to sit and read her father's unfinished book about anarchist thought. All these years she was living in the same apartment with him, but it turns out she barely knew anything about his political beliefs. In a recess in the wall behind his bed she finds a complete run of *Provo*, a magazine put out in the mid-1960s by the Dutch anarchist organization of that name. She flips through them, then starts to read more carefully, almost angrily, trying to crack the code, to find some "message."

"What message?" I ask. "Your dad was writing a book, it's called research."

"But why didn't he ever talk to me about it? You think he was . . . you know, mixed up in something?"

"Anna, don't be ridiculous, he was writing the book right in front of your eyes. He wasn't hiding anything from you."

"Are you saying it's my fault for not taking an interest?"

She cries at the drop of a hat. Because she burnt the toast, because she has to wait in line at the bank, because she thinks I'm implying that she treated Stamatis with indifference.

"I'm sure he was involved in something," she says, wiping the tears from her eyes.

"Well, if so, it's the kind of involvement you should be proud of."

"You know how I feel about anarcho-autonomists, Maria. They have no discipline, and no political vision. They reject power but don't put forward any kind of just solution of their own."

"What on earth does justice mean, Anna? You sound like a mayor, or a minister of parliament."

She frowns at me, then turns back to the manuscript. Every now and then she lifts her head and says something as if thinking out loud: "The Black Panthers were replicating the Maoist Marxism of the third world? Give me a break!" She loses it completely when her father starts to analyze the 1952 public debate between Camus and Sartre in a manner that supports anarcho-syndicalist ideas, which, he contends, are "the only way out between the nihilism of the bourgeoisie and the arbitrary actions of the socialist system."

"But the leftist intellectuals all sided with Sartre back then!" she shouts, stomping her foot on the floor. "It was enough for them that the French Communist Party had the support of the working class. Stamatis always considered Stalinism a necessary evil, even after the invasion of Hungary. I don't understand what changed!"

Everything, everything changed. Even the weather. The Parisian summer slips in through the windows. Anna sits in Stamatis's armchair with the manuscript in her lap, biting her nails. I open the curtains, she closes them again. But the sunlight still sneaks in, lighting her from behind as if she were a Madonna in a fresco, which of course would make her mad, since she despises religion.

Her white eyebrow, the dimple in her chin: a Madonna who's angry at her painter. At her father.

"What do you say, should we go to an island this summer?"

Anna raises her head and looks at me as if I've said something vulgar. Every so often some of her friends from the collective come by. One brings a couple of tomatoes, another a bottle of wine. Beatrice, a girl with a high forehead and sunken eyes, brings roses, which she proceeds to crush into the tablecloth, in a message of consolation and militancy, the way Frida Kahlo did when she first met Trotsky. But Beatrice is no Kahlo, and Anna no Trotsky.

In the newspapers we read about Papandreou's open-heart surgery, about Koskotas's conviction. Such sickness and decay, and I'm here strolling down Parisian avenues? I want to go back to Athens, to reality. I say as much to Anna.

"We've got a whole house to ourselves, merde! It's our childhood dream come true. Why do you want to leave?"

Because if dreams don't come true when you dream them, they might as well never come true.

1989 is a red-letter year for us all. For Anna because she finds the political movement that suits her best—the green movement, the fight to protect nature and the environment. She abandons hardcore communism, returns to art, organizes happenings in Paris involving the spontaneous planting of trees, and of course gets mad when I don't go to help her. For Antigone because 1989 sees the formation of a new party, Synaspismos, the Coalition of the Left. For my parents because they finally buy their plot on Aegina; they plant a palm tree to mark the boundary of their own private Africa. For Aunt Amalia because she goes completely and utterly mad: she hears voices coming from the cooking hood, men saying all kinds of filthy things, and she laughs and laughs. For Kayo because he's been chosen to play a shyster in some low-budget film.

As for me, after the parliamentary elections in June and the formation of an interim government with its project of anti-corruption "catharsis" to clean up the political sphere, I finally have a good idea: I build a metal suitcase with lots of little compartments, load it up with cleaning fluid, Brillo pads, dust cloths, latex gloves, and transform myself into a cleaning lady. I ring doorbells and buzzers, tell whoever answers that I'm doing a performance piece called *Catharsis*, and that I'm offering to clean their bathrooms and kitchens for free. Most of the people I encounter have no idea what performance art is, or conceptual art: they assume I'm crazy and slam the door in my face. The ones who accept my services insist on treating me to something, or on giving me a tip. I throw myself into the scrubbing of sinks and toilets. My hands smell of bleach and latex. A few newspaper columnists mention my piece, I do some interviews, and journalists start to write stupid stuff about the rebirth of political art. One day I ring a bell and the man in the house calls to his wife, "Come quick, Eleni, it's the girl we saw on TV! She came to clean our house!"

No idea lasts long in 1989, in all that madness, in the desperate desire for publicity. *Catharsis* ends then and there, on that couple's doorstep: I turn on my heel and walk away, leaving the man and his Eleni high and dry. I wander aimlessly through the streets, until eventually I set my suitcase down on the ground and sit on it, just like when I was nine years old and the police came and brought me home. I wouldn't be the least bit surprised if they showed up again and told me to move on, that I'm disturbing the peace. The only way not to disturb the peace is to shut yourself up in your house. To listen to the voices coming from the cooking hood.

Merde, I need to find another Ikeja, before I start hearing voices, too.

Seven

I push off the covers. I couldn't possibly get out of bed. My legs are logs, the room is dark, the time impossible to gauge. Am I still in the cave? Is that Gwendolyn pushing open the bedroom door to peer in, or the burglar with the stocking over his head, or the Albanian's ghost?

"Are you sleeping?" Kayo whispers.

What a stupid question. If you're sleeping you can't answer; if you're awake, what's the point of asking?

"You're sleeping," he says.

I shut my eyes. I apparently haven't outgrown my childish stubbornness. That's what happens when a person grows up alongside someone like Anna. Kayo tiptoes over to the bed, pulls the covers up to my chin and tucks me in. Then he leaves the room, half closing the door behind him, and I'm once again wrapped in darkness. I hear voices coming from the kitchen, someone coughs, there's a sound of cups clinking. People are drinking coffee. But that bit of information doesn't help: it could be morning, afternoon, evening. All I know is that it's a time of day when people aren't usually asleep. Which places me automatically in the category of the sick.

That cough again. A smoker's cough. Anna's here.

•

She's perched on the kitchen table, the way Kyria Kontomina used to sit on her desk when we were back in high school. She's wearing high-heeled pumps with ankle straps and a forest green, eighties-style satin dress with puff sleeves. You'd think she was on her way out to one of the disco clubs on the Aegina of our youth. She's smoking, and blowing smoke rings into the air that break one by one on the ceiling. Kayo, Kosmas, Irini, and Irini's younger sister Fiona are sitting in a circle around her, like rapt schoolchildren. Anna doesn't even need words—she speaks with her hands, her eyes, her mouth. Lesson One from Little Wizard: how to hold a magic wand. Half the battle with magic tricks is creating the proper ambiance.

Suddenly Anna hops down from the table. "Oh, my, I remember that blanket!"

I'm standing in the doorway of the kitchen wrapped in the blanket I had as a girl, the one with red flowers. Anna and I used to make tents with it, or play house under it, or whatever else crossed our minds. Later we would wrap it around our legs for warmth, since if you sit still for too long, if you get lost in labyrinthine conversations about the meaning of life, you end up getting cold.

"Are you okay?" Kosmas asks.

"She just fell, it was like . . ." says Irini.

Kayo comes over and rubs my back. "How do you feel?"

"Better."

I'm not really sure, though, I have nothing to compare my current state to. I shuffle out of the kitchen and over to the mirror in the hall, which reflects the following image: a green wig with bangs, slightly askew. Bone-white skin. Purple circles under my eyes. As for the eyes themselves, they're blurry, nearly overflowing with inexplicable tears. I look like a Martian that missed its space-ship. Or a ghost.

"Don't worry, you're still Miss Inner Beauty," Anna says. She's standing behind me. Even in heels, she knows how to glide sound-lessly on her magic carpet.

"Should I fix you something to eat?" Irini calls from the kitchen.

"No, I want to go out."

"I know a place with decent food," Anna says. "Let's all go, we need to get something in your stomach."

Today she's driving Malouhos's Jeep, which is big enough for us all. Anna and Kayo are up front, I'm in back with Irini and Kosmas.

"I've never ridden in a Jeep before," Irini says.

"And you never will again," I say. "Life is hard."

"I'll take you for a ride whenever you like," Anna promises, adjusting the mirror. She wants to keep an eye on me. Apparently she still worries when I'm tired, or angry, or acting unpredictably.

"Why are you here, anyhow?" I ask.

"I was passing by and decided to ring the bell. Sixth sense, I guess."

"You live way out in Ekali and you were just passing by?"

"I'm pretty sure we still have freedom of movement in this country."

Irini is looking at me questioningly. Someday, if I manage to figure out the why and the how, I'll write a novel. I'll tell the whole story, all that we lived through, from my point of view. I'll let Anna have the title, though: *Why I Killed My Best Friend*. If you don't feel like reading it, the cover should be enough, you can skip the story: one friend kills another, big deal, human beings are killing one another every day all over the world. Sometimes, to give a logical structure to these conflicts, they fight body to body,

hand to hand with the police. Or they fall down the stairs in a
metro station without even having been pushed. They'll even fight
themselves, if there's no other worthy opponent around.

They bleed, therefore they exist, as Camus would say.

The car in front of ours brakes abruptly. A toy dog on the dash-
board bobs its head frantically as if agreeing with me, as if signing
my proclamation on behalf of the inanimate world.

"Hold on tight," Anna shouts.

We hold on.

We drive toward Syntagma, slipping between cars as if down a
playground slide. The Grande Bretagne is to our right, Parliament
to our left. As we look for a place to park, they tell me what happened: I fell down the stairs in the station at Syntagma, just before
the demonstration hit its stride. Irini and Kayo carried me outside
and laid me down on the grass.

"I don't know what happened, I just couldn't breathe. It felt like
claustrophobia, or a panic attack."

"Maybe you saw blood?" Anna asks, holding the restaurant door
open for me to go inside. "Maria faints whenever she sees blood."

"What happened next?" I say, ignoring her.

After that the demonstration erupted into a spontaneous party.
Everyone loved the whistles, they were acting like little kids. The
police beat up two teenagers they caught spray-painting something
on the platform wall. They handcuffed a gypsy, who spat at them.
They confiscated as many whistles as they could. They carried
one half-crazed old woman to a police van, with her shouting the
whole time, "You call yourselves men?"

"The question is, what's the long-term effect of all that?" Anna
asks.

"The conviction that we're strong. That's not enough for you?"
Kosmas says.

"And the conviction that we can participate in social life without being controlled by bureaucrats or career politicians," Irini adds.

"Sure, fine, they let you blow off some steam for an afternoon," Anna says. "Look over there, though." A gypsy kid has come into the restaurant, and the waiter runs over to shoo him out. "Just look at how one outcast treats another. We cut off our nose to spite our face."

"Why would you call the waiter an outcast?" Fiona asks.

"The kid isn't allowed to join the meal, and the waiter isn't, either. They're both here to serve us," Anna says. "Over here, kid!"

The gypsy kid dodges the waiter and comes over to our table. He's carrying a bunch of carnations whose stems are mere stubs wrapped in aluminum foil. Probably stolen from cemetery wreaths.

"Do you want a carnation?" the boy asks.

"What do *you* want?" Anna says.

"What's that?" he says, motioning to her plate with his chin.

"Zucchini."

"Can I have some?" the boy asks.

Anna motions for him to sit beside her and feeds him a bite from her fork. Her three young acolytes stare at her, mouths hanging open. Yes, the woman in the evening gown is a bit eccentric. One bite for her, one for the gypsy kid.

"I have to go," the boy says, wiping his mouth with the back of his hand. He runs to the door, stops short, comes back and offers her a mutilated carnation. Anna, protectress of the scorned. A local Frida Kahlo. People at nearby tables are looking at us in annoyance.

"Look at that," Anna says. "We destroyed the illusion of a safe, bourgeois life. And now they've lost their appetites."

Is it really that easy to charm people? Irini and Kostas trust her already, they're opening up and telling her about their lives, their families, their dreams. Fiona, who's usually bored by our meetings, is gazing at her with eyes like saucers. Even Kayo is enjoying himself. He leans over and whispers to me: "She's an eternal nine-teen-year-old." Nineteen? More like nine. Your character is more or less formed by the time you're nine.

I'm beginning to understand the mechanism behind her charm: she does something insane, something out of keeping with her beauty, her image, the way she dresses. Then she uses that conspic-uous act like a blanket: she wraps herself up in it, *becomes* that act. In the eyes of others, Anna is an allegory for generosity, courage, resourcefulness. She does things that occur to other people only fleetingly, enacts scenarios from the realm of instinct. She charms, she torments, she curses, she kills.

Yes, kills.

The face of the Albanian shapes itself for an instant in the bowl of soup before me. His harsh cheekbones flicker in and out of vis-ibility between floating carrots. The broth has the metallic taste of blood. Cave. Metro. Prison. A place that's underground, dark, deep. My temples grow numb, my tongue is dry.

"Anna, we have to talk about it."

"About what?" Anna says.

"That thing. It's suffocating me. I don't know how you can live with it. I—"

She grabs me by the arm and pinches me, hard. "Let's go out-side, merde!" Her voice breaks into a sudden coughing fit. She practically spits her vowels.

"Take a deep breath!" she shrieks when we're out in the pedes-trian street outside the restaurant.

I can't breathe at all.

She rubs my hands between hers. I feel a bit better. We smoke, pacing up and down. The lighted shop windows along the street look like the mouths of whales. All kinds of things seem to have washed up in there: torn clothing, hanging threads, tattered

linings like the one from Aunt Amalia's coat. It's back in fashion.
Meta-punk.

"It was an accident, get it into your head. An ac-ci-dent!" Anna
says. "We've gone over this a thousand times."

"You may have, with your shrink, maybe you're over it now.
But I just dug a hole in my head, dug a hole, do you understand?
Inside me! And now it's all seeping out. It's coming back out, all of
it! Like an overstuffed suitcase that just pops open on its own, you
know?"

"So close the suitcase," Anna snaps. "It's done, it's over."

"I think we need to confess. We need to go to prison."

"Have you completely lost your mind? You want to confess
to the cops? Why don't you go and light a candle at the church
instead, like your mother?"

"I have to do something, I need to figure out how to make
sense of it."

"I could kill you, you know. I've fixed my life, and you come
along and tell me—"

"What do I care? I never fixed *my* life. I've felt dead for a long
time now."

"Forget the drama, Maria. I can't deal with any more drama."

She hugs me in the only way she knows: tightly, asphyxiatingly,
urgently. Her bones dig into mine.

"I know a good psychiatrist," she says.

I know an even better psychiatrist: the National Library. I tell Saroglou I've come down with the flu and won't be in for a few days.
But the truth is I've got another school to go to: the school of
silence—silence, not hysterical aphonia.

I need peace and quiet, high ceilings and a sense of purpose. I
sit at one of the tables devouring whatever I can find about caves,

prisons, even the architecture of metro stations. Anything having to do with underground life, darkness, or the attempt to escape into the light makes my pulse race, though it also holds a certain attraction. I read about Plato's cave, about the prisoners who have spent their entire lives chained to a wall, facing another wall, trapped and immobilized in the darkness, unable to see even their fellow prisoners. The only light comes from a fire burning behind them, lit by their jailers. On the blank wall before them they see shadows cast by objects passing before the fire. The prisoners have no knowledge of what light even is.

My tongue goes dry again, my palms start to sweat. I grab my bag and rush outside, run down the marble stairs of the library two at a time, relieved to be out in the daylight. On my way home I wonder how real the things are that the prisoners see. According to Plato, the prisoners' inability to orient themselves, to understand where they are, is a bondage far worse than their chains.

The next day I find a dictionary of sociology full of terms like society, competition, adaptation—"inherited structural and functional characteristics that increase the probability of survival." I also read about an archaeological excavation in Chiapas, Mexico. The archaeologists who went there back in the 1960s claimed that before the Mayans, a tribe called the Zoque lived on the Rio La Venta and sacrificed children in caves. I'd first heard about this from Antigone, after she took a trip to Mexico with her CEO. I rush back outside. Whenever I'm confronted with the image of a cave, even if it's just a mental image, I want desperately to escape again into the light.

The following day I stumble across Piranesi's imaginary prisons. The name is already familiar—from Malouhos, not from any course on eighteenth-century art. In art school we learned about far more general trends, synoptically, as if centuries were bricks to be stacked one on top of the next. The imaginary prisons are terrifying. The perspective in the drawings keeps shifting. Staircases and ladders that seem to lead upward in fact don't lead anywhere at all. If these were plans for actual buildings, the inspectors would nix construction altogether. Piranesi seems to have devised every possible way of escaping from Plato's cave, but in the end he pushes you even deeper down: into the captivity of an internal landscape, a nightmare with no exit.

Only this time I don't feel trapped. I shut my eyes and travel to the place where Aristomenis Malouhos found safety. I jot down in my notebook: *Is it possible to feel safe in a nightmare? Perhaps, if from the start you treat it as the site of an inner struggle. With Piranesi's sketches you're struggling to escape into the light. Freedom and justice are waiting somewhere inside the ruins he draws. An abyss of options. I like that.*

As the week draws to a close, I read about the caves in Lascaux. A charming story: in 1940 four teenagers found a cave in the south of France with remnants of Paleolithic art, which they discovered by the weak light of a lantern. I can imagine the irrepressible curiosity they must have felt at that age: teenagers taking turns goading one another a bit further, a bit deeper. At first all they could see was a hole, most likely opened by a falling pine tree. Then the most daring of the four suggested they widen the hole by digging, though he probably wasn't the one to start. He would have been more like Anna, a leader telling the others what to do. Soon they encountered a small cavity, and tumbled down onto a pile of stones covering the old mouth of the cave. That led them to yet another cavity, which later came to be known as the Hall of the Bulls. I can picture them holding their lantern up to the walls and seeing paintings of red cows, yellow horses, bulls, deer. How could they possibly have slept that night, and what dreams might they have had? The next day they went back and used a rope to lower themselves down through a narrow passageway. They ended up in the Shaft of the Dead Man, where a painting shows a man with a bird's beak beside a bison with lowered head, in attack position, and what appears to be a rhinoceros. Which figure would each of them have identified with? I myself would have identified, not with either animal, or with the human, but with the particular shade of ochre used in the painting. A faded yellow, like an old jealousy. Odiosamato.

The news spread through the village and beyond. Archaeologists flooded the place. How must those four French youths have felt, having their discovery taken from their hands and transformed into a tourist site? In 1955 the paintings revolted, as Malouhos would say. They started to lose their characteristic colors. People said it was due to the carbon dioxide being released from visitors' breath. Scientists came up with a system to control the release of carbon dioxide, but the damage had already been done: green spots of oxidation started to appear on the walls. The development of the archaeological site had upset the ecosystem, the natural development of the flora and fauna alike.

I jot again in my notebook: *There comes a time when we need to leave the cave in peace. We're guests there, not owners.*

"What's going on with you?" Kayo asks, poking his head through the crack in the door. "Are you painting?"

"Kayo, can you leave me alone for a while? Can you just listen? A-*lone.*"

"Okay, I get it. But Anna's called three times today. She says for you to call her back as soon as you can."

I lock the door of my room and regress to the time when I thirsted for black. Only now, instead of using black paper, I draw in black on a white background. Black, and ochre, too. I sketch the prehistoric animals in the Lascaux caves, as I remember them from the books I pored over at the library. Horses, bison, cows, deer. I practice doing feet and tails for a while, then start to draw little creatures in miniature. Tiny animals entering enormous caves. Or gigantic animals trying to squeeze through the mouths of microscopic caves. The mismatched proportions transport me straight into the realm of fairytale, offering me that particular comfort of children's drawings. As a child, you're presented with a rigid world of predetermined sizes and power relations. You lie down on the floor with a piece of paper and deconstruct it all—you draw blue roots on the trees, people with no fingers, see-through bellies with babies inside; you bestow life and take it away again with your colored pencils. With faith and with rage you change the world.

"Daphne, eyes on your own paper, please. Leave Natasha alone!"

She obeys immediately, a spitting image of the bison: head down, tongue out. Today she's drawing a cave with babies flying all around, like little airplanes.

"Why are the babies flying?" I ask.

"They're not babies, they're storks. The babies come out of their mouths."

"Who did you learn that from?"

"Svetlana. She thinks a stork is going to bring her baby. She doesn't even know how babies are born!"

Daphne has gotten much sweeter since our tea party in her room. She became infatuated with the idea of the cave, of a place where you can hide something that's all your own.

Today the whole class is drawing caves. Daphne has worn out their ears with stories of mud and witches—and children are natural imitators. Natasha, as always, draws rainbows all around her cave. Panos puts his whole family inside and himself outside doing cartwheels. Sandra draws a wild dog at the entrance, barking red bow-wows. Aris draws soldiers with machine guns. The mouth of his cave is full of barbed wire, and land mines are exploding in the background.

Of course none of them draw men with stockings over their faces, or headless dolls, or a child with a severed finger. To each his own cave.

She slaps the desk with her hand and her silver bangles clatter.

"Why didn't you call me?" She's smoking and coughing by turns. I don't answer right away, and she stands there kicking the leg of the desk with one pointed boot.

"I want to be alone for a while," I say eventually.

"What does that mean?"

"What does solitude mean?"

"Can we go for a coffee in that awful place across the street?"

"No, Anna. I'm busy. I'm going home."

"I'll drive you."

"No, I'll take the metro."

"But—didn't you say you'd never go back into the metro? After your panic attack?"

"You're the one who said that, not me."

"I'll come with you, then, in case something happens."

"No."

No. It's the first time I've ever said no to her and stood my ground. The leather of her boot is scratched from constantly kicking at the leg of the desk. It's scary, as if her soul has dropped down into her shoe. As if she's lost something of her shiny self-sufficiency.

I head underground somewhat gingerly. I take the stairs, not the escalator, which is packed with people. I walk to one side, keeping hold the metal railing. *You're one of the prisoners in Plato's cave*, I tell myself. *Don't deny it. Find the limits of your cell.* On the platform my palms start to sweat. A woman gives me a look that manages to be both absentminded and severe. The train is equally severe, rushing toward me at great speed. The platform shrinks and expands, pulsating: a heart, cruelly illuminated by fluorescent lights.

You're in an imaginary prison, I say to myself. *You're Piranesi. You're the one who has sketched this distorted perspective, this overflowing platform. You've drawn in those dark stairs climbing into the sky, you added whatever crossed your mind—corners, curves, labyrinths. Get in the train. Unbutton your jacket if you feel hot. Take the kids' drawings out of your bag and fan yourself with them. Before you can count to ten, you'll have reached your stop. Trouble breathing? Just remember that word from the dictionary. "Adaptation: inherited structural and functional characteristics that increase the probability of survival." You're seeing shadows? That's only natural, the prisoners haven't ever seen light. Hold on, hold on. This is the only way—from captivity to freedom.*

I step out of the train car and set off almost at a run. The light rushes down the stairs to meet me. A warm, comforting light. It's as if the staircase is a mouth spitting me out into the springtime Attic sky. I'm one of the youths in the Lascaux cave, who saw the prehistoric animals and is running to share the discovery with others. Or perhaps not. Not with others just yet. I'm a combination of the kids in Natasha's and Panos's drawings, doing cartwheels outside of the cave, with a rainbow overhead.

Specks of dust and freedom.

"Will it bother you if I go and stay with her?" Kayo reaches out and pulls me theatrically into his arms, as if we're about to break into some impressive dance move. Only we just stand there, motionless. Then we sigh at exactly the same time. It happens to us all the time, and always makes us laugh. We call it our simultaneous orgasm.

"Was I too hard on you, Kayo? I didn't really mean it when I told you to move out."

"I've gotten used to you snapping at me. We've been doing that to one another forever. Don't worry, this has nothing to do with you. Svetlana is having her baby and Anna can't find anyone to take care of Daphne."

"If she thinks she's found a way of keeping tabs on me . . ."

"Why should she want to keep tabs, Maria? Just let it go."

I peel myself from his embrace and open the balcony door. I rest my knee in the gap between the bars. The mark made by my very first rebellion.

"You have no idea," I say softly, as if talking to myself.

He packs a suitcase, whistling some pop song that's all the rage on the radio. It's perfectly clear, he's happy he's leaving. He oppressed me in New York, and I'm oppressing him here. Property is power, what can we do? You give someone a room to crash in but demand emotional ransom in return. And what about me? Am I happy he's leaving? I'm not sure. I've never been alone in my life. There was always family, friends, bodies in motion that occupied space, talked, shouted, watched television, listened to music. Shared space, a communalism I believed in.

He hugs me at the door, suitcase in hand. He's at his goofiest, to keep us both from crying. Deep down I'm afraid Kayo might never come back. He even took his foam Statue of Liberty.

"We're meeting about the Attic Highway. Are you coming?" Anna's voice breaks into one of her theatrical, smoke-infused coughs.

"We? What do you mean, we?"

"I joined your group, if that's okay with you."

"Congratulations. Where's the meeting?"

"At my house. Tonight at six."

"In Ekali? There's a revolution brewing in the trenches of the northern suburbs?"

Anna sighs and hangs up on me.

That afternoon, without knowing why, I toss my old Super 8 in my bag. I haven't used it since art school. There's dust on the lens. Irini comes by in her ancient Autobianchi to pick me up. Kosmas will head straight to Ekali after class.

"Aren't you the one who always says we should be open to others, no matter how different they are?" Irini says, shifting gears. The car shakes, and we shake with it.

"I don't trust her."

"But why? Can't someone who's rich have a social vision, too? Would you prefer for all the rich people to be on the other side? At the very worst, you can take their money and use it to print posters."

"The issue isn't money, it's ambition. Anna's a leader. If it were up to her, she would resurrect May 1968 and make herself prime minister in the process."

Irini sighs. "Fine, and what would you be in that scenario? You'd just be the opposition party."

She's right. We're all tired politicians. And now we're headed for a bipartisan meeting at the prime minister's residence.

We run into traffic on Kifisias Avenue; they've already started when we arrive. Anna is cross-legged on the floor, barefoot in a blue track suit. Kosmas and a classmate of his, Nikos, are sprawled on the sofa. Kayo seems already to have made himself at home—he's in the kitchen, fixing martinis. The martini revolution.

"Okay, let's do a recap," Kosmas says. "Only by taking control of the streets can we have control over the city. That's our basic point, right? The reason we've decided to occupy the Attic Highway is because we want to finally have control of our lives in this shitty town. Are we agreed this far?"

"The Olympic Games are a multinational corporation, and we don't want it to bulldoze our grandmother's house, to destroy her chicken coop," Anna says.

"Her chicken coop? Did we miss something?" Irini asks.

"We're trying to draft a text about the occupation," Anna says, making room for her on the rug. "We're just brainstorming." It's Anna's favorite activity: sitting cross-legged on the floor, surrounded by people and papers, brainstorming.

"Where's Daphne?" I ask.

"In her room."

She's in her cave, wrapped in a comforter with ducks on it. Each of the ducks is standing on a single foot, like a stork, on a tuft of grass surrounded by nothingness. There are markers everywhere, a trail leading from the door of her room.

"What are you coloring?"

"Oh, you came! I want to show you something."

Daphne picks up her piece of drawing paper and holds it directly under my nose. The witch and her apprentice have been shipwrecked. They're sitting on the pointed peak of an island. All around is the sea—blue and slightly torn here and there from Daphne's habit of pushing down hard when she draws.

"What island is that?"

"It's not an island, it's a cave," Daphne tells me, disappointed.

So the cave has come unstuck from solid land and is sailing off blissfully, like a raft on the waves. The witchlet isn't hiding in the cave anymore. And why would she? The rain has stopped.

There's a cloud of smoke over the leather sofas in the living room. I lean on the banister at the top of the stairs and watch as they gesture, smoke, argue about the four million cars produced each year and the pollution created by the capitalist system. The idea is to occupy the last of the shacks condemned by eminent domain along the proposed route of the Attic Highway, before the bulldozers come. To put up a fight.

The younger among us have already gone to visit the people living in those shacks. They've started a discrete awareness-raising campaign. They drink coffee with them, listen to their stories, and dream of the moment when they'll go to live among these aging farmers, in a back room, a storeroom that's been cleaned out for the purpose, under a hanging lantern or some old-fashioned trinket. They're as naïve as I was when I packed my suitcase with roller-skates and eggs.

"Why so thoughtful?" Aristomenis asks from behind me.

I forgot, it's Sunday. Even rich revolutionaries deserve a day of rest.

Aristomenis's office is almost directly across from Daphne's bedroom, and the door is ajar. The office contains two perfectly white desks: a work desk piled with books and architectural plans, and a desk for relaxing, with a coffee pot that's half full, cookies, pipe tobacco, and a plate of sliced kiwi. The last bit of daylight slants through the windows, making the kiwis glow with an even more otherworldly color. Aristomenis moves in the manner of a person who knows how long supplies will last, how many days fruit stays fresh, how much milk to put in a cup of coffee.

"Come on in, sit down and tell me about it."

"About what?"

"You seem disappointed."

"I'm not disappointed, I'm confused."

"Have a kiwi. It's comfort food."

I chew slowly. "It's ridiculous for me to be running around to protests all the time. I'm afraid of blood. What kind of activist faints at the sight of blood? In the metro the other day, I have no idea what came over me, I just fainted, like an old lady. I'd like to start painting again, but I'm too old for that kind of thing."

"Too old?"

"I'm almost thirty-five, I'm not a kid anymore. Either you really pursue something or you don't. You can't just drop things and pick them up again whenever you like."

"Who says? Take your friend. Now that she's found an opening, she's in all the way. She was raised to care, to offer herself."

"To offer herself?"

Aristomenis tugs on his beard when he's thinking. He's shaped his own mental image of Anna, one that's significantly different from mine. He remembers her in the apartment in Paris, for instance, making soup and coffee for everyone. Once he saw her standing on the steps outside the building, talking to an unshaven man wrapped in a blanket. Aristomenis had been moved by how Anna knelt down so as to be at the same height as the man. She pulled him by the hand, telling him to come in off the street to where it was warm. "They'll just put me out again," he said. "Then they'll have me to reckon with," Anna had shot back, putting her hands on her hips to show how tough she was. According to his theory, Anna had been born into a house where people were always talking about revolution. When she wanted ice cream as a kid, she would draw a rocket pop and run to her parents, shouting her own version of the rallying cry of the Polytechnic: "Ice cream, education, freedom!" She would be woken up late at night by voices in the living room, the voices of strangers smoking and talking about democracy. She dreamed of being a heroine from the French Revolution, barefoot and in rags, carrying a flag in her hands. She would pick up bits of conversation, terminology, slogans, and then say whatever came into her head, as long as it included the word "equality." She misinterpreted her father's political theory because her thinking was superficial, she hadn't read enough to understand. For Anna, politics was a way of getting attention and love. After Antigone's death, she withdrew into herself, didn't give a damn about anyone, as if that circle of love had closed. But she was used to getting involved, to working, organizing. She just needed the right opportunity.

"How did Antigone die?"

When she and the CEO parted ways, Antigone went back into action. She was the old, good Antigone again, with an added element: the obstinacy of someone who sacrifices one thing for another that turns out not to be worth the trouble. When she figured out that the CEO didn't deserve her love, Antigone threw herself back into organizing for all kinds of causes—against nuclear energy, for the rights of political prisoners, for refugees in Rwanda and Kosovo. She wrote texts, organized conferences, and eventually pitched a tent outside the university, as parts of a hunger strike for human rights. Though she was participating under medical supervision, she quickly became entirely dehydrated and suffered a shock to her system. She died in the most romantic way, in a tent in a public square with a drip in her arm.

Aristomenis shields me from my annoyed comrades who don't understand why I suddenly want to leave. He says he'll drop me at the metro station in Kifisia. As we drive, Antigones of various ages pass by my window, bony women with anxious eyes. It's in style now for women to be tall and skinny, to look withdrawn. Back then Antigone was alone, an anorexic monster of circumstance. She takes shape clearly in my mind: peeling carrots, smoking her Gauloises cigarettes, giving us ballet lessons, telling us: *It's our duty to remember those who sacrificed their lives for us.* Now that she sacrificed her own life, in a manner of speaking, her words sound almost prophetic. On the station platform I see yet another Antigone pacing up and down. Sad, distracted, a fur stole wrapped around her neck like a scarf. I take the Super 8 out of my bag, record the way she moves: she sways on her expensive heels, a walking advertisement for an untenable utopia. We've written proclamations about this kind of thing—but the Albanian woman in the metro the other day didn't know how to read. So I'll try again, to say something in images.

That night I project the film on the wall of Kayo's empty room. Black and white calves, pacing back and forth. The woman is on her way to a protest, to her own personal insurrection—only she's lost her way.

Eight

"Look at those bums!"

Dad is in front of the TV, watching what's become of the anniversary march at the Athens Polytechnic. Molotov cocktails, fires, overturned police barricades. I feel nauseated. Even televised tear gas makes my eyes sting.

"If only they would hand them over to me, just for a day!"

You have one of them right under your nose, Dad. You're sharing a bowl of pumpkin seeds with her, mumbling "Change the channel," "Fine," "No."

"I just think of their poor parents," Mom sighs.

I'll just bet she does. I get up and go out onto the balcony. I rest my knee in the hole in the railing, from back when I got my head stuck and the man had to cut through the metal to get me out. *You're a handful, eh?* Yes, a handful. More and more of one.

How is it that sometimes, on starry nights, you move backward in time, and feel as if it was only yesterday when you stuck your head between the bars, when you felt powerless and angry and tried to run away, with two cracked eggs in your suitcase and a head full of Gwendolyn's proverbs? *When a ripe fruit sees an honest person, it falls.* Only there's no ripe fruit anymore, and no honest people, either.

It's 1993. PASOK is back in power, the salt is as worm-ridden as it gets. In a few days I'll be turning twenty-six and I'm not afraid of states of emergency anymore, of political unrest. On the contrary, I'm a person who causes unrest.

I bleed, therefore I am.

"Oh, Maria! I'm so glad you guys came."

I toss my backpack on the floor, sink my face into her hair and breathe in her new scent—bergamot and cinnamon. As always, Anna is both tart and sweet: she hugs me tightly, but pinches my arm. She kisses Thanos three times, French style. He doesn't know anything about the French way of greeting and keeps on going, kissing the air after she's pulled away. Anna is blindingly beautiful at the end of her first communist period. She has on Moroccan leather flip-flops and a see-through dress printed with starfish. Her hair is in a bun, held in place by a pair of chopsticks—a blonde version of Antigone. The famous Thierry, barefoot, is slicing tomatoes at the kitchen table. He's tall and attractive, an Aryan Kayo with curly hair down to his shoulders. He winks at me and my heart does a backflip. She's found the best, yet again. In the most beautiful city, in a sun-drenched apartment with half-circle balconies near Buttes-Chaumont. The apartment is all hers now; not even Stamatis's ghost inhabits it anymore. Where the photograph of Poulantzas used to be, now there's one of her as a child, at some celebration after the fall of the junta in Greece: the Arc de Triomphe in the background, Anna's fingers making the victory sign. Unbuttoned pea coat, red cheeks, white eyebrow, dimple in her chin, tortoiseshell barrette in her bangs. The wunderkind of the exiled Greek left.

One of Anna's pieces has displaced the poster about the reality of desires. She's done a whole series: she buys old, romantic landscapes from junk shops—snow-capped peaks, forest streams, houses perched on mountainsides—and alters them with her brush.

She adds bits of an anarchist's city plan, paints in factories or toxic waste, dirties the waters of a lake, ravishes the landscape with acid rain. She's become a romantic again, just as she was with Angelos. She wants to save nature, like a medieval knight fighting to protect a princess who never expressed the slightest desire to be saved.

Thierry is a Greenpeace activist. Anna goes with him on missions to save endangered animals, follows him to Kuwait and Venezuela to protest oil spills. She sends me postcards with laconic messages, signed "with love." But I no longer believe in Anna's love. What she really wants is to show me how well she's doing, moving from one revolution to the next—from sexual freedom to communism, and now to her new tree-hugging routine.

"What's wrong with that?" Thanos asks when we've shut the door of the attic room, which is now the guest room. Anna's charmed him, too.

"Neither one of them cares at all about the slaves who work in the fields all day, handling all those toxic chemicals. They swoop in after the fact and act like stars, play the ecological activists, the official protectors of nature."

"Aren't they just doing their job?"

"That's exactly what I'm saying: Anna and Thierry are just doing their job. The two of them are drowning in money, and they spend so much effort trying to hide it."

"What would you prefer? For them to give it to you?"

"They could give it away. Or just spend it without feeling guilty all the time."

They painted the apartment themselves, and they remind us of it whenever they can, so we don't think they're too bourgeois. They sing the praises of a dirt cheap pizzeria they discovered. After lunch, Anna drags me to a thrift store.

"Well, are you going to tell me about Thanos?" she says, trying on a red kimono with holes at the elbows.

What could I possibly tell her about Thanos? He's a bank teller, the absolute personification of mediocrity. He only goes out on weekends, he lives with his parents, he provides me with the cover I need. If I tell her about Thanos, I'll have to tell her about Camus, too, about who I really am, what kind of life I lead. For the first time since my locking-myself-in-the-bathroom phase, I have secrets from Anna. Only back then it was a personal revolution. Now I'm fighting for others.

"He's good to me," I say.

"Goodness never mattered to you, Maria. If anything, I'd say you preferred to be a little bit mistreated, you always wanted the ones who pushed you away . . ."

"Isn't it amazing how a person can change?"

She frowns. "You're up to something," she says. "There's something you're hiding."

I'm hiding it from my parents, from my art school friends, from the police, and you think you're going to figure it out?

"I'm bored, Anna, that's all. My life isn't as fascinating as yours is."

So this is how we'll live in peace: if you ever start to suspect anything, I'll just break out the passive-aggressive complaints. I've been afraid of her all my life, but it turns out she's a known quantity. She's predictable.

As Gwendolyn would say, a bird doesn't change its feathers when winter comes.

"Senegal is amazing," Thierry says.

I look up from my pizza. "When did you guys go?"

We're eating at the cheap pizzeria, with some French friends of theirs, such colorless people that you'd think Anna and Thierry chose them on purpose, to set off their own personalities, their brilliance, their joy.

"I went alone, Anna didn't come. But I came back with Seidu, a Senegalese who was traveling to Europe for the first time, on a scholarship."

Anna is shaking with laughter. "Do we need this? Do we need that?"

It's apparently a private joke, because Thierry laughs, too. He explains that Seidu was from a remote village in Senegal that didn't have a supermarket. When they first went to pick up a few things for his apartment in Paris, Seidu completely lost it. He didn't know what any of the products were, or what they were used for, and kept asking, "Do we need this? Do we need that?" Seidu, they kept saying, how are you going to go to the bathroom without toilet paper, or cook without oil? And Seidu kept walking, hypnotized, down aisles full of carefully arranged goods.

"Nice joke, guys. It's so funny, isn't it, to make fun of people from the third world?" I say, biting angrily into my slice.

Anna shoots me a piercing glance. "Maria, you don't get it. Seidu's better off, not us. He gets aesthetic pleasure from the washing machine!" Thierry explains that Seidu used to spend hours in front of the washing machine, entranced by the centripetal movement as it spun. Thanos finds that extraordinarily amusing, too. I feel like shoving the entire pizza in their faces.

Anyone who makes fun of Africa is making fun of me.

We're dancing tango at a retro café-theater that Thierry and Anna discovered, somewhere in Pigalle. Two drunk prostitutes walk by outside, blowing kisses through the window. Thierry gestures for them to come inside and they lift their skirts in an improvised can-can. Thanos is dancing in place, a bizarre combination of heavy metal and the kalamatiano. I laugh, forget myself, feel normal for a while. But all it takes is for someone's gaze to linger on me a bit too long for me to freeze in fear. They're following me. They know.

Camus says I've lost it completely. He practically ordered me to go to Paris for a few days. Sometimes I get so scared I think I might stop breathing. It happens at relatively safe moments, like when we're putting up posters in the streets. When things get serious, I forget my fear. I concentrate on my arms, my legs, I turn into a machine that's running, or trampling something, someone.

"Want to go pee?" Anna says. Her hair is a mess, she's bright red from dancing, but she's gorgeous. A tiny vein pulses on her forehead.

She sits on the toilet, I lean against the wall. Our favorite positions.

"Thierry wants us to go and live in Africa," she says dreamily.

No, merde! Africa is mine!

"He says if you don't live where the real problems are, you're a tourist."

"Paris has real problems, too. Unemployment, homelessness, racism . . ."

"We're working toward other goals, Maria."

"Oh, I forgot, none of that's in fashion. This year everyone's wearing aboriginals and ecological disasters."

Anna reaches out a hand and pinches me hard on the arm. "I'll kick you out of the house! You can go and sleep in the metro, with your precious homeless people!"

"Don't bother kicking me out, I'll leave on my own!"

I rush out into the street. The cold Parisian air stings my face, my hands, as if dozens of Annas are pinching me over and over in the dark.

"Are you crazy, merde? Come here!"

She runs after me, catches up, and tosses Thierry's coat over my shoulders. Her ecological worries have sensitized her to the needs of endangered species—even childhood best friends who, if you leave them for too long without food and water, turn feral.

•

We mend our friendship at the kitchen counter with kir royals and stale chouquettes. Thanos and Thierry have gone to bed, the girls are having their own little party. We're listening to old French songs on Stamatis's record player. Anna mimics a few moves from our childhood dance routines, from back when we did arabesques and pretended to leave carnations on the graves of students killed at the Polytechnic.

"Be serious, Anna. We're not nine anymore."

"If you think like that, you'll age before your time."

"Well, I certainly don't feel all that young these days."

"Because you've lost your faith in our friendship, that's why." Anna hugs me tightly and whispers in my ear, "If you think distance always means separation, you'll spend your whole life looking for replacements. I for one am tired of looking for replacements. You're my best friend, and that's that!"

"Forever?"

"Forever!"

Anna strokes my hair, plants a sloppy kiss on my ear and weaves her fingers through mine. We lie down on the cold kitchen floor, wrapped in one another's embrace. An entire Buttes-Chaumont, with its gentle slopes and trees, springs up around us.

Dear Kayo, Paris continues to feel small without you. I miss you incredibly, particularly when it rains. I open my arms and pretend you're by my side. But I'm with Anna. She's changed again: this year she's full of love and in a generous mood. A chic, bourgeois leftist. She reads the same books, but interprets them however it suits her. That's her problem, though, not mine. I can't live in her shadow anymore. For me, that's the worst form of captivity. I tear the postcard into pieces. I'm too old for schoolgirl confessions.

"Come in here so we can do your hair," Anna calls from the bedroom.

We're back in an era of grooming, an acceptance of female beauty. She sits me down in a chair and runs a comb through my hair, as if I were a doll.

"See that?" she says. "You look good with a bit more volume." Is she implying that my hair is thin?

She opens the closet and tells me to choose something.

"I've brought plenty of clothes with me . . ."

"But I want to give you something."

I know these gifts well. They carry a price, she demands emotional sacrifice in return. I have nothing left to give her. My inner world has been flattened, it's one long row of dusty ruins. I read, think, and do only what aids Direct Action.

"Please, Maria."

Just to shut her up, I grab a black striped button-down.

"When you wear black you look sadder, more serious," Anna says.

But I am sadder, more serious than ever.

"What exactly is going on with Kayo?"

She's on her knees, trying to piece together my torn-up postcard.

"Anna, I can't believe you! What right did you have?"

Fortunately the piece with her name on it is missing. She thinks "the worst form of captivity" refers to my feelings for Kayo. I grudgingly tell her his news: Kayo is living with a much older man in Manhattan, doing lots of drugs, pursuing his dream of being an artist, at least to a point: he goes to galleries, hangs out with artists, but in a superficial way, to see and be seen, as if he hasn't figured out how to submerge himself in real life.

"He's jealous of you, that's why. He wants to do whatever you do."

I wonder if she's also describing our friendship.

"Why would he want to do that?"

"Kayo is superficial, a narcissist, a nobody. You've given him the soul he otherwise wouldn't have."

"And you wonder why I don't talk to you! You're harsh. And bossy."

"I'm not bossy."

"Then why are you looking through my trash?"

"I don't know you anymore. These days I'm always going on old information. I want to know how you live, what you think, who you hang out with."

Who I hang out with.

The plane's turbines grind Anna's words as they spin. *I'm always going on old information . . .* It's a relief to be leaving Paris. It's as if I'm emerging from a nightmare full of beautiful people, harsh words, superhuman trials. Thanos is quiet, sad. After all, he's headed back to work at the bank, in the absence of Anna's triple kisses, Thierry's vinaigrettes, the apartment with its half-circle balconies. It turns out he's ambitious. He enjoys having houses and ideas, he's adopted Thierry's way of talking and I'm sure he fantasizes about having Anna beside him in bed.

"I think we need to take a break for a while," I say.

"Mmm," Thanos murmurs, as if daydreaming, draining the last of his soda.

No one has ever pursued me enough, no one wants me for his very own. Whereas everyone tries to get Anna to ride on their motorbikes, to kiss them, to come with them to Africa. Even I want her all to myself, a knick-knack in my heart. Or at least that's what I used to want. It's time I let her go. It's time I said a silent goodbye to them all. It's time I made up my mind.

"They won't leave me in peace. They're watching everything I do!"

Aunt Amalia is chewing the ends of her hair. Her eyes look right through me, as if I'm made of air. I stroke the back of her hand.

"Who's watching you, Amalia?"

"The king, of course!"

"He lives in London, we've been over that. And he's not the king, he's the former king. *For*-mer!"

"Oh, honey, you don't know anything! He has spies everywhere. He has people in New Democracy, they tell him who I'm talking to, what I buy at the supermarket . . . They know every last detail."

Amalia occasionally watches the news, and fragments of reality work their way into the stories her heightened imagination invents. The other day Parliament passed a bill concerning the confiscation of royal assets. New Democracy abstained from the vote.

"Who cares?"

"What do you mean, who cares? He has no money anymore, no estates, no grandeur. Don't you see? He's poor and wants to kick me out of my house so he can live here, with that woman. He's got agents. They ring my doorbell, they threaten me."

She walks over to the television and turns it on. We silently watch the commercials as night falls outside.

"Shhh! Listen!"

What's there to listen to? A blond woman is chopping onions to show how natural and healthy a particular brand of instant soup is.

"Don't you hear what she's saying?"

"No, Amalia, what's she saying?"

"I'll chop you to pieces just like these onions, if you don't do what we tell you to!"

I light a cigarette. Aunt Amalia claps.

"That's the idea, a smoke screen!" She apparently knows her James Bond, too.

I hug her, exhaling the smoke behind her back, down onto an empty candle holder sitting on a side table that looks like a God's eye from above. A proud, unforgiving god, who has completely forgotten his servant Amalia. Forgotten my mother, too.

"Where did you disappear to this time?"

Mom doesn't really enjoy my visits. We spend the whole time discussing my lengthy absences, my indifference toward my family.

"I have something for you." She hands me an envelope covered with little angels and roses.

"Who's getting married?"

"The wedding already happened. Your old friend from Aegina, Martha. I called you for days. Aren't you ever at home?"

"I was in Paris, with Anna."

"One logical individual meeting another . . ."

"How was the wedding?" I know she likes that kind of thing.

"It was nice, lots of people came. We went to the reception afterward, too."

She's talking to me, but looking at the television. Her soap operas have expanded to take over the whole middle of the day. Mom lives a life of weddings and divorces, dastardly deeds of revenge, silk sheets and champagne.

"When are you going to give me that joy?"

On the screen we see a couple in profile, kissing—a redhead with thick, gorgeous eyelashes and a blond guy with a square jaw who's probably gay in real life. The kind of people you want to throw a bomb at.

"You're twenty-six, when are you planning on getting married? Do you want to end up like Aunt Amalia?"

"I don't want to end up like her, or like you, either."

Mom gives me a hurt look, a perfect imitation of the women on her soaps. She doesn't wear makeup or curl her hair, but she's mastered that wounded look of middle-aged actresses watching as their daughters or lovers walk off, leaving them helpless. It makes me want to smash the screen. I don't know anything more satisfying than the act of throwing a television through a shop window.

"Are we going on vacation together this year?"

Anna's voice sounds pinched on the other end of the line.

"What happened?"

"Thierry and I broke up. Won't you comfort your old friend?"

It turns out Thierry was more interested in whales, turtles and oil spills than in Anna. "Merde, he can go live with his turtles, I've had enough!" She tells me that I was right, environmentalism is dangerous, because it distances you from people's real problems. Now she's working for a lawyer, a friend of hers from the collective, who defends large families in Paris from eviction.

"So, should I come to Greece and we can go crazy this year?"

"We'll see."

Vacations are a bourgeois habit that's out of keeping with my new way of life. I tell Camus about my conversation with Anna. "You're overdoing it," he replies. "You're always talking about that friend of yours, Anna, but you're not that different from her, in the end. You let your ideas take over your life. No one throws bombs all the time."

He takes off his shirt. There are no wings sprouting from his back. It turns out he's only human, too. He pulls me down onto the tattered mattress, in the room where he once gave me drawing lessons. His fingers reek of nicotine, his breath of coffee. His smell brings me down to earth with a bang. Usually, for me, Camus is as portable as a slogan.

I bleed, therefore I am.

It's entirely logical for me to sink my fingernails into his back.

"Maria, you're the only one who understands me. They installed a transmitter in my TV and are broadcasting the most terrible words. They curse at me, ridicule me. If I don't escape, they'll drag me naked through the streets to Syntagma, to the guillotine. Where can I go? I have no where to go!"

But she does. She jumps from her third-story balcony, finally headed elsewhere, to some dark refuge. She's in a coma when they take her to the hospital, with contusions in her brain and all her ribs broken. Dad is waving the note in his hand when I arrive. Mom's eyes are red and swollen from crying.

"Our Amalia," she says.

Dad brings us coffee. Mom is holding an old photograph with crumpled edges that she's had in her wallet for as long as I've been alive. She and Amalia are sitting on the stoop of Mom's childhood house in Kypseli, laughing, their mouths open in gap-toothed grins. Their knees are filthy, but their braids gleam. They're each proudly holding a rag doll. "We were like sisters, just like you and Anna." She starts in on the stories: how they grew up on that stoop, swapping those dolls for trading cards of Hollywood actors, and later for actual men.

"You mean she had a boyfriend once?"

"Amalia had more marriage proposals than I could count. She loved to be taken out for walks, to have men promise her this or that. But that's as far as it ever went. She'd found her prince." Amalia slept with the crown prince's photograph under her pillow. It started as a family joke: Amalia was going to marry Konstantinos and on Sundays they would all go out for rides in the palace gardens. Those idyllic daydreams had led to others, about social welfare: Amalia would distribute soup and children's toys to the poor.

She wasn't a royalist, she was a romantic. A proletarian royalist, as Anna always said. Toward the end of her life, a whole army of religious panhandlers had paraded through her house, praying for her and pocketing her pension.

"What happened when you and Dad left for Africa?"

"She cried, begged me to think it over. It was a real drama. I told her to come with us. But she couldn't possibly, because one day her prince was going to come for her. Even at the airport she tried to get me to stay. She said she would die. And now she's made good on that threat!"

"Mom, please. She's not dead yet." Though deep down I don't think Amalia will live, either. Besides, if you jump off a balcony, what's the use in surviving?

We're sitting on an uncomfortable hospital bench, in a narrow hallway with the same harsh lighting you find in butcher's shops, or prisons. Mom and I are finally sharing something, if only the cell of the same emotional helplessness. The women in Mom's soap operas go to the hospital dressed to the nines, their emotions overflowing everywhere—rage, pain, sadness, despair. Mom just silently twists a handkerchief in her hand, one she embroidered back in Africa.

At last they let us into the ICU. They give us masks. We're like aliens, bending over the bed of a relative who's been infected by contact with earthlings. Aunt Amalia, hooked up to machines, with an IV and an unrecognizable face, looks like a martyred saint who's finally at rest. No black dress with doo-dads on it, no buns or curlers in her hair. If I were to say "fart on my balls," would the shock of it wake her up?

I bend over and whisper all the bad words I can think of in her ear, a free association of filth.

"What did you say?" Dad asks.

"A prayer."

"Amen," Mom says, crossing herself. "May the Virgin protect her."

Aunt Amalia has been lying in the same position, eyes closed and with a drip in her arm, for five days. All of Dad's siblings came to see her, and some of her old girlfriends, and Kyria Pavlina, Fotini, Martha. Even Antigone comes. She hugs me, serious and emotional. She's wearing a suit and jewelry. The braid is gone; her hair is short now, with red highlights.

"What's going on?" I ask.

"I met someone." In all the years I've known Antigone, I've never seen her with a man. "It's not the right time," she whispers, catching sight of Aunt Amalia behind the glass in the ICU. "She looks like a caterpillar in a cocoon. Or a baby." Amalia is in fact wrapped tightly in the sheets, her head just barely poking out. Only this caterpillar won't ever turn into a butterfly. And the baby won't ever grow up.

Antigone brought roses. I take them back to the apartment on Stournari and change the water obsessively. If they survive, maybe Amalia will come back to us. For now she's in an in-between state—as she was her whole life long, for that matter: between her world and ours, in a tunnel of voices and darkness.

"I'll take the next plane," Anna says.

There's no need to rush.

Anna, in a white mask, bends down over the bed.

"Wake up, Amalia, we're going out to find you a man," she says, her voice breaking. She wipes away a tear and takes a step backward toward the door.

"We have to do something about this. Write books, I don't know. Ban princes from fairytales. March against monarchy, against the ridiculous consumerist production of dreams. Set them all on fire, merde, on fire!"

Anna kicks the wastebasket. The head nurse gives her a stern look. I bite my lip until the top layer peels—it's the only aggression I allow myself when I don't have a kerchief tied around my face.

"You really want to set them on fire?" I ask.

"More than anything!"

"Fine, then. Come with me."

I take her by the hand and literally drag her out of the ICU.

"Where are you taking me?"

Where she asked me to. Where the fires start.

Camus's eyes shoot daggers.

"How dare you? How stupid are you?"

"Let me explain!"

"Explain what? That you brought your little friend here without giving us warning, just because you felt like it? Who are you going to bring along next time, your dad?"

"But you guys can bring your girlfriends, huh? Did anyone ask my permission? And I sit here and put up with your phallocratic bullshit!"

It's a screaming match; Anna is standing off to one side. For the first time, someone doesn't want her around and I'm doing my best to convince him.

"On a trial basis," Camus says. "Just one meeting. Got it?"

Anna gazes at him in awe, but Camus sends us packing.

"Maria, tell me everything, from the beginning."

We're walking in the Field of Ares, kicking stones. I keep looking around, paranoid that I'm being followed. I don't know where to start. The name of our group is *Amesi Drasi,* Direct Action. Our emblem looks like the anarchy symbol, only the alpha has another line at its base, so that it's nested inside a delta. Our slogan is "I

WHY I KILLED MY BEST FRIEND

bleed, therefore I am," and it comes from a bizarre description of police violence that Camus read somewhere: *The policeman's riot club functions like a magic wand under whose hard caress the banal soul grows vivid and the nameless recover their authenticity—a bestower, this wand, of the lost charisma of the modern self: I bleed, therefore I am.*

No theory is airtight. At some point I tell them we need to talk about feminism, and one of them replies: "Thanks, Emma Goldman, but as they say, when the wise man points at the moon, the fool looks at his finger." They're all men, around Camus's age, so they're apparently the moon, and I'm the finger. The severed finger. Sometimes they bring admirers. I wonder how big those girls' mouths are. Of course we take precautions: we call one another from phone booths, we never meet in the same place twice, we ignore one another if we pass in the street and refer to one another by pseudonyms. Antonis is Bertrand Russell, since he believes that happiness is to be found in idleness. We call Paris Altol, a cross between Aldus Huxley and Tolstoy. We've got our Chomsky, too, otherwise known as Telemachus. Sakis's pseudonym is Debord, because he considers vandalism a work of art. As for Terzis, Camus is the perfect name for him. He offers us a solid philosophical grounding whenever we get lost in nihilistic conversations: anyone who seeks to destroy everything, he says, ends up self-destructing. So I sleep with him every now and then, to keep from self-destructing.

Camus only allowed me into the group after I'd sufficiently earned his trust. At first I thought I'd entered a den of fools. They wanted to march against the cops carrying huge mirrors, the way the riot police carry bulletproof shields. They were going to have their girlfriends dance topless, too, like maenads.

"Are you guys nuts?" I said. "Are you really that naive? All those sensitive cops are going to be shocked by the sight of their own violence? And you're going to ask women to act out the fantasies of men in uniform?"

219

We come from various backgrounds and are always at logger-heads. If we go too far, someone—usually Altol—reminds us that we have a common enemy: the state, the capitalist system. Chomsky always objects that the word "enemy" is too emotionally loaded and we should use the term "opponent" instead, and an argument ensues, until Camus calls us back to order.

"I bleed, therefore I am," Anna whispers conspiratorially. "It's kind of contradictory, to say the least, to believe in a slogan like that when you faint at the sight of blood."

We're walking arm in arm now, like girls from good families, along the path with the statues in the Field of Ares. Where Aunt Amalia first taught me not to use dirty words.

At her first meeting Anna makes coffee. At the second she tries to forge a common front with Chomsky, but he's too much of an anarchist for her taste. At the third, she puts her hands on her hips and shouts, "I don't understand what you've all got against the Soviet Union. Show me another truly revolutionary society!"

"There's no one-size-fits-all solution," Debord retorts. "What's true for the Eastern block isn't necessarily true for the West, and the same goes for Africa. Some people need food, others—"

"Sure, crumbs for the proletariat, art for the intellectuals," Anna cuts him off. "Who cares about literature and the arts when an apolitical history of art is going to come along after the fact and destroy it all—dadaism, surrealism, even situationsim?"

"We're with you on that. The issue is to find ways to have art infuse movements of social change with imagination and creativity."

"Merde, merde, that's never going to happen! The artists will stay right where they are, shut up in their glass tower." My guess is she's not painting much these days.

"Are you by any chance related to Rosa Luxemburg?" Altol teases.

And that's how she gets her name.

Rosa decides our organization could use some organizing. She says we don't meet often enough, have no discipline, can't even make a decent cup of coffee. Her speech is full of annoying words like sacrifice, rage, guilt. She wants us to swear allegiance to a common cause. Common cause? We're just feathers in the wind.

"No!" Anna says. "You can't think that way! Revolution has to effect actual political change, otherwise you're just letting off steam. Why don't you go to a soccer match if that's what you're looking for?"

I have the sneaking suspicion that she chose us, rather than us choosing her.

"It's over."

There's no need for Mom to say more, I understand. Aunt Amalia—whatever was left of Aunt Amalia—is gone. I pound my fist on the table. It used to be where I drew. Now it's covered in paper: books, photocopies, proclamations, articles about the Zapatistas. With a single motion it's gone: I sweep the telephone, my pencils, the papers all onto the floor. Suddenly the table is empty and clean. All that's left is the marks from my X-Acto knife.

"What happened?" Mom shouts. Her voice is coming from the floor, through the tiny holes in the receiver.

"Something fell," I say, stretching out on the floor next to the phone. Something fell, yes. I can see Amalia now, falling from her balcony in slow motion so as to escape the spies with their burning eyes. I picture her in a long cotton nightgown, though I know she was wearing her black and white dress when they found her. In the movie in my head, she's a cartoon hero: she bounces back up into the sky as if the sidewalk were a trampoline, bursting into a fit of laughter. The tears won't come. My emotions just lie there on the floor, amid the piles of paper: overturned, indefinable.

At the funeral, Dad leans down to dust off his shoes with his hand. Mom blows her nose into an embroidered handkerchief. Antigone is wearing huge Jackie Onassis sunglasses. Anna cries for us both. If there's an afterlife, Stamatis, too, is surely hovering overhead in a velvet armchair with wings, pipe in his mouth. Camus stands a little ways off, next to some other grave. He's pretending not to know us, and smoking like a chimney.

"He loves you," Anna says, wiping her eyes.

Merde, there goes another one. She'll steal him, too.

"Antigone is completely nuts. She's going on vacation on a yacht."

"Aren't you happy she's happy?"

"Are you serious, merde? Happy with the CEO?" Anna makes a face. Happiness is meaningless if it's not the kind she approves of. Her mother has fallen in love with an upper-echelon executive of a multinational corporation. We see them in magazines hobnobbing with members of the administration. Antigone is always looking away—"out of guilt," Anna claims. The executive has a baby face and white hair and is always wearing a tie. You'd think they grabbed him right out of grade school and threw him into the thick of it. I've never met him, but he's left his mark everywhere. The bookshelves in the living room, which were always in utter disarray, are somewhat more presentable now. A woman from northern Epirus comes and cleans the house in Plaka twice a week. The lithograph by Tasos has given way to a painting by Kostas Tsoklis. Antigone travels with her new man to Mexico, Buenos Aires, Morocco. They come home laden with rugs, copper pots, maté gourds.

"There was a time when she would have walked her shoes to pieces to meet Subcomandante Marcos. Now she slips into heels, neat as can be, and goes down to breakfast at the Intercontinental."

"You're too hard on her, Anna."

"Am I, or is she insensitive? Who would have expected it? She's no better than your mother these days."

"What do you mean? My mom doesn't have a boyfriend, and hasn't bought a new outfit in years."

"I mean that these days Antigone cares about what people think, what people say."

Antigone used to have a false braid! Wasn't that caring what people thought? I wish I could say something. I wish I could find a way to offend her, the way she offends me.

The crickets are shrieking.

"Listen to this," Anna says. *"One must deliver politics from the tyranny of history, in order to return it from the event."*

She's re-reading Alain Badiou on the rocks of Amorgos. She's found a walking stick, too, like a present-day hermit. This year she's wearing a blue kerchief over her hair, and new espadrilles. A cheerful worker all in pastels.

"What does that mean?"

"That in practice, communism is entirely active, kinetic, anti-state." Everything that comes out of her mouth is a quote. I go on cutting up a peach with my penknife.

"Want some? It's juicy."

"Why are you avoiding the conversation?"

"I'm not avoiding anything. I just like dealing with tangible things—the sun, a peach. When you were going through your environmental phase, you liked things like that too."

Anna's gaze drills right through me. "My environmental phase?" She suddenly leaps to her feet. I'm afraid she's going to pinch me, but she walks right by, preparing herself for one of her theatrical dives. She slices into the water; a few moments later her head appears in the distance like the head of a pin. I reach for her book and scan the phrases she's underlined: *"the emigration of victory," "with that orphanhood of the real," "in order for the impossible to obtain its historicity."*

What precisely is she looking for? As the years go by, I find Anna harder and harder to comprehend.

Her hair is done up in a loose braid, her shoulders smell of vanilla-scented moisturizer. She has her back to me in bed, as if we're a quarreling couple. She's gathered the sheet up so that it's dividing her part of the bed from mine, the way she used to divide our desk down the middle at school. This year we rented a room, we're too old for campsites. We want our own bathroom.

From the other side of the wall come the sighs of a man and woman having sex. The regularity of the sounds seems almost silly when you're not involved. We eavesdrop; we both miss being in a long-term relationship. These days I see Camus only rarely, and Kayo remains an untouchable dream. For a moment I imagine that the cries are coming from Camus and Anna. It's not hard to picture them twisted into revolutionary poses on his tattered mattress. Is something going on between them? I'll never know. These days Anna is careful.

I pull her braid. She throws a pillow at me. Scratches, elbowing, tickling. We dissolve into laughter, fall to the floor, our faces bright red. Anna mimics the couple's sighs and we laugh until our bellies ache. Our friendship is like a balloon: we blow and blow until it bursts in a flash of disappointment, then we mend the holes and start all over again from the beginning.

"Want to go get something to eat?" I say.

Whenever we're very sad or very happy we head for the fridge. These days we don't make up by peeing, but by eating. We order double portions at all the tavernas on the island. The owners treat us like walking advertisements: two toothpicks who eat for five. We wipe our plates clean with chunks of bread and sigh.

"No one knows me the way you do," Anna says, wiping her mouth with a paper napkin.

We're in our classic posture of reconciliation: face-up on our towels, Anna's head on my stomach. My head is turned toward the rocks, my eyes are closed, my lids burn in the sun. I hear footsteps and half open my eyes: high up on the rocks, a man is standing with his hands on his hips. He hisses at us as if we were cats.

"Get lost, you fool!" Anna shrieks. She sits up and puts her hands on her hips, too, ready as ever for a fight.

The man starts climbing down in our direction. He's moving quickly, practically at a run, aided by the downward slope. The sun is at his back, which makes it hard for us to see him clearly. It's not until he's just five meters away that we can see he's a foreigner, probably Albanian, and of that indeterminate age of men who work hard under the sun. He has a sunburnt forehead, bright green eyes, and an enraged look in his eyes. He seems to think I'm the one who shouted at him. He rushes at me and grabs my wrists, the way my mom used to when I was little.

"Who did you call a fool?"

"Let me go!" My wrists hurt.

"Let go of her right now!" Anna shouts. "You pig, you jerk!"

The man is beside himself. He grabs me and drags me to the very edge of the rock; my head scrapes against the ground, my back is bleeding. Anna rushes at him, leaps onto his back, clings to his shirt. The man elbows her hard in the ribs and she falls onto my towel, as if she were a pesky lizard he'd flicked off his arm. He heads for me again, threateningly. His shoes are caked in tar and sand.

"Who did you call a fool?"

His hands—thick, callused red fingers—are curled into fists. I close my eyes and see three stocky men at the mouth of a cave.

They have stockings over their faces. Behind their backs stretches a beach with rusting suya grills. The air is thick, humid. It's the rainy season in Nigeria.

Someone kicks me hard in the nose. Hot blood gushes. Instead of fainting, I open my eyes wide: the man is standing above me, ready to kick me again, this time in the ribs, and maybe spit on me, too. His nostrils flare with rage. Anna rushes at him again, this time with her walking stick. She takes aim as if she were a pole-vaulter and plunges the stick into his gut. The man loses his balance and falls off the rocks into the sea. He growls, swallowing water with loud gargling noises, then shouts something incomprehensible, struggling against the waves.

"Run!" Anna shouts.

We start running up the hill like madwomen. At the top we stop to catch our breath beside a bicycle with a rusted chain—it must be his. I turn back toward the sea. My heart feels as if it might explode.

"Anna, look!"

My voice sounds distorted, I'm holding my nose with one hand to stop the blood. Her eyes turn instinctively to where I'm pointing: the Albanian's body is floating, face-down. His printed shirt has ballooned out like a parachute over his back.

The sun is hot, but our inner temperature has dropped.

"Are you sure he drowned?" She keeps asking the same question every five minutes, as if any second now he might come back to life, swim to shore and crawl from the sea like a creature out of some horror movie thirsting for revenge. Deep down we wish we were in that kind of movie. We wish he would crawl out of the water and attack us again; we wish he would give us a second chance.

Sitting on the bed, we take turns tending to one another's wounds and crying. My back is badly scraped, and my nose won't stop bleeding. The worst was when we had to go back down to the shore and gather our things, clean the blood from the rocks and get rid of the stick. The whole time we could see the Albanian, floating, out the corner of our eye. Motionless, his shirt filled with water, like a deflated raft. Blood was flowing from somewhere, diffusing steadily into the sea. He had probably hit up against the rocks.

"We're murderers, murderers!" Anna hisses. Her eyes are wider, bluer than ever.

"It was self-defense, he attacked us!"

"How was I supposed to know he couldn't swim?"

"The real question is, what do we do now?"

We don't sleep at all that night. At the smallest noise in the hallway we're sure that they've found our fingerprints. That they've come to arrest us.

"I saw this strange image," I whisper in the middle of the night, nestling my head against her shoulder. Anna is drenched in sweat, her hair practically dripping. The moon casts a macabre, yellow-ish light on her eyelashes, her cheekbones, the dimple in her chin. "Right before he kicked me, I saw these men in a cave. They were holding me hostage. It was so strange . . . as if . . ."

Anna sits up, wrapped in the sheet. "What happened next?"

"There was no next. That's all I saw. Three men with stockings over their faces."

"But what then?" Anna hugs me, and a shiver runs through me.

"I told you, that's all I saw!"

"Remember, try to remember," Anna whispers, gently stroking my hair, as if I were a child.

Gwendolyn is ironing, I can see her clearly. The tropical rains have started, which is why she hasn't set up the ironing board on the veranda. She irons as if she were dancing, shifting her weight this way and that, in the big basement room where the cleaning supplies are, next to the storage room. Yes, Gwendolyn—her heavy, square body with its smell of salt and humidity; her unruly bun, with tufts of hair always escaping, the softest thorns I know; the whites of her eyes flash each time she raises her head to look at me. Lying on my stomach on the floor, I'm drawing our house with colored pencils. I put banana trees all around. They're not there in real life, but my picture looks happier with all that yellow. Every so often my eyes drift shut, and I doze on my papers while Gwendolyn's iron slides back and forth over the ironing board with soothing regularity. The room smells like my father's shirts, my mother's embrace. I slowly sink into a dream that's a faithful copy of my drawing. Suddenly a window up on the ground floor breaks, jolting me awake. Gwendolyn freezes in place, standing there with the iron in the air.

"It's the wind," I tell her in English.

"Shhh," Gwendolyn hisses.

We hear footsteps overhead, furniture being moved. Did Mom come home from Mrs. Steedworthy's? But she wouldn't ever come in through the window. Dad usually stays at work until late. And the hobgoblins in fairytales who sneak into stranger's homes to get warm never break windows, they just slip in on tiptoe. Gwendolyn grabs me and shoves me into the storage room, behind Dad's wine rack. "Not a peep out of you," she says. Only in her anxiety and confusion, she trips over a crate of soft drinks and the whole tower of them comes crashing to the floor. The noise on the ground floor stops. Gwendolyn rushes to the telephone; two men come running down the stairs and overtake her. They have women's stockings over their faces and are holding knives. They're not very sharp knives, but Gwendolyn starts shrieking anyhow. I come out of my hiding spot to help her; no one would hurt a little kid.

A third man grabs me and hefts me onto his shoulders as if I were a sack of flour. He's so scary, with his nose and lips smushed by the stocking! His eyes are squinted partway shut, his cheeks are swollen. The men argue with Gwendolyn in African, probably telling her to hang up the phone. Gwendolyn is crying. I've never seen Gwendolyn cry before. The men growl, their voices distorted by the stockings. One of them is carrying Mom's jewelry box of carved wood. Another grabs a few bags of rice from the storage room. The third has me. We all pile into a van. Gwendolyn runs out into the rain after us. The man who had me over his shoulder shoves her and she falls to the ground, in the muddy water. I watch through the window of the van as she gets smaller and smaller, until she disappears altogether, along with our front gate. The men make me lie down on the back seat so that no one will see me. The van—a wreck, smelling of burnt rubber and sweat—bounces around in the mud for a long time. Eventually I forget about the three strange men with stockings over their heads. My eyes wander to the torn cloth on the roof of the van and I listen to the sound of the rain. I start to laugh. I'm thinking about how mad Gwendolyn gets when I say, "Gwendolyn, listen! It's God peeing!" At some point, the sound of the struggling motor stops. I raise my head. We're on a deserted beach with a cave at one end. They tell me to go into the cave and sit there. Their English is terrible. All they know how to say is, girl, here, sit here.

"Are you alone?" Anna asks.

"No, there's another little girl."

"A little girl?"

"She's very small. She's expecting me to save her. But I can't. They cut off her arm and her head and throw her into the sea . . ."
A wave breaks inside me, then another. My eyes fill with tears.

"It's not another little girl, Maria, it's your doll!"

My doll! Bambi! She has silver hair and a necklace around her neck, a bronze chain that gave Gwendolyn the idea for the story with the two friends. Bambi is no ordinary doll: she talks nonstop.

Whenever my parents or Gwendolyn or Unto Punto come into the room, she plays dead, but when we're alone she purses her tiny red lips and whispers that I'm her savior, that my love broke the spell of her boring doll's life. I cover her with a blanket my mother made out of an old woolen shawl. I kiss Bambi's pink cheeks and tell her, "Don't worry, I'll protect you." Bambi comes with me into the storage room, nestles in my arms at the dinner table, sleeps on my pillow. She has straight hair, like Anna's, blue eyes, and dark, shiny eyelashes. And she's naughty. She always wants us to do naughty things, like climb up onto the roof of the house, or climb the trees in the garden, or hide in the laundry room and jump out to scare Gwendolyn. Sometimes she overdoes it. She says, "Pour your milk down the sink, it's gross! Blech!" Or, "Grab one of the goldfish by the tail, let's see how long it can last out of the water." The goldfish flops around while Bambi begs me to hold it just a little bit longer. But I'm good to the fish, good to all God's creatures—I toss it back into the water and wipe my hands on my school uniform. Bambi has a uniform, too. Mom made it for her out of leftover fabric from my white summer school smock. Bambi is always getting dirty, just like me. "Oh, Bambi, what have you gotten yourself into this time?" I say. "Come here, I'll clean you off." She likes to roll on the grass, in the dirt, and sometimes goes for a swim in the goldfish pond. Then I have to dry her uniform with the hair dryer. I kiss her on the forehead and forgive her. I always forgive her.

Yes, Bambi is with me when I'm drawing on the floor, when Gwendolyn pushes me into the storage room, when the men with the stockings on their heads shove me into their van. And she's with me in the cave, too. "Let's get out of here," she says to me. "These are bad guys! Quick, let's run away!" We take off our shoes—Bambi's are red patent leather with a little strap, mine are black and full of sand. We run across the muddy beach, under the rain, toward freedom. Neither of us realizes that the men are running after us—until they grab us and whisk us up into the air. It's easy as pie for them, bad guys always run faster than good guys. My bad guy, the one who slung me over his shoulder, grabs Bambi, pulls off her arm and tosses it into the sea. "Don't, don't!" I cry. Then he pulls off her head. I rush at him and bite his arm, but instead of behaving, he throws Bambi's head far off into the waves. Then he hands her back to me, headless, missing one arm, as if he were the judge in Gwendolyn's story, and I'm the jealous friend who wanted the necklace. "That's what we'll do to you if you try to run away again," he says to me. And to scare me even more, he pulls the stocking off his head. He's white! The very worst bad guy is white! I would have preferred him to be black, it would be more like Mom's stories, about how being poor makes black people so crazy that sometimes they do bad things.

They lead me back to the cave. I put my head in my hands and cry and cry. And since it's raining, it's as if all of Ikeja, all of Africa, is mourning with me. Bambi, Bambi, you can't talk anymore? Did they kill you? Did you turn back into a doll? I dig a hole in the sand and bury her, the same way we buried our baby.

"What baby?" Anna asks. She's still stroking my hair.

"My little sister."

She was a tiny baby, like a worm. Before she was born she seemed enormous. She would stretch her legs in Mom's belly and Mom would put my hand on her belly button and ask if I felt her kicking. "Why is she kicking?" I'd ask. Dad would say that that's how babies are, they do naughty things, but I should set a good example. I couldn't wait for her to finally be born, so we could play together in the garden and draw houses and banana trees and peeing gods. In the end she was born prematurely. "She couldn't wait to meet us, either," Dad said. In the hall outside the emergency room I kept standing on tiptoe to see our baby better: she looked like a sleeping cat. I made up stories in my head: we would play hide-and-seek with Unto Punto, we would sneak into the storage room and put one another's hair in ponytails. But the baby wanted to sleep forever. Mom said she went up to heaven to be with the angels. Gwendolyn said they put her in a nice white house, with photographs of us, and lollipops, candies, and teddy bears, and lowered her deep into the ground. "Why?" I asked. "Because the light of Africa hurt her eyes. She was used to the darkness in your mother's belly." Mom started to believe more and more in God, and to cry and get fat. Dad stayed at work later and later. Gwendolyn talked more than ever about salt and worms. Mrs. Steedworthy brought me Bambi so I'd have someone to play with. I couldn't save our baby, but I made Bambi talk, and she told me all the time how I'd saved her from her boring doll's life.

"It's not your fault," Anna says, and hugs me so tightly I think I might break into a thousand pieces. I'm not paying any attention to her. After all these years I'm right back in that cave. Night falls; Bambi is buried in the sand; the men gesture, argue, smoke. I'm little, they won't see me in the dark. I'll just go as far as the main road, some car full of good guys will stop and pick me up and give me a blanket so I'm not cold. We'll go to another beach far away, we'll light a big bonfire to dry my clothes, they're gypsies, they'll tell me stories, and I'll tell them about my adventures with the burglars and our baby, and the gypsies will have lots and lots of kids, so many that they won't mind giving me one to be my little sister. In the morning we'll eat bananas and then they'll take me back home to Ikeja, and Mom and Dad will cry with joy. We'll all give the gypsy baby a bath and teach her Greek and English and the salt won't ever get worms again.

I get up and start to walk. I'm not running as I was before, just walking to go meet my gypsies. But the bad white man catches up with me. "What did I say would happen to you if you didn't listen?" he shouts in my face, and before I can say a word, he slices off part of my little finger. Just a little bit, not even half, but there's blood running everywhere. The other two, the black men who aren't as bad as the white man, punch the white man in the face. One tears off part of his shirt and wraps it around my finger and says, "Sorry, girl, sorry." Then all three of them leave, disappearing into the dark.

The blood has seeped through the shirt of the better bad guy. It hurts a lot and I'm crying. Eventually I run out of tears, and my voice is gone, too. I sit and listen to the wind howl. The sand is cold from the storm and looks like the crystallized sugar we have in our storage room. Mom will yell at me for not bringing a coat. Something moves in the back of the cave. Is it a snake? A dragon? A hobgoblin? In the end it's a cricket. It climbs up on my knee, and I play with it, I ruffle its wings. I'm very hungry. What if I ate it? I bite into it and chew as quickly as I can. It tastes good, like a potato chip. The sound of the cricket in my mouth is reassuring, like company.

They find me in the morning. First the Ikeja police come and wrap me in a blanket, since my teeth are chattering and I'm trembling. They ask me about the white man. Then my parents show up in the Mercedes. Mom runs toward me with open arms and kisses me all over, even my eyes and ears. "I was afraid I'd lost my other child, too," she whispers. When she sees my finger, she lets out the loudest scream! Dad pounds his fist in his open palm like he's beating himself up. The police say that the white man is an American from the base who went crazy, and that the burglars didn't think anyone would be home. They took me with them for ransom, and when I tried to run away they panicked. They didn't know what to do. "Well, I know exactly what I'll do!" Dad shouts. He curses all the blacks in the world and says we're going to get out of Africa as soon as we can.

"But, Dad, the murderer was white!"

"What murderer?"

"He killed Bambi."

I show them where I buried her. Mom is sobbing. Dad asks, "What is that?"

"A piece of cricket, so she has something to eat in her grave. I didn't have any candy or lollipops." I made a mistake, again. Bambi's head is in the sea. She has no mouth to chew with.

This year Walkmans are all the rage. At the beach you see girls with headphones drumming their fingers against their knees. They tap their feet to the rhythm, whistle or sing off-key, in a world of their own. And when they take the headphones off, they look surprised, dazed by the sudden onslaught of reality. That's how I've been living all these years: with headphones on. And then Anna, who always knows better, who's always one step ahead, comes along and yanks my headphones off: "It's not another little girl, Maria, it's your doll!"

"How did you know about any of that?" I ask. It's past dawn now, and we're lying in bed, wrapped tightly in the sheets. Exhausted mummies.

"Your mother told Antigone, back when we found you on the beach in Aegina. You know, after Angelos and I . . . She was crying because you were eating crickets and grinding your teeth, just like back then."

"She told you about that, too?"

"How could you eat crickets, Maria?"

"Think of it as practice, for prison."

"You really think they'll put us in jail?" She wraps herself even tighter in her sheet, curling into the corner of an imaginary cell and looking at me despairingly. The room smells of mildew, just how I imagine a jail cell would smell. I picture Antigone and Mom sobbing during visiting hours. Anna and I in rags, gnawing on crusts of bread, plagued by guilt. Direct Action has been discovered and the media are distorting our cause in light of our crime. They describe us an anarchist fringe group whose members include fanatic nationalists. They blame us for the recent attacks on Albanians. "Young people with confused ideas and no vision for the future," the newscasters declare.

"We have to split up," Anna says. She's pacing up and down in the room, biting her thumb.

"What?"

"We have to leave here right away, and never speak again."

"You mean to one another?"

"Yes, to say goodbye forever. Abandon Direct Action. Forget it all. It's the only way."

We have to dig a hole in our heads, as Aunt Amalia would say. Put in the Albanian who didn't know how to swim. And then we'll bury one another, too. I'll bury Anna in her *marinière*, holding her drawing of Patty Hearst. And she'll bury me in my school uniform with the Mao collar and my Savings Day prize.

Anna leaves first. She packs silently, shoving her clothes into her duffle bag as if they were dirty laundry. She makes a vague gesture with her hand. She doesn't kiss me, doesn't hug me; for once there's no drama. She just stands in the doorway long enough for some parting words: "You know what Mayakovsky said? That a true revolutionary burns all bridges behind him." And then she shuts the door.

I sit on the bed, I don't know for how long. Hours. A whole line of Annas parade by me, at all ages, striking pose after pose, making faces, with their white eyebrows, the dimples in their chins, those big blue eyes, deceptively calm. Then I pack my suitcase as hurriedly as she had, tossing in books and clothes. I understand the plan: she'll head to Paris and never look back. I, meanwhile, need to go someplace where Direct Action won't find me. Somewhere with sand, heat, tropical rain.

For a start, Aegina will do.

"I want to ask you something. But I want a french fry first."

Martha gets up from the sofa in a funny way: first her stomach, then her. She chooses a french fry off the plate—she prefers the underdone ones—and bites into it with pleasure, with her front teeth, like a beaver. A butterball beaver that purrs, rubbing its belly. She has on a loose dress of gray flannel and tattered cotton socks. She's turned out exactly as I would have guessed: she and her husband live in what used to be her family's summer home, that two-story house with the stuccoed walls, sliding doors and watercolors of angry seascapes on the walls. The only thing she's gotten rid of is Kyria Pavlina's flypaper. And their goat has long since died of old age. Her husband is so shy he blushes whenever you talk to him. He's a notary public who works in Pireus.

Martha used to work at a travel agency by the port, but now, about to give birth and naturally chubby to begin with, the most she can manage is to stand up and sit back down again. She has no one to help her. Fotini is living in Thessaloniki with an out-of-work actor, the absolute opposite of the Harlequin romances the two sisters used to read. Kyria Pavlina is confined to her bed, suffering one kidney stone after another. As for Angelos, he married an Italian, Romina, and took over the management of her family farm somewhere outside of Sienna. They smile at us every day from a gold-framed photograph, brandishing muddy shovels as if they were tridents.

All day long I fry potatoes. Martha has a weakness for fries. The smell of hot oil makes me queasy, but it suits the melancholy familiarity of this house, with the television always on in the afternoon, a housewife curled up on the couch.

"You're going to stay with us, right?" Martha asks the same question every afternoon while I drink my coffee and she eats her fries. Nanny, governess—now there's a job that never crossed my mind. The older I get, the closer life brings me to Gwendolyn. "You'll have your own room, you can do your art in there and play with the baby, right?" Ever since she was little Martha has spoken almost exclusively in questions. She opens her eyes wide and looks at you as if the end of the world has arrived.

"We'll see."

My room is Angelos's childhood room. There are still pencils and erasers in his desk from when he was a teenager and would shut himself up for hours, before he started breaking girls' hearts. There's still something masculine in the air, a lingering smell of stale aftershave. Martha brings in roses from the garden and little pots of basil, but to no avail. Only when winter has finally come and in place of those flowers Stella's toys sprout one by one do I forget that I'm sleeping in Angelos's old bed.

At first I don't go near her crib. I'm afraid of those tiny fingers that shape themselves into fists, afraid of the furrowed skin, the tongue that paints her toothless gums with spittle. Then she starts to make the most thrilling sounds: deep vowels full of existential doubt, guttural noises that sound like attempts at a laugh. I could watch her for hours on end and never get bored. Now that the hole in my head has opened and let out the cave and the burglars, Stella is a comfort, a replacement for lost siblings, dolls, and childhood friends.

Martha senses it, and has stopped asking.

"You'll stay," she says.

•

I knit socks and hats for Stella. The only art I still remember is this circular form of fencing: knit, purl, slip stich. I knit until my needles spark. Beside me on the sofa, Martha is nursing the baby, watching her afternoon shows out the corner of her eye. The baby drinks greedily, eyes closed, like a cat. For an instant I feel like I've returned to my childhood house and am watching my mother nurse my little sister. I'm afraid I might be losing it. It wouldn't take much, just a few more holes in my head to unbury themselves all at once.

I miss Anna. She visits me now and then in my dreams, smacks kisses on both of my cheeks, so hard that my cheekbones shatter as if they were made of glass. I guess we didn't say a proper goodbye. We buried each other hurriedly, so that afterward we both simply stood up from our imposed graves and shook off the dirt. This Aztec pattern with the orange zigzags I'm knitting would look good on her. I could send her a hat in the mail. Or I could call.

No one picks up at the apartment in Paris. I try every half hour, it becomes an obsession. It seems to me that the phone is ringing directly in Anna's gut, in her heart, and that she's not picking up because she no longer cares. She'd rather pretend I don't exist. I remind her of the weakest, darkest part of herself. As she does for me: if I shook myself like a tree, whatever still clung to the branches would have something to do with Anna. All the heaviest, saddest things. And heaviest of all would be the dead body of the Albanian. The corpse of our friendship. He did turn out to be Albanian, after all—brief articles buried in the back pages of the daily papers said it was probably a crime perpetrated by the Albanian mafia. He appears regularly in my dreams, too, or in my nightmares, face-down in stagnant water. His shirt pops like a balloon and giant crickets crawl out.

I devote myself wholeheartedly to Stella. We have vowel competitions, play airplane on the sofa, count how many hops the bunny of my hand takes to reach her neck for a drink of water. In early summer Martha goes back to work at the travel agency and Stella starts to confuse me with her mother, the way I once did with Gwendolyn. For the umpteenth time in my life, I have something that I also don't have. I had and didn't have a sister, a doll, a friend. I had and didn't have a personal revolution. I had and didn't have Angelos, Kayo, Camus. I'm sure Camus is still chain-smoking in his apartment. Kayo is living his fake life in New York. As for Angelos, he now belongs to a classic Italian wife who is unrepentantly Catholic and jealous.

These are the kinds of thoughts I think as I push Stella's stroller down to the wharf. We stay there awhile, I sing a lullaby, the baby stretches her arms out to grab the sun—"thun." My ears are numb from the heat, my heart numb with borrowed happiness. I've lost everything, but Stella gives me the illusion of a new life.

Until one day, on our usual walk, something sticks in my throat, my heart contracts. The sun, the soft, steady breaking of the waves, Stella's smile—nothing can calm me down. I turn my head, pretending to be looking for something I dropped. Twenty meters behind me a man is walking and smoking, a newspaper under his arm. I don't need to look a second time. The quiet rage in his eyes, the invisible revolutionary's wings sprouting from his shoulder blades. And his fingers, yellowed for sure. I bleed, therefore I am.

He found me.

I wonder how fast a person can buy a ticket for New York.

Nine

PROTESTING THE SYSTEM

With slogans and . . . laundry hundreds occupy the Attic Highway

"This is not a protest. I repeat: This is not a protest. These are artists and students. Over." The message being broadcast over the walkie-talkies in patrol cars yesterday at the height of the demonstration on the Attic Highway wasn't entirely correct. Artists, students, and workers flooded the highway near the Sorou exit in Marousi, carrying colorful banners with slogans such as "The streets belong to us, not to the cars," and, "Resistance is the secret to happiness." Alongside them marched some of the rowdier action groups, such as the infamous Bears, who lent a carnivalesque tone to the protests, wearing furry masks and banging on pots and pans. Their goal was to impede the work crews that had come to bulldoze the remaining residences in the area—most of them illegally built shacks.

For the demonstrators, however, what matters isn't so much zoning laws as the symbolism the highway encapsulates, at least in their view: "In the name of progress, modernization and the Olympic ideal, the average Greek citizen has been led to believe that the swift Europeanization of his daily life, in the service of rabid profit-seeking, is the only way to proceed." These are the words of twenty-year-old mass media student Irini Mantoglou, who is helping to construct a tunnel through the shared walls of the shacks that will unite the individual dwellings and facilitate communication among demonstrators.

Asked why they're destroying the very buildings they are fighting to save, the demonstrators reply, "This isn't destruction, it's a return to an older form of neighborliness, of mutual support and interdependence that we've shut out of our lives in the name of parliamentary democracy and political representation. We refuse to continue to leave our fate in the hands of politicians who might as well be investment bankers, industrialists, or corporate lawyers."

At present several hundred demonstrators and spectators have gathered at the site of the protest. At night they throw impromptu parties with loud music, and in the morning the street is transformed into a "neighborhood" with laundry hung out to dry. The occupation is raising serious concerns in the administration, largely because of how rapidly it has grown in the past twenty-four hours, and the attention it has drawn from ordinary citizens and mass media alike.

Dimos Hatzidis
The News

•

OUTRAGE ON THE ATTIC HIGHWAY

It's an outrage! A few hundred anarchists have once again managed to wreak havoc on the law-abiding citizenry. Where's the state? Where's our police force? Hippies, remnants of days gone by, dazed-and-confused kids like the ones we see roaming around Exarheia, have disrupted our lives by hanging laundry out in front of houses along the Attic Highway, painted with ridiculous slogans inviting people to take part in their "anti-establishment celebration." My question is: Don't these children have parents? If not, isn't our police force capable of dispersing them? Does the footage we've been seeing on television project the image of a civilized country? Bulldozers and digging machines at a standstill, lined up in front of youths flailing around to the sounds of rave music and the banging of pots and pans?

We say we want to stamp out terrorism. Then why don't we start with these small, everyday instances of terrorism perpetrated by a ragtag army of spoiled brats? Why does our society, at a moment of prosperity, continue to put up with this sort of false revolutionary rhetoric? Perhaps in doing so—all in the name of protecting individual liberties and freedom of expression—it actually fosters the development of a more widespread and dangerous terrorism, one born of the collective, wide-spread hatred of the wealthy, the powerful, the American, the police officer, the system?

> From the column "In Athens" by Emilios Laspas
> *The Free Press*

•

ABANDONED STAGE SETS

As the days pass, the Attic Highway is looking more and more like a stage-set for utopia, a microcosm of liberated ecological culture that isn't aiming to please us, coming to us only as an outlandish spot on the nightly news. And really, what have we done to deserve a simple, honest life? What basic values did we ever protect?

Dragging furniture out of houses, hanging old ladies' blankets out to air on the wire fencing of the work site, fixing coffee and sweets for the last remaining inhabitants of the area, who will inevitably see their homes destroyed in the name of progress, the students occupying the Attic Highway are creating a new installation, a new piece of performance art with every day that passes. A life installation, life *as* installation, along the lines of what the Luddites did in the nineteenth century when they conducted raids on factories, dressed as women—actions later imitated by the Paris Commune and then again in May 1968. It's the kind of piece we admire in international biennales yet fear won't ever have any real effect, since the theatrical, performative message of such works is ultimately undeliverable when presented in a taxidermied, museum-friendly form.

In 1970 the artist Gordon Matta Clark bored a hole through a house and Walter De Maria filled a room with dirt; more recently, Rachel Whiteread created a concrete replica of a condemned Victorian house in situ in East London. The young people on the Attic Highway are digging a cylindrical tunnel to connect the shared walls of the houses slated for destruction. In my opinion, it's an important gesture. It reminds us of how much we've lost, and how much more we're willing to lose, in the name of progress, of consumption, of that hotly desired "privacy" that gets packaged and sold as a luxury item, yet actually prevents us from living together, united.

"The street is a place for us to live, eat, talk, sleep," these young people say. "The street has a history of its own," people of our generation used to sing at anti-dictatorship protests in the '70s. But who remembers that slogan today? The street has become an abandoned stage-set that we hurry across without the least twinge of emotion, on our way somewhere else, alienated from our own footfalls, from the urgent situation of the present moment. Public squares have become sites for the deafening hubbub of festivals organized by city officials, supposedly "for the people." But when the festival is spontaneous and improvised, decentralized and unpredictable, then it becomes an annoyance. A danger, even. The images of riot police standing by, of bulldozers lined up face to face with the bonfires of the young people's jubilant celebration brings to mind moments in this country's past that we simply don't want to relive.

Op-ed column by Gerasimus Pantazis,
Professor of Sociology at Panteion University
The Daily Post

•

TRAGEDY ON THE ATTIC HIGHWAY
Thirty-five-year-old mother fights for her life

It was as if there were a war on. Tear gas everywhere, a battle scene. At the height of the clashes on the Attic Highway, at one in the morning, a few policemen fired shots in the air to disperse the crowd. One bullet, which seems to have gone astray, ended up in the temple of the unlucky Anna Horn, an artist who played an active role in organizing the demonstrations, and the mother of a six-year-old girl. She was rushed by ambulance to a hospital in Kifisia, where doctors have been struggling to keep her alive. The next twenty-four hours, they say, will be critical. The wounded woman is the wife of successful architect Aristomenis Malouhos, known for his office complexes along Kifisias Avenue, and the daughter of well-known philosopher Stamatis Horn, who lived and worked in Paris during and after the dictatorship.

In the wake of this tragic event, the protestors dispersed. The demolition of the remaining homes will commence tomorrow morning. Apart from the buildings themselves, workers are now faced with the piles of trash left by "environmentalist" protestors, who fought for a better tomorrow with beer cans and paper bags . . .

Bela Psaraki
The Afternoon Post

•

A FAREWELL TO ANNA

Who was Anna Horn? An everyday saint whose name was unknown until yesterday? An incurable romantic who fought for a
better tomorrow? Over the past few days we've seen her on the
news, infinitely repeating the only statement of hers which—to
their great luck—television crews had recorded, so that they are
now able to give a face to the name of the woman murdered
in cold blood by a policeman's bullet. "We all have to show
courage and faith in our ideals," she said. "We have to literally embody our emotions if we're going to act politically. New
technologies have marginalized the body. There's nothing more
dangerous than that. We here are going to fight with our bodies, because it's the only thing we have left."

And Anna Horn did in fact fight with her body. Beautiful
militant, mother and intellectual, her multifaceted image has
already been so thoroughly circulated as to end up a stereotype.
Old photographs from her days as an art student in Paris, state-
ments from friends and acquaintances, even some of her father's
writings about the anarchist movement in Europe have been
deployed. But what lesson can we learn from Anna? What did
she leave behind, apart from a young daughter and an adoring
husband?

What Anna Horn left behind is a deep distrust of the Greek
police, and by extension of the entire state apparatus—a state
apparatus that once again reacted to tragedy in a way that can
only leave us speechless. A press release by the Minister of
Public Order reads, "We must learn from this mistake. It is in
our best interest as a nation not to dwell on a single event, but
to consider and assess the overall effort." This "overall effort"
apparently refers to the muzzling of thousands of protestors
(roughly 2,500 were present on the night of the shooting) who
had come to express their anger and bitterness at the way the

state machine is organized, at the passivity of political life. To express, too, their nostalgia for a way of life they are being asked to abandon in order to make way for the forces of progress and prosperity signaled by the grand Olympic building projects.

What else did Anna teach us? That we still have bodies, which we can use as political tools. That an overexposure to mass media achieves precisely the opposite of bodily political action: we watch instead of taking part. That the ideology of the lone revolutionary no longer applies, that there isn't just one form of revolutionary thought. Beneath their kerchiefs, behind their names, the young (and not-so-young) demonstrators on the Attic Highway taught us the postmodern political language of the masses, taught us to accept states of contradiction, taught us that the era of solitary leaders is over. No more tidy marches organized by trade unions, no more dogma, no more replacing of one power structure with another that's even worse. The biggest challenge faced by anti-globalization movements is an internal one: if the reformist left prevails at the expense of these grassroot, anti-establishment trends, then we'll simply continue to breed cosseted unionists with no real impulse to fight the reigning institutional framework of representative "democracy." In which case every radical attempt at regeneration will fail. All that will remain in a hierarchy of this sort will be the leisurely demonstrations of the middle class (who have money to travel to the places where World Bank summits are held) and the occasional quaint little article in the daily paper . . .

Something else that Anna taught us: that the act of occupying the street at this particular historical moment is the end result of multiple processes—and while rapt art historians and theorists have noted the theatrical value of this act over the past several days, it also has a certain pragmatic value, which lies in the (albeit temporary) disruption of the work crews, and in the difficulties created for the system, if only for a few days.

If we all become romantic troublemakers, Anna Horn won't have to feel alone.

From an op-ed by Despina Arvaniti
The Free Press

•

THE REAL REVOLUTIONS
OF ANNA HORN

I've known Anna Horn since we were kids. We used to play together during recess. What times those were! Dressed in school uniforms, we swapped hair clips and zodiac crackers. It was 1977. No one could resist the charm of our new classmate who arrived from Paris and spoke to us with such aplomb about the Café de Flore and real butter croissants. Petros Misiakos, today the director of a major software company, wanted to marry her. Maria Papamavrou, whose installations have in the past decade breathed new political life into the art world, was content to live in her shadow. And me? Anna taught me lessons of radical elegance—I begged my mother to buy me tortoiseshell barrettes, which in those days you could only find in major European cities.

The newspapers are calling Anna a great revolutionary, which in my opinion is a distortion of her personality. Anna was a cheerful aesthete who knew how to make you feel she was a rare diamond, even in jeans. Our paths crossed twice in the past year: once at a reception at the prime minister's residence, and once at a charity fashion show. And no, Anna Horn didn't breathe a word about politics. She was a radiant bohemian, looking for a French-speaking governess for her adorable little girl. I'm sure she went to the Attic Highway as enthusiastically as she came to these charity events, moved by her desire to give back. I'll always remember her as a lively woman who knew how to have fun, who would grab her husband, Aristomenis Malouhos, by the arm, to fight with him side by side in the only real trenches we have left: the trenches we dig in the struggle against gloom and doom.

In this issue you'll find the best of the military look that will dominate the catwalks this winter. My recommendation? Don't give up the fight for the masterful Christian Lacroix backpack. Long live the revolution!

Editor's note, Geli Kotaki
Vogue Greece

•

ALONE AT HOME,
EATING BLACKBERRIES AND BREAD

Night falls;
it's nice to feel you're missing nothing by staying in
—the river, the mountain, the city that calls to you.
You turn inward, curl up on your inner branch;
outside it's at least as dark as in.
A woman walks through the apartment upstairs,
a man nails something to the wall you share.
Night falls—a little bread to help the berries go down.

Yes, they nail into you, walk over you,
you can trust yourself to strangers' hands.
Door locked, alone, blackberries and black bread.
You eat and are eaten, watch and are watched.
You unfold what you are and take a good look.
Day breaks again, objects harden into shapes.
The tree is a tree, the bread bread, and the berries

small and moldy at the edge of the plate.
The woman left for work,
the man surely has a seascape, now,
in his living room.

Naked and repellant, those inner branches,
and the day calls to you again.

Anna Horn
Paris, April 1981

•

ADIDAS CLASSICS

On the way home from my evening walk I passed by your house.
Lights on, windows open
and the sound of your life from the attic room
—a chair being dragged
    a woman's laugh
    or perhaps you left the TV on again?
I can live with these things, I'm getting used to your absence.
What I can't bear
are your sneakers outside the door,
worn at the heels, with muddy laces,
placed so neatly side by side
as if your mother were still alive, and pleading:
    "son, some order, please."
Your shoes remind me of all we never had—
a house, children, double-bed sheets, the TV playing.
The geography lesson of any couple:
memories to the east, boredom to the west.
Your shoes say,
    "He's not yours anymore, accept it."

I stand in front of your locked door and accept it:
the white, worn leather
    is the last sign of your existence
at the moment when your body, your airy heart,
your black t-shirt
are journeying from the attic to the sky.
Then, at the corner,
your shoes suddenly disappear,
everything disappears.
As it should.

When you have nothing, you know exactly what it is you want.

Anna Horn
Summer, 1981

•

FARMING

Am I scraping at the earth or is it scraping at me?
Am I weeding or is something inside me being uprooted?
Am I tidying hoes and watering cans in the garden shed
or is someone telling me to shut up already and go to sleep?

I have no idea what happens in nature, who does what.
Usually nothing happens.
The earth is silence.
When day breaks, I go back to weeding
flies buzzing over all my actions
in recognition of their significance and difficulty.
I tear open seed packets
to make sure the supplier hasn't tricked me.
In the afternoon I water and listen.

Dampness is silence.
"And if it prefers to dry up?"—I wonder.
"If it got tired and wants to die?"
I'll never know.
Silence is silence.

Anna Horn
Summer, 1984

•

PIZZA NAPOLITANA
for Maria

A large group—how many, twelve?
You're at the far end, in a bad mood,
barely looking my way.
I look when you're not looking, and when you're looking, too.
I keep hoping you'll come over and give my cheek
a sudden kiss in this crowd of strangers.
But your sharp teeth are busy
with something else:
they're devouring a slice of napolitana.
Is that tomato sauce on your upper lip
or a new, fresh wound?
Should I come over to see or would that not be wise?
Your cheeks say no.
They're filled with something hard
something you keep replacing with something else
even harder.

But I want to be your mouthful
and the next
and the next after that.

I want to be your digestion and your hunger, too.
Look: tomato sauce stains my lips, like yours.
You bite me and make me bleed.

Anna Horn
Paris, 1989

•

It's been a week since the memorial service and the same electrified silence still reigns in the office of the house in Ekali. I've pulled the shutters closed to admit no light, to block out the trees—the nature Anna described in some of her youthful poems. This is how I punish myself for not being there, for not saving her. Sitting on the floor, I'm putting her papers in order under the cold white light of Malouhos's lamp. Every now and then tears come. The strange thing is, I don't cry over the things you'd expect—the poem she dedicated to me after our heated discussion in that awful pizzeria. I cry at the phrase *fought for a better tomorrow with beer cans and paper bags*. Or, *not a protest, over*.

The letters she never sent to me are stored in shoe boxes, along with piles of other unsent letters. The ones to me all begin with the same harsh invocation of my name—a plain *Maria*—and end with an urgent *write to me*. And now I do really feel the need to write her one of those torrential, twenty-page letters we used to exchange back when we were teenagers.

Anna, it would begin, *you betrayed me and I betrayed you countless times. Today I found a huge stack of letters you wrote to Michel, in which you call him your only love. To me you talked about exercises in courage, about bourgeois habits, when what you were really trying to say was love. What kind of friends were we, anyhow? Years later, when I told you I'd seen Michel in Berlin, you asked me how he was, what he was up to, if there was a woman in his life—but you couldn't even hint at the truth.*

You loved whomever I loved—Michel, Angelos, Camus—probably because you loved me, too. That's something that never crossed my mind. Sincere, passionate, oppressive love. Odiosamato. Was that it? Then why didn't you say so? Or perhaps you did, in your way, and I just didn't want to hear. I thought that people who love too passionately must be lying, maybe even on purpose. That's something you never understood about me. My reserved nature wasn't an indication of my distrust toward you, but toward life.

You were always storming off in anger, and then coming back again. I always thought those returns were the fruit of my tireless efforts to win you back, but you would have come back anyway. You needed that cycle of emotions in order to exist: enthusiasm, betrayal, anger, despair, forgiveness, then back to enthusiasm again. Only then, only thus, were you Anna. You were afraid of earthquakes, afraid of the end of ideology. What else were you afraid of? Of your own hands, perhaps, which were capable of going so far to protect me, of pushing a man into the water, of bringing an end to ideology, of causing the earthquake that would destroy the safety of the world?

Another long cycle and you came back entirely refreshed, with new blood, new resilience, a husband and child—what better suit of armor? Now I can see it clearly: you came with a plan. You wanted us to organize the revolution we'd abandoned in the middle. When you saw me withdrawing, when I stopped being involved with the preparations for the occupation of the Attic Highway, when I became a "sheep," as you called me right before you hung up the phone on me for the very last time, you decided to teach me a lesson. You went on television, supposedly addressing yourself to the world, but really you were talking straight at me. I've memorized what you said, I don't need a reporter to quote it: "We all have to show courage and faith in our ideals. We have to literally embody our emotions if we're going to act politically. New technologies have marginalized the body. There's

nothing more dangerous than that. We here are going to fight with our bod-
ies, because it's the only thing we have left." In essence, you were warning
me. If I didn't show courage, you'd show me how a body can be used as
the ultimate weapon. For all those years I thought you were the one who
was killing me bit by bit, with your attitude toward me. That without you
I could finally become the person I dreamed of being. Whereas in fact I was
killing you, too.

And now that you no longer exist, I sit here wallowing with you in an
absolute nothingness. Or perhaps I'm playing the worst role of all: that of
your ghost. Malouhos won't let me leave, on the pretext that your papers
need to be put in order by the person who knew you best. Daphne clings to
me like a leech, her hands shake my hips, punishing me for not saving you.
It was bad timing, the worst timing: you see, I was trying to save myself.
And part of that attempt was the decision to keep my distance from you for
a while. I wanted to montage the video of women who look like Antigone;
I wanted to make them walk to the tune of the Internationale. I wanted to
finally look for a gallery where I could show my work.

Now I miss you desperately and regret all that. There are times when
I'm gripped by the morbid desire to open your closets, to touch all your
clothes from this final phase of your life, these clothes that rustle gently, and
to comfort myself with your smell—the heavy, womanly perfume you started
to wear after Antigone died. Were you trying to replace her? And yet you
followed her fate down to the letter. You may have acted like one of those
girls who are in love with their fathers, but all along you clung pathologically
to your mother's skirts.

So, then, we lied to one another constantly. Silly, heroic lies. I never
told you about my little finger, but then again did I tell anyone else? Even
myself? Perhaps that was the hardest thing of all: you knew more about me
than I did, and you made me spit it all out, one detail at a time, like half-
chewed insects, as day broke on Amorgos. And when I'd finally realized
who I was and how I'd gotten to where I was, you opened the door and left,
because Mayakovsky said that's what real revolutionaries do. You'll never

know what it means to finally tell your deepest secret and have your only witness walk out the door, leaving you at your own mercy.

"You'll never know": I'm talking to you as if you exist, as if you just went into the kitchen for a minute to fix a round of martinis. The shock of your death is something I have no experience of, nothing to compare it to. I didn't go to the memorial service, or even to the funeral: as your casket was being lowered into the ground, I was at home drawing, like the insensitive brute I am—drawing pitch-black caves. Malouhos came by the apartment afterward and cried like a child, grabbed me by the shoulders and said, "Let me hold you, there's even more of Anna on you than there is on me." He practically dragged me here to the house in Ekali. Kayo was standing stock-still and expressionless in the middle of the living room. Daphne was curled up in her cave. Your cigarette butts filled an ashtray in the bathroom, your satin pajamas were on the bed, though it had been a week since you last slept there. I imagine you in full gear at the occupation, sleeping in your clothes, making coffee and sweets and cursing me, the coward, for ruining your plans. Are you satisfied, at least? Deeply, existentially fulfilled? I'll never know. I only started to understand you after you left us, and the further away you get, the more unconfirmed my theories will remain. If I keep going like this, I might invent an Anna who bears no relation to the real one.

But I owe you a real Maria. After you hung up the phone on me, I went to the rector's wife and told her something that I just as easily could have told myself—I simply needed an audience for the promise to stick: I want to make art, to take photographs, to wander station platforms with a Super 8. Do you know what I'm most afraid of? I'm afraid that all the newborns in the world might die and leave a deep wound in their mothers' hearts; I'm afraid of blood, I still have nightmares about severed fingers; I'm afraid of pretending to be brave when art is the only thing that gives me courage. Art is my revolution, the embodiment of my emotions. I know it won't change the course of history, but not all of us are cut out for grand gestures. And even your grand gestures got distorted. Our old classmate

Angeliki (who goes by Geli, now, it turns out) described you as an aesthete who frequented charity balls. I'd have thought you would rise from the grave to give her a black eye. One leftist columnist wrote that you taught us "the postmodern political language of the masses, the acceptance of paradox and the end of leaders." You, the bossiest leader I know.

What am I supposed to do with you? For starters, I need to settle our unfinished business. I killed you just as you killed me. I didn't push you from an open window, the way people do in movies. And besides, you're still alive—vague, elusive, the eternal Anna. When I'm overcome by a need for explanations, I'll read your poems, where the real you can't hide. In those poems you make mistakes and admit it, you love and forgive without fear. Perhaps you should have tried to write poetry instead of chasing my dream of making art. And perhaps I should have told you right from the start that only when I'm covered in paint am I truly happy.

Write to me,
Maria

A bird flies through the garden. I prefer to think it's a good spirit flitting through the room. A witch, set free.

Daphne comes into the office, rubbing her eyes. Those eyes don't belong in her face: they're adult eyes, serious, red, surrounded by wrinkles and folds.

"Don't do that, sweetheart."

"Why not? It makes me see colored circles. Do you know any stories about colored circles?"

I tell her whatever comes into my head. That the colored circles are soap bubbles coming from a witch's mouth, because her little apprentice witch was very mischievous and tricked her into eating a bar of magic soap.

Daphne's mouth drops open. When she's surprised, she looks just like her mother. "Soap? That little witch is even naughtier than I am!"

Yes, the apprentice witch is mad at all the other witches, she wants to take away their magic so they turn back into people.

"But won't she turn back into a person, too?"

Yes, she will. But she's tired of living in caves and riding on broomsticks, she wants a simple life, a house with a yard, where she can sit on the grass and talk to the goldfish in the pond, and work the simple magic of everyday life—like whistling, for instance.

"And the caves?"

Well, the caves can become museums about magic, where we'll put broomsticks and magic soap, and when the former witches buy a ticket to go in, they'll feel a slight dizziness in their heads, but only for an instant, since they will no longer remember the time when they could do anything they wanted.

"How does the story end?"

Oh, but the story doesn't end. Show me even just one person who will manage in the course of this life to visit all the caves there are.

TRANSLATOR'S ACKNOWLEDGMENTS

Translation is always a work of collaboration, but this particular book is the result of a closer collaboration than most. *Why I Killed My Best Friend* is a coming-of-age tale rooted in a succession of particular historical moments. It is uncannily prescient of the current crisis in Greece, while also hearkening back to a series of earlier crises, from the exile of many Greek citizens during the dictatorship of 1967–1974 to the AIDS crisis of the 1980s to the continual, internal ideological crises of the Greek left. The dizzying array of cultural and historical references in the novel kept me running to internet resources, to Greek historians, to countless friends in Greece and elsewhere, and of course to the author herself.

In addition to exchanging any number of email queries and responses, drafts and corrected drafts, Amanda Michalopoulou and I were fortunate to spend a week in residence at Ledig House in fall 2012, in the company of four other translator-author pairs working together in well-fed isolation. I am grateful to D. W. Gibson and the folks at Ledig House for providing this invaluable opportunity, and particularly to the other translators in residence— Neil Blackadder, Lisa Dillman, Tanya Paperny, and Joel Streicker—for the many conversations and inspirations small and large. I am also immensely grateful for Amanda's close cooperation during that week, and for her eagerness to use this translation as an excuse to revisit and even revise the original itself. (Careful readers familiar with the Greek may notice some larger-scale changes than translators usually allow themselves; these were all made with Amanda's consent and involvement.) As strange as it may be to dedicate a translation to the author of the original, I would like to dedicate this translation to her.

Other thanks are also in order: to my parents and brother, David, Helen, and Michael Emmerich, faithful readers and supporters of everything I write and do; to Evi Haggipavlu for the many meals and so much else; to Panayiotis Pantzarelas for never tiring of my questions; to Dimitri Gondicas, always. Thanks also to Chad Post at Open Letter for believing in this book, and to Kaija Straumanis for her careful editing. And a very sincere note of gratitude must go to the FRASIS program of the Greek Ministry of Culture, which in this bleak economic moment still believes that the contemporary literature of Greece deserves a chance at life abroad.

Amanda Michalopoulou is the author of five novels, two short story collections, and a successful series of children's books. One of Greece's leading contemporary writers, Michalopoulou has won the country's highest literary awards, including the Revmata Prize and the Diavazo Award. Her story collection, *I'd Like*, was longlisted for the Best Translated Book Award.

Karen Emmerich is a translator of Modern Greek poetry and prose. Her recent translations include volumes by Yannis Ritsos, Margarita Karapanou, Ersi Sotiropoulos, and Miltos Sachtouris. She has a Ph.D. in Comparative Literature from Columbia University and is on the faculty of the University of Oregon.

Open Letter—the University of Rochester's nonprofit, literary translation press—is one of only a handful of publishing houses dedicated to increasing access to world literature for English readers. Publishing ten titles in translation each year, Open Letter searches for works that are extraordinary and influential, works that we hope will become the classics of tomorrow.

Making world literature available in English is crucial to opening our cultural borders, and its availability plays a vital role in maintaining a healthy and vibrant book culture. Open Letter strives to cultivate an audience for these works by helping readers discover imaginative, stunning works of fiction and poetry, and by creating a constellation of international writing that is engaging, stimulating, and enduring.

Current and forthcoming titles from Open Letter include works from Argentina, Bulgaria, France, Iceland, Latvia, Poland, South Africa, and many other countries.

www.openletterbooks.org